the
further
adventures of

SHERLOCK HOLMES

THE WAR OF THE WORLDS

THE WAR OF THE WORLDS

MANLY W. WELLMAN
& WADE WELLMAN

TITAN BOOKS

THE FURTHER ADVENTURES OF SHERLOCK HOLMES
THE WAR OF THE WORLDS
by Manley Wade Wellman & Wade Wellman

ISBN: 9781848564916

Published by
Titan Books
A division of Titan Publishing Group Ltd
144 Southwark St
London
SE1 0UP

First Titan edition: October 2009
10 9 8 7 6 5 4 3 2

Visit our website:
www.titanbooks.com

What did you think of this book? We love to hear from our
readers. Please email us at: readerfeedback@titanemail.com, or
write to us at the above address. To receive advance information,
news, competitions, and exclusive Titan offers online, please
register as a member by clicking the 'sign up' button on our
website: www.titanbooks.com

A CIP catalogue record for this title is available from the British
Library.

Printed in the USA.

Two Authors' Notes

In the summer of 1968 I was fortunate enough to see *A Study in Terror*, a splendid movie involving Sherlock Holmes pitted against Jack the Ripper in London around 1890. This is the only film I have ever seen in which the magnificent speed of Holmes's thinking is brought to life with full effect. So effective was the portrayal of Holmes that, as I saw the film for the first time, I suddenly began to ask myself – wondering, indeed, why I had never thought of it before – how Holmes might have reacted to H. G. Wells's Martian invasion. I determined to write a story on this subject and, since I am primarily a poet, felt obliged to ask for assistance. My father agreed to collaborate, suggesting that another Doyle character, Professor Challenger, be included. Our collaboration, 'The Adventure of the Martian Client', was published in *The Magazine of Fantasy and Science Fiction* for December, 1969.

I then felt that more could be done with the idea and suggested a sequel. Our second story, 'Venus, Mars, and Baker Street', appeared in the same magazine for March, 1972. After it appeared, I decided that the account of Holmes's activities in the first ten days of the invasion was far too brief, and that a third story, a sort of inverted sequel, must also be written. By the time this was purchased, we determined to turn the saga into a book, which we now offer to the public, with some additions and revisions.

Incidentally, it seems evident that Wells's *The War of the Worlds* was to some extent influenced by Guy de Maupassant's 'The Horla', although the influence has never, to my knowledge, been observed by a critic. Readers of this saga should take notice of an excellent moving picture, loosely based upon de Maupassant's tale, *Diary of a Madman*. The bad title has damaged the film's reputation, but the title character, superbly played by Vincent Price, is a man who outwits and destroys a superior being in a fashion well worthy of Holmes. Two motion pictures, then, have played their parts in the various inspirations for these five tales.

I dedicate my part of the saga to my friend Bob Myers, in warm appreciation of the courage, resolution, compassion, and humor which are so nobly outstanding in his character and personality.

Wade Wellman,
Milwaukee, Wisconsin

My partner in this enterprise says he found inspiration while pondering two motion pictures, which I have not seen and cannot judge. But he vividly imagined Sherlock Holmes in *The War of the Worlds* for both of us. We have seen publication of our short stories about it, and we feel that the whole story was not told. Here is the effort to tell it.

Wells's novel was serialized in *Pearson's Magazine*, April–December, 1897, and published as a book in London and New York the following January. But Wells spoke from a time in the then future, dating the invasion as "six years ago". My partner, a better astrologer than I, pointed out that the only logical year of the disaster was 1902, in June of which year Mars came properly close to earth; which supplies for us the necessary dates for the other corridor of time in which these things happen, including Wells's view-point as of 1908 and publication presumably late that year or early in 1909.

All our labors would be plagiarism, did we not make positive and grateful acknowledgment to Wells's *The War of the Worlds* and his short story, 'The Crystal Egg', which is a supplement to the novel; similarly to the whole Sherlock Holmes canon and to Doyle's *The Lost World* and other stories about the fascinatingly self-assured George Edward Challenger. Sherlockians both, we have also consulted with profit numerous works in the field and have found particular value in William Baring-Gould's exhaustive and scholarly *The Chronological Holmes*.

If I may dedicate my share of the present work, let me do so to the memories of the inspiring Sir Arthur Conan Doyle and Herbert George Wells.

Manly Wade Wellman,
Chapel Hill, North Carolina

Introduction

The distinguished career of Sir Edward Dunn Malone in journalism and literature, as well as his brilliantly heroic service in both World Wars, is too well known to need review here. The present volume contains certain of his previously unpublished writings, recently brought to our attention by his literary executor.

His account of some aspects of the so-called "War of the Worlds", anonymously published some years ago under the title of *Sherlock Holmes Versus Mars*, now proves to be a greatly modified and abridged version of the original essay found among his private papers. Sir Edward's private correspondence reveals some displeasure at that modification, and it would seem that his fear of similar treatment dissuaded him from offering for publication two other studies of the same event. We have therefore decided to publish the three essays – two of them never published before, the other one presented only in condensed form – as a connected narrative.

It has been thought appropriate to add to them two other accounts by John H. Watson, M.D., which also were previously published in abridged and modified form. In the interests of making the collection more or less complete, there is further included Dr Watson's letter to Mr Herbert George Wells, which first appeared as a postscript to the anonymous *Sherlock Holmes Versus Mars*, but which we here offer as the final section of the volume, in the interests of historical continuity.

I

THE ADVENTURE OF THE CRYSTAL EGG
BY EDWARD DUNN MALONE

One

It was one of the least impressive shop fronts in Great Portland Street. Above the iron-clasped door was a sign, ART AND ANTIQUITIES. In one of the two small windows with heavily leaded panes a card said RARE ITEMS BOUGHT AND SOLD. The tall man in the checked ulster gazed at this information, then walked in from the cold December afternoon.

The interior was like a gloomy grotto, its only light a shaded lamp on a rear counter. The shelves were crowded with vases, cups, and old books. On the walls hung sooty pictures in battered frames. The tall man paused beside a table strewn with odds and ends and bearing a placard reading FROM THE COLLECTION OF C. CAVE. From an inner door appeared the proprietor, medium-sized, frock-coated, partially bald. "Yes, sir?" he said.

"I hope to meet someone here, Mr Templeton," said the other. His hawklike face bent above the table. "What are these articles?"

"Another dealer in antiquities died two weeks back. I took these things when his shop was sold up."

The visitor picked up a crystal as big as his fist, egg-shaped and beautifully polished. A ray from the lamp kindled blue flame within it. "What do you ask for this?"

"Cave priced it at five pounds."

"I'll pay that for it." A slim white hand flung back the ulster and from an inside pocket of the gray suit drew a pocketbook and produced a five-pound note. "Don't bother to wrap it."

As the purchaser stowed the crystal in his ulster pocket, another customer came through the front door. He was short and shabby, with truculently bristling gray hair. He stopped and stared at the tall man with suddenly wide eyes.

"Templeton," he blurted out, "did you bring Sherlock Holmes here?"

"I came of my own volition, Hudson," said Holmes coolly. "You have conjectured that I had come to anticipate you. Your powers of deduction, though slight, should tell you the reason for my presence."

"This is Sherlock Holmes?" Templeton was stammering. "Hudson, I assure you I did not know—"

"Nor did Morse Hudson know," interrupted Holmes. "I sought him here on behalf of young Mr Fairdale Hobbs, whose Cellini ring was stolen."

"You can't prove I took it from him," blustered Hudson.

"My small but efficient organisation has helped me trace it to your possession. Mr Templeton here should be wary of receiving stolen goods, and I will relieve him of such an embarrassment. I see the ring on your forefinger." Holmes extended his hand. "Give it to me at once."

Hudson swelled with fury, but he tugged the ring free and handed it over. "You're a devil, and no other word for it," he muttered.

"I am a consulting detective, which may mean the same thing to your sort," said Holmes, sliding the ring into the pocket of his waistcoat.

Hudson blinked at Templeton. "Where's that crystal egg?" he demanded. "I heard from a Mr Wace about it."

"I have just bought it for five pounds," Holmes informed him, smiling. "I wonder, Hudson, how a man of your wretchedly dull esthetic sense could see the beauty of that object."

"You know about it," charged Hudson, glaring. "Shall I tell Templeton here some interesting private matters about you?"

"Do so, if you want me to tell the police some interesting matters about yourself. Suppose you keep silent and hope that I do likewise. I have recovered my client's property so easily that I feel disposed to let the matter rest."

He walked out. Hudson bustled after him into the chilly street.

"I demand that you sell me that crystal for five pounds, Mr Holmes."

"You're in no position to demand anything of me, Hudson," Holmes said quietly, "but let me give you a word of advice. If ever again you prowl this close to Baker Street below here, for whatever reason, that day will see your shop filled with coldly suspicious men from Scotland Yard, and you will watch its sun set through the bars of a cell. Is that sufficiently clear? I daresay it is."

He signaled a hansom and got in, leaving Hudson to glower helplessly in the wintry air, and rode to the lodgings of Fairdale Hobbs in Great Orme Street near the British Museum. Hobbs was a plump young man, wildly grateful for the return of the ring. It was a family heirloom, he said, and had been promised to the girl he meant to marry. "You recovered it in less than twelve hours," he chattered as he paid out Holmes' fee. "Marvellous!"

"Elementary," Holmes replied, smiling.

Back at his rooms in Baker Street, he rang for Billy, the page boy, and gave him a handful of silver. "Circulate these shillings among the Baker Street Irregulars and give them thanks for tracing that lost ring."

"We've learned something else, Mr Holmes," said Billy. "Morse Hudson has moved into a new shop. He was heard telling old Templeton that he wanted to get away from your investigations."

"Once I suggested that move to him," nodded Holmes. "Amusing, Billy, how even my enemies act on my advice."

Billy hurried away. Holmes hung up his ulster and took the crystal from its pocket. He had thought of giving it to Martha for Christmas; she loved beautiful things to put on her shelves. But why had Hudson been so interested? Sitting down, Holmes studied it. Again he saw a gleam of misty blue light within it, shot through with streaks of rosy red and bright gold. This way and that he turned the crystal. At last he drew the curtains to darken the room and again sat down to look at his purchase more narrowly.

At once he found himself sitting eagerly forward and straining his eyes to see better. The blue light had grown stronger, and it seemed to stir, to ripple, like agitated waters. Tiny sparks and streaks of light moved in it, brighter red and gold, with green as well, swirling like a view in a kaleidoscope. Then there was a clearing of the mist, and for a moment Holmes glimpsed something like a faraway landscape.

It was as though he looked down from a great height across a plain. Afar in the distance rose a close-set range of blocky heights, red as terracotta. Closer, more directly below, stretched a rectangular expanse, as though of a dark platform. To the side he made out a sort of lawn, light, fluffy green, through which the reddish soil was visible. Then the misty blue returned, blotting out the vision.

A soft knock at the door, and a key turning. Quickly Holmes leaned down to set the crystal in the shadows beside his chair and rose. His landlady came in. She was tall, blond, of superb figure and her red lips and blue eyes smiled. He moved toward her and they kissed.

"Dr Watson is gone to the theatre," she said, "and I thought I would bring in dinner for the two of us."

"Excellent, my dear," said Holmes, drawing her close with his lean arm. "I have been thinking about Christmas for you. I have even decided what I shall give you."

"This first Christmas of the new century," she said. "But should you tell me so far ahead?"

"Ah," and he smiled, "you are breathless to know. Well, that Cellini ring I found for Mr Fairdale Hobbs is a striking little jewel. What if I should have it duplicated for you?"

"You are too good to me, my darling."

"Never good enough. All right, fetch us our dinner."

She was gone. Holmes went to the telephone and called a number. A voice answered. "Let me speak to Professor Challenger," said Holmes.

"This is Professor Challenger," the voice growled back fiercely. "Who the devil are you, and what the devil do you want?"

"This is Sherlock Holmes."

"Oh," the voice rang louder still, "Holmes, my dear fellow, I had no wish to be abrupt, but I am in the midst of an important work, irritating in some aspects. And I have been bothered by journalists. What can I do for you?"

"There's a curious problem I would like to discuss with you."

"Certainly, any time you say," bawled back Challenger's voice. "You are one of the few, the very few, citizens of London whose conversation is at all profitable to one of my mental powers and professional attainments. Tomorrow morning, perhaps?"

"Suppose we say ten o'clock."

Holmes hung up as Martha Hudson fetched in a tray laden with dishes.

Next morning Holmes took a cab to West Kensington and mounted the steps of Enmore Park, Challenger's house with its massive portico. A leathery-faced manservant admitted him and led him along the hall to an inner door, where Holmes knocked. "Come in," came a roar, and Holmes entered a spacious study. There were shelves stacked with books and scientific instruments. Behind the broad table sat Challenger, a squat man with tremendous shoulders and chest and a shaggy beard such as was worn by ancient Assyrian monarchs. In one great, hairy hand was cramped a pen. He gazed up at Holmes with deep-lidded blue eyes.

"Let us hope that I am not interrupting one of your brilliant scientific labours," said Holmes.

"Oh, it is virtually finished in rough draft." Challenger flung down the pen. "A paper I am going to read at the Vienna meeting, which will hold up to scorn some of the shabby claims of the Weissmanist theory-mongers. Meanwhile, I am prepared to devote an hour or so to whatever problem may be puzzling you."

"As you were able to help me so splendidly in the matter of the

Matilda Briggs and the giant rat of Sumatra."

"That was nothing, my dear Holmes, a mere scientific rationalisation of a fortunately rare species. What is it this time?"

Holmes produced the crystal and told of his experience with it the night before. Challenger took the object in his mighty paw and bent his tufted brows to look.

"There does seem to be some sort of inner illumination," he nodded, frowning. "Will you pull the curtains? I think darkness will help."

Holmes drew the heavy draperies, plunging the room into deep shadow, and returned to look over Challenger's mighty shoulder.

"It has the appearance of a translucent mist, working and rippling," said the professor. "Almost liquescent in its aspect."

"'Charmed magic casements, opening on the foam of perilous seas, in faerie lands forlorn,'" said Holmes under his breath.

"Eh?" The bearded face swung around. "What are you saying? What has that drivel to do with the matter?"

"I was quoting a poem," said Holmes.

"Which strikes me as singularly lacking in merit."

Holmes smiled. "It is by John Keats."

"Indeed?" sniffed Challenger. "Well, I have never pretended to critical judgement in matters of that sort. In any case, we have no seas here, but a terrain. Look, Holmes."

He had taken a dark cloth from a drawer and cradled the crystal in it. Again the soft radiance of the mist had cleared, and they looked on the landscape which Holmes had seen the previous night.

It was like peering through the wrong end of a telescope, a view small but vivid. There was the great stretch of ground, the distant red-brown bluffs and, below in the foreground, an assembly of rectangles that seemed to be vast, flat roofs. Things moved there, and among the tufts of shrubbery on the sward alongside. Straight ahead, in an ordered row, sprouted up a series of lean masts, each tipped with a glare of radiance, like a bit of sunlit ice.

"Beautiful," said Holmes, enraptured despite himself. "Unearthly."

"Unearthly is an apt description of it," muttered Challenger. "No such scene exists in any land upon Earth that ever I heard report of."

The vista fogged over a moment, then cleared again. Now they were aware of what the moving things were. On the ground they seemed to creep like gigantic beetles with glittering scales, while closer at hand, on the roof, several small rounded objects moved here and there. Then, among the masts straight ahead, a flying something, like a moth or bat, appeared. It swooped close, and suddenly a face looked from within the crystal.

Holmes had the impression of wide, round eyes staring deeply into his. Next moment it was gone, and the whole vision with it. Only blue mist churned in the crystal.

"Did you see it, Holmes?" said Challenger, springing up to draw back the draperies.

"I did indeed. Here, I'll write down what I saw on this pad. You might do the same."

Holmes drew a chair to the table, sat down and wrote swiftly. Challenger snorted over his own hurried scribbling. Both were silent for some moments, then exchanged pads. Each read the words the other had put down.

"Then it was no illusion," said Challenger. "We saw substantially the same objects. Perhaps my eye is more scientifically trained, better qualified to observe, but you have written down the rooftop and the remote system of cliffs and the presence of moving, living things. It is now our task to rationalise what this crystal has shown us."

"Some representation of another planet, I increasingly suspect," said Holmes.

"I am tempted to the same suggestion." Again Challenger turned the crystal over and over. "If this is an artificial semblance inside, like those Easter eggs children love to look into, it is an amazingly elaborate and impressive illusion."

"Keep turning the crystal in various positions," said Holmes. "See if the viewpoint remains the same."

They experimented for some time, with varying success. It became evident that by turning the crystal they could somewhat change viewpoint, shifting the direction here and there above the great expanse of flat roofs and across the surrounding landscape, but visibility blurred, then blurred again. At times it faded completely.

"Would things be more visible if we had complete darkness?" Holmes wondered.

"Possibly so. I'll try to achieve that condition later on. At present, I am considering your suggestion that the scenery is extraterrestrial. I can neither confirm nor deny it."

"I remind you that it is only a suggestion, not a deduction," said Holmes. "Wherever the place may be, however, it seems certain that we are looking down upon it from one of the tall masts, at the very end of the row."

"I have a similar impression," agreed Challenger.

"I fear I must leave you now," said Holmes rising.

"My presence is required elsewhere. But let us make further studies, by all means."

"That was unnecessary to urge upon me."

As Holmes went out, Challenger crouched above the crystal in almost a fury of concentration.

Holmes took a cab to Scotland Yard, where he was able to offer considered opinions on two difficult cases. Returning to his rooms, he busied himself with making notes on the two problems, pushing the crystal to the back of his mind. He and Watson had dinner together and talked in friendly fashion, but Holmes said nothing of the crystal.

Next morning, Watson departed to make several professional calls. Holmes visited Scotland Yard again and conferred with two inspectors. When he returned home early in the afternoon, he found Challenger in the sitting room, tramping up and down as though frenzied with excitement.

"Your landlady let me in when I assured her of the enormous importance of my visit," Challenger greeted Holmes. "Extraordinarily fine woman, that landlady. The sort with a gift of deep feeling – brilliant feeling, I should judge. There are brilliances of feeling as there are of mind."

"Yes," said Holmes quietly.

"But I am here to report concerning our crystal," Challenger hurried on. "Holmes, you were right. I have vindicated your suggestion that the scenes it shows are extraterrestrial. I have even identified the planet."

"Amazing, my dear Challenger!" cried Holmes.

"You will find it elementary, my dear Holmes. The suggestion that I study it in absolute darkness proved a fruitful one. I took a black cloth such as photographers use and draped it so as to shut out almost all the light. I saw more clearly than when you were there this morning. Night had fallen over that landscape, the stars were out – and that is when a highly important truth, nay, a staggering one, revealed itself."

"And what was the truth?" asked Holmes.

Challenger drew himself up dramatically. "The stars were out, I say, in the sky above that roof with the towers. I made out Ursa Major, the Great Bear. What does that suggest to you?"

"That, if it is on a world other than ours, it is close enough so that the same constellations are visible."

"The constellations are the same, yes, but what followed was vastly different and conclusive. Two moons presently rose above the horizon – not one moon, but two. Both were very small, markedly jagged, and one of them moved so swiftly that I could see its progression. As they rose high, they vanished from sight." Challenger drove a fist into the palm of his other hand. "Do you see what that means?"

"I believe I do," said Holmes gravely. "If you saw the Great Bear, you saw the skies from within the solar system. And two moons – the only planet near us that has two moons is Mars."

"You are right, Holmes," nodded Challenger energetically. "This is proof that we are able to see a Martian landscape."

"'Proof palpable as the bright sun,'" said Holmes. "You must forgive me, Challenger, if I quote Keats again – this time from *Otho the Great*."

Challenger sat down heavily and puffed out his bearded cheeks. "You will do me the justice of believing that I have read and appreciated poetry in the past, before the direction of my researches came to demand so much of my time. Of the Romantics I preferred Shelley, precisely because of his own interest in scientific subjects. Even in my literary tastes, I have cultivated the purely scientific mind."

"And I have aimed rather at the universal mind," said Holmes, "But you are right, Shelley was the most scientific in his interests among the Romantics."

"He was keenly interested in astronomy, and the subject now before us is certainly astronomical."

A knock at the door. Billy looked in. "Someone to see you, Mr Holmes," he said, and Templeton entered, carrying a shabby top hat in his hand. He seemed nervous and apologetic.

"If you are engaged at present, Mr Holmes–" he began uneasily.

"I can spare you a moment. What is it?"

"It's about that crystal, sir. I've found out that it is worth far more than the five pounds you paid me."

"You accepted five pounds," said Holmes bleakly. "You have come a bit too late to raise the price."

"But Morse Hudson tells me that others will bid high for it," pleaded

Templeton. "A Mr Jacoby Wace, Assistant Demonstrator at St Catherine's Hospital, and the Prince of Bosso-Kuni in Java. Hudson says they both have money. If we get a profit from one or the other, you and Hudson and I could divide it."

"Templeton," said Holmes sternly, "you endanger yourself by associating with Morse Hudson. Had he not surrendered the Cellini ring to me in your shop, you might have been guilty of receiving stolen goods. As for the crystal, be content to realise that it is no longer in my possession."

"Mr Holmes is telling you the truth, my good man," rumbled Challenger.

Templeton gazed wide-eyed at Challenger. "How am I to know that, sir? I do not believe I am acquainted with you—"

"Does this fellow doubt my word!" roared Challenger, bounding to his feet. "You are addressing George Edward Challenger, sir! Here, Holmes, stand aside while I throw him down the stairs."

Templeton flew out through the door like a frightened rabbit. Challenger sat down again, his face crimson.

"So much for that inconsequential interruption," he said. "Now, Holmes, it is our duty to consider all implications. First of all, we must speak of the crystal to nobody."

"Nobody?" repeated Holmes. "You do not want other scientific opinions?"

"Bah!" Challenger gestured impatiently. "I have had experience of such things. A revolutionary new idea stuns them, impels them to make ridiculous, offensive remarks. At present, keep it our secret."

"My friend Watson is a doctor, has scientific acumen," said Holmes. "I have always found him respectful and ready to be enlightened. Some day you and he must meet."

"No, not even your friend Watson. I shall not tell my wife. And I trust you will not tell your landlady."

"Why do you admonish me about that?"

Challenger's blue eyes regarded Holmes intently. "I give myself to wonder if you cannot best answer that question yourself. But meanwhile, we must continue our observations, checking each against the other. When can you come to Enmore Park?"

"Later this afternoon," said Holmes.

"Shall we say four o'clock? I have an errand, but I can dispose of it by then."

Challenger donned his greatcoat and tramped out. Holmes sat at his desk, brooding. He picked up a pen, then laid it aside. A knock at the door, and Martha entered.

"You haven't had any luncheon, my dear," she said.

"A correct deduction, but how did you know?"

"Because I know your habits. You never take care of yourself when you are deep in a problem. Before I bring the tray in, will you tell me what you and Professor Challenger were discussing?"

"We spoke about poetry, among other things," replied Holmes.

She smiled. "You have written some poems to me. Beautiful poems."

"At least inspired by a splendid subject."

She went out and returned in a few minutes, bringing their lunch. Holmes was writing at the desk. He laid down his pen, put away his notes in a drawer, and joined her at the table.

Three

At Enmore Park later that afternoon, Holmes and Challenger sat down at the table in the study with the crystal before them. Over their heads they drew a closely woven black cloth that excluded nearly all outer light. At once the crystal glowed with its inner blue radiance, lighting up Holmes' intent profile and Challenger's bristling beard. Challenger carefully maneuvered the crystal between his hands.

"There," he said softly. "Do you see the mists clearing?"

The strange landscape was coming into view. They could make out the distant tawny-red cliffs, the great platformlike expanse below them. Then, as details grew sharper, they saw the row of lean, towering masts with their points of radiance. A clear, pale sun shown in the deep blue of the cloudless sky.

"That sun is but half the diameter of ours," said Challenger. "At its closest approach, Mars is about thirty-five million miles beyond Earth's orbit. If we take the Sun's apparent diameter into consideration, we may arrive at some scale of dimension in what we see here."

"I would judge the visible terrain to be many miles in extent, and this rectangle of roofs below the masts to be fairly large," said Holmes

"We may go on that assumption," said Challenger. "Now, watch closely." He shifted the crystal with painstaking care. "We are able to see in another direction now, as though we moved a viewing glass."

It was true. They looked downward past the straight edge of the platform and gathered a sense of a perpendicular wall below it. The ground showed, lightly covered with green as with a lawn, and feathery shrubs or bushes grew in clumps here and there. Among these clumps moved dark shapes. They seemed like distant bulbs of darkness, furnished with spidery limbs.

"It is as though we are above the closely set roofs of a city," said Holmes. "I would hazard that our point of view is the top of the mast at the end of this row we have seen. And down there on the ground are what must be the residents. I wish we could see them closer at hand."

"Perhaps we can." Again Challenger shifted the crystal. "Now, observe the rooftop immediately below. I can discern others."

At the foot of one of the nearer masts moved several of the creatures. Seen nearer at hand, they displayed oval bodies, dark and softly shining, holding themselves erect on tussocklike arrangements of slender tentacles.

"They strongly resemble octopoid mollusca," said Challenger. "But see, Holmes, some of them can fly."

One of the shapes on the roof suddenly rose into the air. It soared, or skimmed, on what appeared to be ribbed wings. Higher it rose, growing larger to their view.

"It does not move its wings," said Holmes.

"They seem to be simple structures."

The flying creature changed direction and swooped toward the top of the mast nearest the point from which Holmes and Challenger seemed to watch. Its two sprays of tentacles twined around the mast and the body drew close to the shining object at the apex.

"It has brilliant eyes, there at its lower part," Challenger half-whispered, his voice strangely touched by awe. "Those eyes, when I have seen them, have stared with a marked intensity. Now it is looking into that shining object, it gazes fixedly."

The creature clung there for long moments. Silently the two observers studied it. At last it relaxed its hold and came floating toward them in the crystal, growing in size, growing in detail. Close at hand they saw its gleaming eyes, and suddenly those eyes came as though against the opposite side of the crystal, the substance of the creature blotting out all the rest of the scene. Then, abruptly, the mist came stealing back, obscuring everything.

Challenger flung aside the cloth. He gazed at Holmes.

"We are in communication with Mars," he said dramatically.

"Communication?"

Challenger's hand scrambled for a pad of paper. He jabbed a pen into the inkwell. "Before another moment passes, we must both record what we have seen," he pronounced. "There are materials for you."

Silence, while both of them wrote. At last they finished and looked at each other again.

"A city, a Martian city, has been revealed to us," burst out Challenger. "And we have seen living Martians. I have written here," and he drummed his notes, "that they seem to be of a vastly different species from ours. Perhaps something to be referred, for comparison's sake, to the arthropods – the insects."

"Why the insects?" asked Holmes.

"Their form, for one aspect. Many thin appendages and soft muscular bodies. And you have seen that some have wings and some have not."

"From my limited observation, I would not be surprised to establish that some of them at least can fly. But they may all have that capacity."

"No, manifestly the power of flight is far from universal," Challenger flung back impatiently. "Indeed, the presence or absence of wings may well be a difference of the sexes – the females may be winged, and the males not."

"I have no basis of argument as yet, but I wonder if the Martians have not evolved to the point of sexlessness," said Holmes, studying what he himself had written. "The wings may be artificial."

"Nonsense!" exploded Challenger. "If they are artificial, would they not be attached with a harness? I saw nothing like that, nor, I suggest, did you."

"They may well have other ways of assuming their flying apparatus than with a visible harness," said Holmes quietly. "Reflect, Challenger, that this is another world on which they live, apparently with a tremendously complicated culture of their own."

Challenger subsided, locking his shaggy brows in thought. "You may be right, Holmes," he said at last. "It is not often that I feel obliged to retreat from a position."

"You are generous to give way," replied Holmes smiling. "Earlier today, you spoke disparagingly of other scientists who cannot do that. But let us consider another point for the moment. Our view seems to be from the top of a mast, and twice we have seen one of those creatures coming near and seeming to look into our very faces, as it were. We have also noted the glints of light on the other masts. Might it not follow that on top of our mast is some device similar to this very crystal we have here? And that a view through that crystal gives them a look through this one at us, as a view from this one gives us a look at them?"

"Indeed, what else?" demanded Challenger triumphantly, as though he himself had come up with the theory. "It is no more than sound logic, Holmes. On top of that mast on Mars is a contrivance which in some way is powered to observe across space to the area where this crystal is located on our own planet – to this very study."

"As one telegraphic instrument communicates with another, although the procedure is far more subtle than that," said Holmes. "And these creatures on Mars may be far ahead of humanity, in more than mechanics."

Challenger grimaced in his beard. "Next you will be suggesting that they are a biological advance on the human race, an evolutionary development."

"What I have seen suggests that something of the sort has happened on Mars, over a long period of time. You saw them, Challenger. Those oval bodies must house massive brains. And their limbs, two tufts of tentacles. Might these not be a latter-day development of two hands?"

"That is brilliant, Holmes!" Challenger's fist smote the table so heavily that the crystal rocked. "You may well have the right of it," and he began to scribble again as he talked. "Specialised development of the head and the hands. Nature's two triumphs of the superior intellect. Yes, and a corresponding diminution of other organs, less necessary to their way of life – atrophy of the lower limbs, for instance, as has occurred with the whale." He looked up again. "Truly, Holmes, I begin to think that you would have done well to devote yourself to the pure sciences."

Holmes smiled. "Instead of devoting myself to life and its complexities? I have trained myself to the science of deduction, which develops an ability to observe and to organise observations."

Challenger cocked his great head. "I must repeat, Holmes, we must keep these matters to ourselves for the present. If you will let me develop my reasons for insisting–"

"No, permit me to offer one of my deductions," put in Holmes. "You hesitate to confront your fellow scientists lest they jeer at you, charge you with reckless judgements, even with charlatanism."

Challenger's stare grew wider. "I may have hinted something like that, but your interesting rationalisation is perfectly correct."

"It offered me no difficulty," said Holmes. "In my ledgers at home, under the letter C, are several newspaper accounts that deal with your career. One of the most interesting of them describes your emphatic resignation in 1893 as Assistant Keeper of the Comparative Anthropology Department at the British Museum. There was considerable notice, with quotations, of your sharp differences with the museum heads."

"Oh, that." Challenger gestured ponderously. "That is water under the bridge, of a particularly noisome sort. At any rate, I have not quarreled with you. Now, suppose we ask my wife to give us some tea, and then we will return to our observations here."

Tea was a pleasant relaxation, and Mrs Challenger proved a charming hostess. Half an hour later, the two were in the study again, their heads draped with the black cloth. They gazed at what the crystal showed them of the rooftop, the masts, the lawn below, and the strange creatures that moved here and there. Repeatedly they saw different Martians leave the ground to fly. Finally one of them discarded its wings in their sight. Challenger uttered a loud exclamation.

"You are right, Holmes!" he cried. "The wings are artificial. I am fully convinced."

"Which disposes of them as sexual characteristics," said Holmes.

"Yes, of course. And I can observe in them no physical differences such as denote sexual differences to the zoologist." He breathed deeply. "But why was this crystal sent here to Earth?"

"And how?" asked Holmes in his turn.

Challenger threw back the cloth. "By some strange method we cannot understand, any more than African savages understand a railroad train."

"For what purpose?"

"Manifestly to watch us," said Challenger. "It was a triumph of extraterrestrial science, sending it thirty million miles or more across space."

"If it could cross space, might not living Martians follow suit?"

"An expedition here?" said Challenger. "For what purpose?"

Four

"I wonder," said Holmes slowly. "I wonder."

Their observations that day, and on subsequent days throughout December and on into 1902, developed their awareness of that strange distant, shifting Martian scenery. Holmes found himself involved in several criminal investigations, two of them in connection with Scotland Yard, but when he could spare time from these duties and his personal affairs he visited Enmore Park to gaze into the crystal and make careful notes of what he saw. Challenger spent far more time in observation. He dodged his wife's inquiries and put aside the treatise which he had been writing, to sit long hours in the study, his great head draped to shut out the interfering light.

The two jointly gathered increasingly clear, consistent impressions of the top of the city, wide and long and apparently of considerable height, set upon a level expanse of reddish soil with sparse lawnlike vegetation that extended to the bluffs on the horizon. That city bore something of the aspect of a fort, with its solid construction, its few openings for entrance or exit, and its location in open country as though to make a secret approach impossible. Neither Holmes nor Challenger could estimate the number of the inhabitants, but they seemed to appear by dozens, even by scores. On the green-fluffed plain around their massive dwelling moved metal vehicles of varying sizes and complexities.

"I am baffled," confessed Challenger at one point. "We are like African savages, intelligent enough in their own culture, but unable to understand a train or a steamship."

"Yet African savages, if trained and educated can understand and operate such mechanisms," said Holmes. "Your comparison may be too optimistic."

"Then what comparison would you offer?" inquired Challenger.

"I defer answering that until I am more certain," said Holmes. He smiled inwardly. He saw no point in risking Challenger's wrath by implying that Challenger might, by comparison to the Martians, be an animal inferior in both physical and mental development.

Challenger returned to his study of the scene. "The smallest and most agile of their machines seem to be unpiloted," he said. "I would suspect that they are intelligent mechanisms, possessed of their own powers to act."

"Some of them may well be of that class," agreed Holmes. "Yet they may be operated, at a distance, by thought processes of their operators."

The scene in the crystal faded as they talked, then reappeared, with no mechanisms visible. The bulbous, tentacled beings moved here and there on roof or lawn, walking on their handlike tufts of tentacles or assuming wings and flying above the roofs. Several of the flyers observed the glittering points on the masts or soared away out of sight, on missions difficult to guess. Challenger talked more than Holmes. His manner was that of a classroom lecturer, expounding propositions to students who must pass examinations on the subject. At last he shifted the crystal very painstakingly, to get a view well to one side. He almost shouted in excitement.

"Mars is a planet with only the smallest amount of water to be detected on its surface," he burst out, almost as though Holmes had suggested the contrary. "Of course, there has been all the idle talk about canals, ever since 1877. The notion sprang up because Schiaparelli professed to have seen *canali* – he employed his native Italian. The word means simply channels. But various arbitrary fools, presuming to encroach on the outer fringes of scientific thought, have mistranslated and babble about 'canal', as though they were true waterways."

"Yet there may be some truth in their mistranslation," said Holmes. "A canal, I take it, is an artificial engineering device. And just what sort of waterway is the one we now see in the crystal?"

For a stream was visible, at a point in the plain well to the left of the buildings. A curious bridge spanned it.

"I wonder about it," Challenger admitted. "Perhaps it is an artificial canal, as you seem to suggest. But it could never have been seen by even the most powerful telescope on Earth, and can hardly be related to Schiaparelli's purported discoveries."

Holmes frowned. "Yet what we are seeing may well relate to the strange disturbances, possibly signs of gigantic construction, which were detected on Mars at the opposition of 1894."

"I paid little attention to that," Challenger confessed in a tone of embarrassment. "My attention was occupied with an impudent challenge to my theory of – well, no matter for that."

"If 1894 was a year of construction activity upon Mars, may that not have been the time that our crystal was somehow sent to Earth?" said Holmes.

"An interesting theory," said Challenger, "but, as such, best kept within limits."

"True," said Holmes. "Theorising, in my experience, is dangerously apt to limit the progress of logical deduction. It should be used sparingly, like poetry in a scientific discussion."

He drew his head from under the black cloth and quickly made notes on his pad. "Discourse further, Challenger. Your scientific learning and comprehension are utterly without peer and almost without rival."

"Almost?" grumbled Challenger, but the compliment pleased him. He, too, emerged from under the cloth, smiling fearsomely in his beard.

"Astronomy has not been one of my principal preoccupations," he began to lecture again, "yet I have always tried to notice the findings and conclusions of those who make it a specialty. Mars is a red planet, blotched here and there with greenish areas and capped at its poles with expanses of white that have the look of ice or frost. The green areas, argue some, are vegetation, perhaps of a primitive sort like moss or lichen. Here, at hand," and he cradled the crystal in his fingers. "we have some vindication of that argument. But no water has been detected by the most powerful telescope, and the atmosphere is thin – perhaps as thin as that to be found at the summits of Earth's highest mountains. And the spectroscope reveals only the very smallest proportion of oxygen in that atmosphere, though it stands to reason that oxygen must exist in water and water vapour."

All this he uttered in his characteristic tone of high authority.

"Man, of course, could never survive under such conditions," Holmes offered.

"No," said Challenger, shaking his head emphatically. "On the basis of that oxygen-poor atmosphere, it has often been asserted that life upon Mars is an impossibility. But you and I, Holmes, know better."

"The argument should say, life as we know it upon Earth. What we have seen is life of a very different sort indeed. But as to the redness of the planet's surface, our crystal agrees with our astronomers' findings on this point. Why, do you think, is it so rusty red?"

"I can be only speculative and hazard the conjecture that it is a soil similar to clay."

"Clay," repeated Holmes weightily. "I have given some time to studying various soils. In several instances I have solved crimes by taking note of dust or sand of distinctive sorts on clothing or shoes. Clay, says the old textbook, is of hydrated silicates of aluminum and can become plastic when wet and can be made into bricks, tiles, and pottery. Redness in its colour indicates the presence of oxidised materials."

"What you say is true, if somewhat banal," said Challenger in a tone of lofty concession. "And where are you trying to lead us?"

Holmes leaned back in his chair and placed his fingertips together, his habitual pose when deep in a problem.

"It could well be that the soil of Mars has absorbed, over many ages, the oxygen that was once fairly rich in the atmosphere."

"Hum!" Challenger grunted. "That possibility has occurred to others before you. I do not perceive its relevance here."

"If a mineral deposit contains oxygen, a proper chemical action could release the oxygen again."

"By heaven, Holmes, I begin to see the direction of your reasoning." Challenger's teeth glinted in a smile. "Your association with me is a profit to your mental processes, my dear fellow. The buildings that we see in the crystal make up a group of considerable dimensions. They could house intricate mechanical and chemical equipment, and these creatures dwelling there might be able to produce a localized atmosphere that is breathable and can support them."

"Something keeps them alive, even if my specific suggestion here is at fault."

Challenger reached out and took Holmes' hand to shake it. "My congratulations. You are a colleague worthy of George Edward Challenger. Much more so in fact, than a number of professional scientists I could name."

"I will try to merit that high endorsement," said Holmes, bowing. "In order that I may do so, let us return to our studies."

Again they draped their heads with the cloth, and for some time they pored over the crystal in attentive silence. Challenger turned it this way and that, finally bringing it into position for a line of vision commanding the row of masts.

"Here we see those points of light at the respective apexes," he said. "Now one of the Martians, equipped with wings, is approaching to study, even as we do. But he is at another mast than the one from which we see. Again I feel more or less assured that each of those masts is furnished with a crystal similar to ours and so empowered as to provide a view of some faraway place."

"Perhaps also on Earth?" Holmes wondered. "As this crystal we have can communicate with their crystal on the farthest mast in the rank, might there be other crystals also projected across space, also communicating?"

Lines of thought deepened on Challenger's massive brow. "It may well be so. The speculation begets others. Among them, the question of how this crystal, and perhaps similar ones, made the journey to Earth."

He flung back the drapery and gazed at the gleaming crystal egg, turning it over and over.

"Its construction and operation seem to have no analogy with anything in our own civilisation," he said slowly. "The transmitted power may well be electrical, but that is merely a guess, not worth our discussion at present. Now, if they sent it to Earth in 1894, as you have suggested, they have been watching us for seven years. How much can they have learned about us in that time?"

"A considerable amount, I would hazard," said Holmes. "Far more than we might deduce about them in a comparable period."

"And what do they make of us?"

"That would be interesting to know," said Holmes. "But you and I agree that they may well be planning an expedition here to Earth. The concept of interplantary travel is not a new one. It has been a subject of imaginative tales for centuries. Now you and I face it as a reality; thus far, only you and I."

Challenger fondled the crystal, his beard jutting above it.

"Fate did well to put this problem into my hands," he said. "Aided a trifle by yourself."

"Perhaps it was not fate, but the Martians themselves, who put this into our hands," said Holmes soberly. "What if they guided it into our possession to see how our rational minds would react to it? They might realise that men like you and me have unusual mental ability, and so arranged that it would come into our possession instead of that of a fool and a philistine."

Challenger glanced sharply at Holmes. "You yourself are beginning to romanticise. Just why did you buy it?"

"I decided, on the spur of the moment, that it might make a suitable Christmas present for my landlady. However, she has not seen or heard of it as yet."

"Which is for the best," said Challenger, "You will, of course, make her a suitable gift of some other sort."

"Of course," said Holmes.

Five

L ate in the afternoon of the last day of January, Holmes sat playing softly on his violin. A timid knock sounded at the door. Holmes rose and opened it to a slight, black-haired young man who took off his hat and fumbled with it timidly.

"Is Dr Watson at home?" he asked.

"He's gone to a meeting of medical colleagues," said Holmes. "If you care to leave a message, I will be glad to give it to him."

"Are you Mr Sherlock Holmes, then? I came looking for Dr Watson – I have the honour of some slight acquaintance with him – to ask him to introduce me to you. My name is Jacoby Wace; I am assistant demonstrator at St Catherine's Hospital in Westbourne Street." The young man shifted his feet on the rug. "I scarcely know how to begin."

"Begin by sitting down and explaining."

Wace dropped into a chair and nervously related his story. He had known Cave the antiques dealer, and had often studied the crystal with him. To Cave, more than to Wace, the crystal had shown its secrets – Wace said that Cave had fairly clear impressions of the extraordinary scenes reflected within its depths. And Wace had been almost crushed when he found that, upon Cave's death, the crystal had gone with other objects from the dead man's shop to that of Templeton and there had been sold to someone whose name Templeton said he had forgotten.

"I put advertisements in several collectors' papers," said Wace. "There has been no response whatever. But I am convinced that a great scientific truth can be yielded by that crystal, and I appeal to you to help me trace it."

Wace's manner was becomingly diffident, Holmes reflected. It would flatter Challenger. The thought gave him an inspiration.

"Suppose we consult a scientist of distinguished reputation and accomplishment, Mr Wace," he said. "Just a moment while I telephone."

He rang the Enmore Park number. Challenger's booming voice answered.

"Holmes here, Challenger. I have just been talking to a new client by the name of Jacoby Wace, whose difficulty had best be presented to yourself – for reasons which will quickly be apparent," said Holmes guardedly. "May I fetch him over?"

"Does this have any bearing on the crystal?" asked Challenger, his voice falling to a guarded hush.

"Yes," said Holmes briefly.

"Then bring him here immediately."

When Holmes and Wace arrived, they found the professor bulking behind his table. The crystal was nowhere in sight.

"You may be seated, Mr Wace," granted Challenger. "Now, explain this difficulty of yours."

With stammering uneasiness, Wace again described his acquaintance with Cave, his own rather blurred observations of the crystal, and his agony of disappointment at its loss. Challenger heard him out, occasionally jotting down a note.

"And to whom besides ourselves have you spoken of this?" he inquired when Wace had made an end.

"I talked about it to Mr Templeton, the dealer," said Wace, "and I heard that the matter will soon receive some publicity. Templeton said that Mr H. G. Wells, the distinguished author, is now preparing a magazine article on the subject. Both Templeton and another dealer, Mr Morse Hudson, have given him information."

"Hudson?" repeated Holmes. "I have some slight acquaintance with Hudson. I'll be interested in reading the article when it appears."

"I, too," nodded Challenger. "Wells has some rather sketchy scientific background, along with a bizarre imagination. Now, Mr Wace, have you made any efforts to trace the crystal besides inquiries to the collectors' magazines?"

"I wrote letters to the *Times* and the *Daily Chronicle*. Both were returned to me, with suggestions that I was trying to perpetrate a hoax. Indeed, the editor of the *Chronicle* advised me to drop the matter, saying that publishing such material might well damage my career at St Catherine's."

"A typical journalistic judgement," pronounced Challenger. "Yet, to some degree, I agree with the editor's advice. You will do well, Mr Wace, to be prudently quiet about the whole affair, leaving it in the capable hands of my friend Mr Holmes. Will you give us your promise to that effect?"

"Yes, sir," agreed Wace at once. "Thank you, Professor Challenger."

He took his departure. Challenger saw him to the front door and returned, to fix Holmes with earnest blue eyes.

"There you have exactly the response we could expect should we try to interest the press or the scientific faculty in our researches at this point," he rumbled. "Disbelief and ridicule."

"Yet apparently one popular magazine is taking an interest," said Holmes. "I look forward to reading Wells' article, if only to see how honest Hudson and Templeton have been with their information. And reflect, Wace did not have the crystal to show to skeptics, an advantage which we possess."

"There is more than that to our policy of secrecy," said Challenger. "We are agreed that this crystal embodies a means of communication with another planet. If we were to share it with other scientists, what clumsy efforts would they make to establish a rapport? No, Holmes, I would never trust so gravely important a problem to limited mentalities, dulled with years in classrooms and museums. The achievement of articulate exchange with these creatures on Mars must be referred to the only mind on Earth with the requisite intelligence and method – aided in certain ways, of course, by yourself."

But in the months that followed, most of the observations, as well as earnest efforts to evoke a response to signals, fell to Challenger alone. Holmes found his time occupied with a series of criminal investigations.

Inspector Merivale of Scotland Yard asked for his help that March. The police had discovered a widespread circulation of forged crowns and half-crowns, and the man suspected of coining them persuasively denied the charge. He was a respectable shopkeeper in Seven Dials, that man insisted, with no blot upon his reputation. He added that he knew his legal rights, would demonstrate that he had been falsely accused, and would instruct his solicitors to lay action for damage to his character. Holmes managed to obtain some of the accused man's clothing for study, and from the fold of a cuff recovered tiny particles which, under the microscope, proved to be filings of zinc and copper. Confronted by this discovery, the man broke down and confessed.

Officials in high places praised Holmes' method of uncovering this evidence. He thanked them modestly and telephoned Challenger. But Challenger was unwontedly cryptic. "Please wait until you hear from me," he said. "For the present, I want to work entirely alone."

Again, late in April, Holmes was asked to help in another seemingly baffling investigation. A policeman had been murdered in the St Pancras area, and his fellows fiercely yearned to find and punish the killer. The only clue was a cloth cap found near the body, and again a suspect was brought in, a maker of picture frames. But, like the coiner, he steadfastly denied the crime, saying that he did not own the cap and knew nothing of the murder.

The cap was brought to Holmes on Monday, May 5, about the time the mail included a letter from one James Mason. This man was a trainer of racehorses at the ancient manor of Shoscombe Old Place, and he wrote rather guardedly to say that he would come to discuss with Holmes a matter of great importance. Holmes was up betimes on the following day, ate breakfast quickly, and sat down to transfer certain particles retrieved from the lining of the mysterious cap to a microscope slide. Adjusting this in his instrument, he began to make his examination. He could detect tiny fibres, evidently of tweed, and it was known that the suspect habitually wore a coat of that material. There were also small brown blobs, puzzling at first. Becoming fatigued, he left the microscope and sat in his easy chair. He selected a smooth Havana cigar and opened a book. Watson entered and began to eat his own breakfast.

"Extraordinary," said Holmes after he had been reading for several minutes. "My conversational French is no more than passable, yet reading in French is much easier than speaking or writing it."

"What is your book?" asked Watson, stirring sugar into his coffee.

"A collection of the writings of Guy de Maupassant. The section I am reading is a chronicle – it is almost like non-fiction – in the form of diary entries."

Watson's mouth drew thin under his moustache. "Maupassant was a man of dissipated life," he remarked austerely. "I have always thought that he preached immorality in his stories."

"I fear I must disagree with you," said Holmes. "Maupassant, as I think, has always striven for objectivity. In any case, much of what we consider immoral is merely pathological. Oscar Wilde, for instance, was imprisoned under our English laws for a morbid aberration. He would have been shown more mercy in France."

"But what is this particular chronicle you are reading?" asked Watson.

"It is entitled 'Le Horla,' fully laying bare the soul of the diarist. It tells how he came under the power of some unknown, invisible being. Apparently the power departed, for the writer in the last entry is threatening suicide in despair, yet there is no evidence that the threat was carried out."

Watson bit into a buttered crumpet. "Maupassant died a hopeless madman. I've read that Horla story you mention. It struck me as complete proof that he was losing his mind as he wrote it."

"No, Watson, it is too well organised for that. Even if we choose to read the story as fiction, as a highly imaginative tale, I must argue that only a clear, sane mind could have conceived it so artistically, written it so vividly. Here, let me read you an entry in this diary, under date of August 17 – the year 1886, I deduce. Forgive my offhand, amateurish translation."

His eyes on the page, he read aloud:

"No moon. The stars in the depths of the dark heavens darted their rays. Who inhabits those worlds? What forms, what living creatures, what animals, what beings are out there? Those who think in those distant worlds, what do they know more than we? What can they do more than we? What do they see that we do not understand? Will one of them, some day or other, traverse space, will it not appear on our Earth to subjugate it, as the Norsemen crossed the seas to enslave feebler peoples?" Holmes looked up from the book. "Confess, Watson, is that not a fairly sane and rational proposition?"

"If it is fiction, I consider it high-flown, fanciful writing," said Watson stubbornly. "I remember, incidentally, that the diarist burns his house at the end of the account. Wasn't Maupassant's house burned?"

"It was burned, as a matter of fact, but Maupassant never admitted to setting the fire, unless in this account," said Holmes. "If he is confessing that act, we may take the whole as offered for fact."

"Suppose it is factual and sane," said Watson. "If beings such as the Horla did actually exist, do you think that you could be subjugated by one of them, like Maupassant or his fictional diarist?"

"Perhaps not," said Holmes. "A man of sufficient intellect and will might resist such subjugation, or find a way of defeating it."

Holmes marked his place with a pipe cleaner and set the book aside. Returning to the microscope, he resumed his examination of the slide.

"It is glue, Watson," he cried triumphantly. "Unquestionably it is glue. Have a look at these scattered objects in the field."

Watson came to adjust the eyepiece and gaze through it while Holmes explained about the cap picked up beside the dead policeman and pointed out visible factors of the brown blobs. "The accused man denies that the cap is his," he said. "But he is a picture-frame maker who habitually uses glue."

The question resolved, he poured another cup of coffee and turned the conversation to horse racing. Watson, a devotee of the turf, was able to inform him of the racing stables at Shoscombe Old Place and of the Shoscombe kennels where prize spaniels were bred. In the midst of their talk, Billy knocked to announce John Mason, a tall, clean-shaven man of intensely worried manner. He pleaded that Holmes come and discover, if possible, the reason for mysterious happenings at Shoscombe Old Place and in particular the enigma of the strange behavior of Sir Robert Norberton, the proprietor. Holmes agreed to take the case and found Watson eager to accompany him. Before noon they boarded a train for Shoscombe, carrying fishing tackle to simulate carefree anglers on holiday.

A day and a half sufficed to expose a melancholy story, involving the death of Sir Robert's sister and his effort to conceal the corpse. The big, blustering sportsman made trembling explanations and pleaded for sympathy. Coldly, Holmes said that he must inform police authorities, but that he would recommend compassion. Watson took pleasure in the assurance that Sir Robert's splendid colt, Shoscombe Prince, would run in the Derby on May 21, and as he and Holmes journeyed back to London he vowed he would be present at the race to venture a considerable sum on Shoscombe Prince to win.

That night, as Holmes sat alone in his quarters, Martha came in.

"You are alone, dear?" she whispered.

"Watson is visiting his old friend Stamford."

She sat down opposite him. Her rosy face looked earnest.

"My dear, I know that something is weighing on your spirit. Is it some case you are investigating?"

"A most unusual case, Martha. How well you diagnose my behaviour."

"It is only that I have never seen you so wrapped up in a thing, to the exclusion of all else. Of course, I never ask you to confide in me–"

"And that, my love, is one of your thousand or so charms. Let me say that the present case concerns happenings at a great distance."

He tried to sound light and cheerful, but her eyes widened, as usual when she felt worried.

"I have never interfered with your work," she said. "But let me ask, will this investigation make you go travelling far away?"

He shook his head, smiling. "No, I venture to predict that I can conduct all possible observations here in London. Travelling far enough to be away from you is always unhappiness to me."

"And to me." She put out a hand to take his. "You have never said it so strongly before. My dearest, they say that as people grow older their love cools, but ours remains constant and warm."

"It will always remain so," Holmes assured her. "And we are not old, we are in our prime. I am forty–eight – a trifle older than you, several years younger than Watson – but the good Watson avers that many an agile and athletic man of forty is slower and more breathless than I am."

"You respect Dr Watson's medical judgement."

"I do, of course."

He rose, and so did she. They kissed warmly.

"And now," said Holmes, "let me say that last week I was able to find a bottle of Beaune, of an excellent year, across the street at Dolamore's. Suppose we have a glass together, and I promise to forget for a while this curious problem on which I am working."

Six

For the next several days, Holmes was busy talking to officers at Scotland Yard and to Sir Robert Norberton's creditors and solicitors. All of these listened to Holmes' sober suggestion that compassion be shown to the desperate sportsman, whose fine colt was bound to run well in the Derby and bring his master money enough to settle a vast indebtedness. On such terms the case was settled, and on the evening of May 10 Holmes was grateful to find himself with no pressing duty. He sat in his easy chair while Watson scribbled away at the desk.

"Another of your flattering accounts of my cases?" asked Holmes.

"Only notes, to add to my files for the Shoscombe Old Place matter, and something on a professional event," said Watson. "I have been asked to conduct a seminar on tropical diseases at London University."

"Which you will do well, I am sure." Holmes reached for the Maupassant volume, but instead picked up a current magazine and leafed through it. His eye was caught by the title at the top of a page 'The Crystal Egg'. He began to read with deep interest:

There was, until a year ago, a little and very grimy-looking shop near Seven Dials, over which, in weather-worn lettering, the name of 'C. Cave, Naturalist and Dealer in Antiquities', was inscribed...

"More recently than a year ago, I should think," mused Holmes aloud.

"What did you say?" asked Watson, looking up.

"I had begun to read a story by Mr H.G. Wells."

"Wells," repeated Watson, with something like asperity. "A sensation-mongering hack, suspiciously revolutionary in his notions."

Holmes smiled. "You dislike him as you dislike Maupassant."

"Not in the same way." Watson shook his head emphatically. "Maupassant, I told you, is objectionable because of his deplorable private life. Wells I dislike for his manifest disapproval of our civilisation and our government. Of his private life I know nothing. Perhaps it is best not to inquire into it."

"Not inquire?" repeated Holmes, smiling more broadly. "A man in my profession does not hear such things happily. But I won't interrupt you again."

Watson resumed his writing. Holmes read 'The Crystal Egg' through. It seemed offered as fiction, but the names of Cave and Wace appeared in it, and there was mention of "a tall dark man in grey" who had vanished with the crystal. Plainly neither Templeton nor Hudson had dared identify Holmes when questioned.

Holmes pondered the matter, then and on days to follow. He hesitated to interrupt Challenger with further questions. The study of the crystal egg might have advanced as far as possible, unless the Martians could be induced to give and receive signals. And Challenger had seemed irritated when Holmes had suggested that to view the Martians only as of a more advanced culture, comparable to that of terrestrial humanity as a

European city might compare to a savage community, was too optimistic. Increasingly Holmes felt that mankind was a race of creatures much lower in evolution than the Martians.

The problem was unpleasantly perplexing. He made no progress in solving it alone. On May 13 he sat moodily at breakfast while Watson read a newspaper opposite. Suddenly Watson leaned across the table.

"What do you make of this, Holmes?" he asked, pointing to the page.

The headline read: STRANGE ERUPTION OF MARS, and underneath:

> An observatory in Java reports that a sudden eruption of glowing gas was seen on the planet Mars at about midnight. Dr Lavelle, who compares the phenomenon to "flaming gases rushing out of a gun", reports that the spectrograph showed it to be a mass of superheated hydrogen, moving toward Earth with tremendous speed. The light became invisible in about fifteen minutes.

"Singular," said Holmes, with strained calm.

"So I thought. But excuse me, I must not be late at my seminar."

Watson departed. Holmes telephoned Challenger.

"I was on the point of putting in a call for you," came back Challenger's great voice. "Can you come here? I have summoned Stent, the Astronomer Royal. I think it is time that we acquainted the world with what we have discovered."

Holmes caught up his hat and strode into the hall. Martha met him there. "You are disturbed about something," she said.

"No, my dear, I am only in a hurry. I shall be back for lunch with you."

Outside, he took a hansom for Enmore Park. Mrs Challenger herself opened to him.

"I hope you can calm George," she said tremulously. "He's in a furious mood—a quarrel with a visitor, I don't know why."

Holmes entered the study. Challenger stood there, bearded face scowling. He tramped and swayed like an angry elephant.

"Stent!" he snapped out. "How such an imbecile was named Astronomer Royal is beyond even my comprehension. Some political chicanery, I would not be amazed to find out. His refusal to accept my word—"

"Was Stent here?" asked Holmes. "I deduce that he was, from what you are saying."

"I had telephoned him before you and I spoke together. That ejection of gas on Mars impelled me to do so. I told him that I had information of a nature that would astonish the world, or at any rate that part of the world capable of grasping its implications. He came, and then—" Here Challenger drew up his shoulders seeming to spread them like the hood of a cobra. "I showed him the crystal — our crystal, my dear fellow — and what do you suppose that insufferable as said of it?"

"I am eager to be told," said Holmes.

"He accused me of mechanical trickery, mentioned the names of stage conjurors like Alexander Hermann, Robert Houdin, this new fellow Kellar." Challenger's mighty hands opened and shut convulsively. "He smiled and thanked me for what he called an amusing experiment in misdirection. He spoke of raree-shows and magic lanterns, and when I protested, he left, he fairly ran out of the house. It was a highly undignified exhibition, but only to be expected of such a subhuman intellect, such an insolent, spiteful, jealous nature."

"You protested, you say."

"Naturally. I rose to my feet to do so."

"And did you threaten violence?" suggested Holmes.

"I may have conveyed some impression." Again the mighty shoulders heaved. "All this confirms my earlier assurance that no scientific pedant can be entrusted with our secret."

Holmes walked to the table. The crystal egg lay there, softly glowing.

"It is hard to understand how he could look on that landscape and not be impressed," he said.

"He did not see the landscape. There was another view, entirely different. It seems to be some sort of interior chamber. But see for yourself."

They sat down and covered their heads with the black cloth. Challenger took up the crystal, turning it carefully. "Now you may verify what I told you."

The luminous haze cleared. Holmes saw a dimly lighted enclosure of sorts, its contents showing faintly among shadows. There was a girdered bulkhead, against which were ranged complicated mechanical assemblies. One or two reminded him of things in previous viewings. On the decklike floor sprawled several Martians. Glad for this view, the closest view of them that he had ever had, he studied them thoughtfully. Their silent, bladdery bodies were brownish-grey and shone like wet leather.

"Observe that dampness of their bodies," said Holmes.

"I suppose it to be perspiration," said Challenger.

"Perhaps, but I wonder if it is some excretory secretion from the skin. These Martians differ enormously from us in physical structure. Their entire digestive and excretory functions may be utterly alien to our experience."

The Martians lay utterly motionless, but their eyes seemed fixed and brilliant. Holmes wondered if they ever slept at all. The two sprays of tentacles of one of them lay upon an intricate mechanism, some sort of keyboard.

"Their communication device, the one formerly on the tall mast, has been moved," Holmes suggested.

"Obviously," said Challenger.

"We see a compartment, perhaps inside a vehicle of some sort."

"Exactly," Challenger's head wagged under the cloth. "Holmes, they are in a travelling ship or car, heading toward Earth, and they have taken their own crystal to guide them. You have not told me your conclusions as yet."

"Have you a theory?"

"One I am not ready to divulge, even to you; but the clear fact is that they are travelling across space to us."

He emerged into the light. "I would have thought this fact evident to the dimmest rationality, but I never counted on a rationality so dim as that of Stent."

Holmes, too, threw off the drape and rose. "He might have been convinced had he seen the landscape we saw. This drab interior, with no motion or sign of life, is less convincing. Did you explain to him?"

Challenger's chair creaked as he leaned back. "There was no time. We spoke warmly to each other. Had I not remembered my reputation for dignity and restraint, I might have thrown him bodily into the street."

"But what is the purpose of this Martian expedition?" said Holmes.

"Two possibilities occur to me. Remembering that they regard us as civilised Europeans regard the most primitive savages, we can surmise that either they propose to civilise and benefit us, or conquer and exploit us. In my judgement, either program will amount to almost the same plight for humanity."

"I will tell you a theory of mine at some appropriate time. But as of now, I incline to your suggestion of hostility. How can the world be alerted?"

"Impossible," boomed Challenger. "My experience with Stent proves it is impossible."

"Surely others might prove more reasonable."

Challenger rose ponderously and paced the floor. "My dear Holmes, let me tell you a doleful truth about so-called scientific authorities, proven through the ages. They cling to ancient theories and disdain new truths. Galileo was forced, under threat of terrible punishment, to deny the heliocentric system of astronomy. Darwin's theory of evolution was attacked as a tissue of blasphemies. Pasteur, when he demonstrated that disease was caused by germs, was laughed to scorn for years. And I—" He flung out his arms, as though to sweep his three rivals away. "I suffer the same fate as those other pioneers, I must meekly bear the ridicule of mental Lilliputians like Stent, the Astronomer Royal!"

"We might call in Watson," offered Holmes. "He is better acquainted than I with scientists. He might suggest someone more receptive."

"Not as yet," said Challenger suddenly. "Stent's reaction is but a sample of what reception we would get."

"The Martians are on the way," said Holmes. "With them comes vindication."

"And we must hope that their intentions are peaceable. Then they will seek to communicate with us. And who has the intellect, the method, to establish that communication?"

"You want me to nominate you?" asked Holmes.

"Modesty forbids me to suggest it, but I accept."

"The nomination is not forthcoming as yet," said Holmes. "I do not insult you, my dear Challenger, when I say that I doubt the possibility of any communication."

"We shall soon know. Leave all in my hands, and wait for me to notify you of any new developments. Agreed?"

"Agreed," said Holmes.

That midnight, astronomers saw another fiery flash on Mars. Next midnight another, and the next. Holmes visited Challenger again. The crystal revealed only the girdered chamber. But as they peered into it, the face of a Martian drew close and looked steadily, as though meeting their own gaze.

"It must want to tell us something," suggested Holmes.

"Tell us what?" demanded Challenger. "Have you a theory?"

"Call it rather a fancy. What if I acted under some sort of direction in buying the crystal and giving it to you for joint scrutiny? What if this

Martian is trying to say that? Perhaps thought waves come through the crystal; perhaps they came to me in the shop."

The Martian drew away.

"His face was expressionless, at least to us," said Holmes, "but at last interest was shown in our reactions."

"If they do have mental contact with us, they must gather that my intellect is unique on this planet," said Challenger gravely. "Your own is, of course, sufficiently exceptional to be worth their recognition. I must profoundly regret that Professor Moriarty – the one adversary worthy of you in all your deductive career – is not here to observe with us."

The crystal went dim. They sat back in their chairs. "We can only wait for them to arrive," said Challenger.

Each midnight thereafter, precisely at twenty-four hour intervals, new flashes were reported by observatories throughout Europe. The newspapers reported various speculations about volcanic explosions on Mars, impacts of meteors, once a suggestion that Martians sought to signal Earth. Watson was interested, but set aside his astronomical surmises to journey to the Derby at Epsom on May 21, there to wager heavily on Shoscombe Prince and applaud loudly as his choice came home a winner. He stayed away that night and the next, May 22, on which morning the press reported the tenth flash from Mars.

After that, no more explosions. Challenger telephoned several times to say that the crystal gave no new information. "We can only wait for our visitors to arrive," he said curtly.

The first of June brought a minor case for Holmes to study. He successfully concluded it by Thursday, June 5. Next morning he wakened early, to find Watson packing a bag.

"I must go at once, Holmes," he said, putting on his hat. "Poor Murray – my faithful servant, who saved my life in Afghanistan – is critically ill, up at his lodgings in Highgate. I have promised to go and care for him."

He hurried out. Holmes was at breakfast when Billy brought in a telegram. It was from Sir Percy Phelps of the Foreign Office:

HUGE CYLINDRICAL PROJECTILE FELL NEAR WOKING THIS MORNING SCIENTISTS REPORT LIVING CREATURES INSIDE COME WITH ME THIS EVENING YOUR HELP NEEDED

Holmes, too, went out hastily, straight to Enmore Park. Mrs Challenger met him at the door.

"George has gone to Woking," she said. "A number of scientists are gathering there. Do you know what it is about, Mr Holmes?"

"I am going there myself," said Holmes

Back at the flat, he found Martha waiting for him with the door open. She ran to his arms.

"Has Sir Percy Phelps called?" he asked.

"He was here and said he wanted you to take dinner with him at Simpson's. Sherlock dear, please don't go with him into danger."

"It's my duty to go Martha," he said, patting her shoulder. "The government wants me there."

"It may be dangerous," she said. "Take care of yourself, my love. Don't be reckless. Only think how lost, how alone, I would be without you."

"I never forget that," said Holmes. "And I shan't forget it now."

He spent the afternoon arranging some papers and meeting with several scientific writers. These talked eagerly about the cylinder at Woking and offered a variety of glib theories. He met Phelps at Simpson's for an early dinner, and at six o'clock they boarded their train at Waterloo Holmes was silent and thoughtful, Phelps happily excited.

"Men from Mars!" he cried. "How shall we greet them, Holmes?"

"I suggest we wait and see how they greet us," answered Holmes darkly.

II

❧

SHERLOCK HOLMES VERSUS MARS
BY EDWARD DUNN MALONE

Seven

B y evening of that warm, bright Friday in June, throngs had moved out upon Horsell Common, the heathered expanse that divided the pretty suburban town of Woking from the neighbouring hamlets of Horsell and Ottershaw. Almost midway between Woking and Horsell on the Basingstoke Canal some three miles to northwest, near the road through both towns and to Chobham beyond Horsell, a great craterlike pit opened.

That was where the mighty cylinder had fallen from the sky and had unscrewed its top to reveal bizarre passengers. It was like a place where an explosion had happened, with upthrown banks of turf and gravel ringing the hole many yards across. The first sight of the creatures emerging had somewhat daunted a flow of curious people from Woking and from Horsell in the opposite direction, so that they milled around at a considerable distance. But their curiosity was roused anew by a mirrorlike disk that was pushed upward on a rod to turn shakily.

"I wonder if they can watch us with that," said someone.

On the evening train from Waterloo Station in London had arrived Sir Percy Phelps and a tall stranger in grey. Now they, too, came out from Woking to mingle with the crowd of onlookers. Several acquaintances greeted Sir Percy and gazed curiously at his companion.

"I suggest that we do not approach the pit at once," said the tall man to Sir Percy. "Here, we can see well from behind this sandy rise and make deductions."

Sir Percy stood with him in a depression on the far side of a heather-tufted knoll. A nearby bicyclist joined them and told of seeing the creatures of the cylinder.

"Like an octopus," he described them.

"No, more like a big spider," suggested another man a dozen feet away.

The tall stranger wrote on a note pad. Ogilvy, from the nearby college observatory, came to speak to Sir Percy, who introduced his guest.

"Has Professor George E. Challenger been here?" asked the tall one. "His wife said he had come. A short, heavily built man with a black beard."

"Yes, he was here," said Ogilvy. "It was my first acquaintance with him, and I shan't care if it turns out to be the last."

"Why do you say that?" asked Sir Percy.

"He began by saying he had seen these visitors on Mars, and he added that they might not be Martians at all."

"Indeed?" Sir Percy looked blank. "What, then?"

"I fear we never got to anything like sane, considered discussion. Stent, the Astronomer Royal – there he is, yonder with Henderson, the journalist – said something appropriate, about not offering mere conjectures and imagined evidence."

"And Challenger?" prompted the tall man, smiling slightly. "What was his reaction?"

"I cannot exactly quote his unrestrained invective," said Ogilvy, shaking his head. "He talked as though Stent were an impertinent schoolboy, bade him to go to the devil, and went walking away somewhere. I'm glad he's gone. But you, gentlemen, will you join our deputation to communicate with these Martian visitors?"

"A deputation, eh?" repeated Sir Percy. "Why, as to that, since I'm from the Foreign Office, I suppose that I should–"

"You are from the Foreign Office, and that is an excellent reason for you to stay apart for the time being," broke in his companion. "Reflect, Sir Percy, scientists may confer with those creatures if it is possible, which I do not wholly admit. But you are with the British Government and I am but a private citizen. Thank you for your flattering invitation, Mr Ogilvy, but we will stay where we are just now."

Ogilvy left them. At a distance he conferred with Stent, a tall fair man with a rosy face. They moved away, followed by several others. On the far side of the pit, toward Horsell, the deputation formed itself. Stent and Ogilvy took position at its head. Close behind them, the journalist Henderson carried a white flag on a pole.

"That was a wise thought," commented Phelps from behind the mound. "The Martians will know that we offer them peaceful welcome."

"I take leave to wonder about that," said the other gravely. "All these descriptions, though sketchy enough, suggest a race of beings vastly different from ourselves. A white flag may mean nothing at all to them, or it may mean the exact opposite of what it means to us. And creatures who can travel across space may not regard us and our overtures with any particular respect or deference."

The deputation walked closer to the pit, and closer. The more distant watchers all around stood in silent expectation.

Then something seemed to stir in the pit beneath the mirror, something dark and dome-shaped. It hunched upward into plainer sight. Upon it rode some sort of superstructure, brassy brown and shaped like a hood. This object swiveled around as though to face the approaching group. Henderson lifted his flag above his head and dipped it to left, then to right.

Something else came into view. It was a metal arm, seemingly jointed, that bore at its upper end a strange housing, smaller than the hooded superstructure. This, too, shifted position as though to face and observe Stent's party.

"Perhaps—" Sir Percy began.

He got no further. There was a spurt of green vapour from below, a momentary, blinding flash of light. A wail droned in the evening air, and the men of the deputation seemed to burst into flame, all at once. They staggered and writhed, then fell this way and that, motionless and cinder-black.

The hood turned from them, and so did the arm with the ray-throwing instrument. Another flash, rather than a visible beam, swept through the groups of on-lookers in the direction of Horsell, ignited a tuft of trees beyond them, and jumped to more distant houses at the edge of the great open common. Flames burst out everywhere that it touched.

Sir Percy Phelps cried out wordlessly and turned as though to run. His companion shot out a lean arm, caught his shoulder and dragged him powerfully down behind the sandy rise, himself falling flat as he did so. The flash was passing over them, and the wail of sound rose again in the evening air. Others in the groups nearby, less fortunate or less quick, burst into incandescence like grotesque fireworks and went slamming down upon the turf. The flash abruptly died away. The two prone men behind the rise glanced upward. The first stars had begun to wink into view in the darkening sky.

Elsewhere on Horsell Common rose quavering screams of terror. The tall stranger raised himself on his hands until he could peer over the low ridge toward the pit. The dome-like contrivance still hunched there, with the mirror on its slender rod above it. All across the open space people were running, except for those who could run no more. Heather and clumps of furze burned smokily, and trees were aflame. Two miles away to the northwest, the roofs of Horsell blazed redly against the evening sky. He dropped quickly flat again.

"Move away, but keep low," he said to Phelps. "See here, there's a dip in the ground just behind us, toward town. That's our line of retreat, but keep out of sight. Never give them a chance at you."

Crouching so low that they almost crept on all fours, the two made their way into a shallow saucerlike depression, fully a hundred yards across. The strange fire-weapon had not kindled the turf here. Sir Percy trembled, but came along at his companion's touch until they were able to slide behind some bushy trees, burning and crackling but affording a screen. Keeping that mask between them and the thing in the pit, they gained the Chobham Road, rose and ran along it, and so into Woking.

Trees and houses at the edge of town had also been stricken by fire. Along the street beyond these, people huddled at windows or peered in terror from doors. Nobody seemed to move in the streets except the two who now made their way toward Briarbrae, Sir Percy's beautiful home. They entered at the door and came into the study, where they conferred; Sir Percy still shaken, his companion earnest but calm.

Sir Percy scribbled a telegram and sent a servant running with it to wire to London, then dashed off others and sent a second man with those. At last he held out a shaking hand to his guest.

"I haven't had time to say thank you," he said in a voice that could barely be heard. "Out there, when things were happening as though in a nightmare, you knew what to do, you kept us both safe and brought us away."

"Knowing what to do has been my lifelong study," said the other. "At the time, I was thankful that they brought no worse weapon into play than that flashing beam."

"What weapon could be worse?" asked Sir Percy.

"I should think they have it at hand. The ray might be compared to a pistol, something for short range and direct fire, for it could not reach us behind our dune. But very probably they are provided with something that can strike a target under cover, comparable, perhaps, to a rifle in human hands."

"What would it be like?"

"There you call on me for a guess, and I am not prepared to make it. But I think your servants are setting out something for us to eat."

They went into the dining hall, where a supper of cold meat and bread and salad had been laid out. As they ate, a man arrived with a message from London. Troops were being sent to augment the sketchy units already on the scene. The night went on, at about one o'clock word arrived that another cylinder had landed at nearby Byfleet.

"Two cargoes of horror have come to us across space," Sir Percy half moaned. "What next?"

"A third cargo next," readily answered his guest, "and, after that, a fourth. Eight more in all making a total of ten."

"Yes, yes, there were ten flashes from Mars, were there not? I had forgotten."

"It would be well to bear it most faithfully in mind."

At last they sought their bedrooms to rest as well as they could, and were up at early dawn of Saturday. They dressed quickly, drank hot coffee, and walked together to the Woking railroad station to catch the first train for London. Sir Percy stopped to speak to the grizzled postmaster.

"More troops will be coming here, with trained observers and heavy weapons," he said. "Information on all that happens here is to be wired to my office by Brigadier Waring or various members of his staff. Now, here are my urgent orders to you personally. Any message addressed to me is to be sent in duplicate to my friend here."

"Don't I know this gentleman, Sir Percy?" asked the postmaster. "I seem to remember that he visited you here in '88."

"Yes, he came to help me in a confidential matter that concerned the Italian naval treaty. This is Mr Sherlock Holmes, and his address in London is 221B Baker Street."

Eight

Sherlock Holmes hailed a cab when he got off the train at Waterloo Station and was in Baker Street by seven o'clock. He went upstairs to 221B, but did not enter his own flat. Instead, he touched the bell above the doorplate that read Mrs HUDSON. In a moment his landlady opened to him. She was a stately blonde woman with a rosy face, smiling in happy welcome.

"Has Watson come home?" he asked quickly.

"No, he telephoned last night. He says he must stay with his poor old servant Murray until tomorrow, perhaps longer."

"Then we are alone."

Holmes stepped into her sitting room as he spoke and closed the door to the hall. They kissed, holding each other close, her rich curves pressed against his sinewy leanness. "My dear," she whispered against his cheek, "I have always loved you."

"Let us not say quite always, Martha," he amended, smiling. "Not until we met at Donnithorpe, when I was an undergraduate beginning my work as a consulting detective and you were a poor, troubled village girl."

"You are always exact, even when you are kissing me."

"Yes, call me a precisionist in that, too."

Expertly their mouths joined again.

"You solved my troubles then," she said, after long moments. "You set me free from Morse Hudson."

"It was then that I decided what my career would be."

"And you helped me find this place in town, and then you came to live here. You found Dr Watson as a fellow lodger, so that between you, you could pay the rent I must have." She released him at last and drew back, relishing him with her eyes. "But have you had breakfast?"

"Only a quick cup of coffee with Sir Percy Phelps."

"Then here, all ready for you."

She stepped to a table and lifted a silver cover from a chafing dish. Holmes smiled again as he sat down. "Curried chicken," he said approvingly. "I often say, my dear, that you have as sound a notion of breakfast as a Scotchwoman."

Happily she served his plate and he ate with good appetite, telling her of what had befallen on Horsell Common outside Woking.

"How fortunate for Sir Percy that you were there with him," she said. "Only you would have thought to move so quickly and rescue him. Your mind has never moved with such magnificent speed as in that moment of danger last night."

"I'll never tell Watson about it," said Holmes, eating chicken. "Sometimes he embarrasses me with his praise. You never embarrass me with anything, because I love you."

Her blue eyes were wide with worry. "But however did these Martians come here, over those millions and millions of miles?"

"The press gave us notice of that. Midnight after midnight, a flash of light on Mars like an explosion, ten of them in all. Each flash propelled a cylinder into space, aimed here to seek us out. The second cylinder has already arrived, and a third should be here by tonight."

Her hands clasped in admiration, like a girl happy with her first love.

"You are so well-informed of everything. But once Dr Watson wrote that you know nothing of astronomy."

"Oh, I told Watson that as a joke, in the first days of our acquaintance, but I do my best to learn something about everything. Only lately I reread Moriarty's *Dynamics of an Asteroid*, and found new stimulation in it."

"Let Dr Watson think what he will," she said. "I believe that you have truly learned everything possible."

"Not I," he demurred. "The greatest thing any of us can learn is that we can always learn something more." He put down his fork and rose. "Yes, Moriarty's study stimulated me, and I am stimulated by your excellent cooking. Thank you, my dear."

He went quickly down the hall to his own quarters. A letter was stuck in the frame of the door. He opened it and read:

Friday morning

My dear Holmes,

Nobody, naturally, reflects that these invaders of Earth at Woking came prepared to be violent. If you have planned to join me there, I urge you to stay clear. I might be killed, and in that case mankind would doubly need your intelligence, which is not greatly inferior to my own, to help it in meeting this manifest danger.

Yours truly,

George Edward Challenger

As he finished the letter and put it away, a messenger knocked and gave him a telegram:

MARTIANS UNDER OBSERVATION FROM SAFE POSITIONS WILL FIRE AT FIRST HOSTILE MOVE

SIR PRETERICK WARING KCB

BRIG COMM

Through the open window drifted the long-drawn cry of a newsboy. Holmes hurried down and bought a newspaper. STRANGE REPORT FROM WOKING, said the headline equivocally, and beneath this was a garbled account of the things he had seen and knew at firsthand. He sat at his desk and wrote rapidly:

My dear Challenger,

I went to Woking on Friday before receiving your letter, but did not find you. I saw no Martians myself: however, descriptions tally with what we observed in the crystal egg I left with you.

Like you, I was prepared for hostility, and this weapon people are beginning to call the heat-ray is disaster to face. Nor do we know as yet what more terrible armament they may have.

Without indulging too greatly in surmise, I suggest that these are pioneers of a mass migration across space, with more to arrive when Mars and Earth are next in opposition, in 1904. Very likely they consider us lower animals, to be exterminated as pests or possibly to be exploited in some way.

Keep the crystal in your possession. Its properties seem to include interplanetary communication. The Martians may try to recapture it. What if we could trap one of them in the attempt and learn more about how to oppose him and his fellows?

It occurs to me that health on a strange world may be one of their problems. You may enlarge on the supposition.

With warm regards,

Sherlock Holmes

He sealed the sheet in an envelope and rang for Billy.

"See that this letter goes to Enmore Park, in Kensington West, by special messenger," he said.

"What's all this about these Martian people, Mr Holmes?" asked Billy. "You were there, weren't you? The paper says they can hardly creep about in that pit of theirs."

"Never trust such newspaper reports, Billy. They have complex machines to fight with, and undoubtedly to travel with. By the way, where does your mother live?"

"Why, in Yorkshire. She went there last year, to raise a market garden."

"Here, my boy," Holmes held out a pound note. "After you have seen that letter on its way to Professor Challenger, you may take a holiday to visit your mother."

Billy pocketed the note, somewhat slowly. "But I'd rather stay here in London, sir. Things sound like excitement hereabouts, they do."

"Excitement is exactly the word, Billy. But there is apt to be disruption, too, and very likely dangerous disruption. I would feel better if you were at a safe distance."

Billy departed. Holmes returned to his desk and looked through a great sheaf of his hasty notes, making fuller and clearer organisation in writing. Several excited callers came to his door with news, rumours mostly, of heavy fighting in Surrey. That evening, Martha appeared with a veal and ham pie and a fruit compote for their dinner.

"You're troubled," she ventured as Holmes opened a bottle of Beaune.

"And quite accurately deduced, my dear Martha," he said. "A terrible fate seems to have befallen those unfortunate communities in Surrey. I have a special kindness for that country; it was there that I solved a puzzle at Reigate and explained a mystery at Wisteria Lodge, besides helping Sir Percy Phelps when he thought he had lost the naval treaty. Yet, bad as things are in Surrey, they may become bad here in London." He considered that statement. "Worse," he amended.

She ate slowly. "But the people out there on the street do not seem particularly frightened, my dear."

"Because they have not taken thought. Their minds are incapable of grasping the implications of this strange invasion. But I find myself talking like my respected friend, the professor, who holds the intellect of the entire human race, except for his own, in utter scorn. I wish I could talk to him. Yes, or to Watson."

She was able to smile at that. "You have always laughed at Dr Watson when he is unable to follow your own reasoning."

"Yes, I have had my fun with him, but his mind has a good, sound scientific organisation, and again and again he has proved his great courage and dependability. Now," he said, rising. "I must go to the telegraph office, but you may expect me back shortly. By the way, I sent Billy on a holiday to his mother in Yorkshire. Where is your maid?"

"I let her go home to Cheltenham for the weekend."

"Then I hope she stays there, well away from London. But let us think of ourselves for a moment or two." He went to take his violin from its case. "Before I go, how about a little night music?"

She sat and listened happily as he played a Paganini melody, then a wilder, more haunting strain.

"What is that?" Martha asked.

"I learned it from a gypsy. It was all he could pay for my help when he was falsely accused of picking pockets. I think it is beautiful."

Again he changed key and mood. She sat up straight and alert.

"I remember that, my dearest," she said. "You played it long ago, at the Trevor house at Donnithorpe. I heard you from outside the window. Who composed it?"

"I did," he told her, smiling in his turn. "Once I had ambitions to play sweet music, to be thanked and renowned for it. But as you know, I took another way of life, and am content not be so greatly celebrated for my labours."

He returned the violin to its case and went out on his errand.

That night, and on Sunday morning while the church bells rang, Holmes interviewed refugees from the towns in Surrey. In shaky voices they told him of troops wiped out wholesale by the flashing reflector devices that by now were called the heat-ray, and of gigantic machines like "boilers on stilts", on the swift move everywhere below London. By Sunday noon, Holmes gathered that whole communities had been effortlessly destroyed and that military forces – horse, foot and artillery had proved helpless against those stalking, merciless fighting-machines. Back in his sitting room that afternoon, he made two copies of all he had learned and his own estimate of the desperate situation.

"And I have had no further word from either Watson or Challenger," he caid to Martha. "Small wonder – the telephone service seems completely disrupted by a great flood of calls. Well, I shall leave one copy of my notes here."

He stuck them to the mantelpiece with a jacknife. Martha winced as the point of the blade drove into the varnished wood, but he did not seem to notice.

"The third cylinder's arrival has been reported," he went on. "It fell last night, again in Surrey. Apparently they are able to concentrate their landfalls within a few miles of each other and consolidate a position from which to operate."

"At least they have not come to London," offered Martha, though with no great optimism.

"But it takes no great deductive reasoning to see that this hopelessly one-sided war of the worlds will move toward us," he replied. "They are well aware that this is the largest city, the largest center of population on Earth, and they mean to capture it."

"But London," she said. "Great, powerful London. How can London fall to them?"

"That, my dear Martha, you and I shall not be here to witness. Both Billy and your maid have gone to safe distances, and so shall we go. Pack some things, my dear while I do the same."

"Yes, yes," she agreed quickly, "but where shall we go?"

"If you approve, we shall take our own holiday up at Donnithorpe, where we have not been for almost twenty-five years. You told me that your uncle is now landlord of the inn there, and my old friend Trevor is justice of the peace, like his father before him."

Yet again he went to the post office, where he read more tersely wired reports of Martians on the move. Five of them, it seemed, came with each cylinder. That meant fifteen thus far, with more on the way. One of their fighting-machines had been smashed by an artillery shell at Weybridge, though the batteries there had been promptly obliterated by its comrades. Descriptions of those fighting-machines were exaggerated and sometimes incoherent passages, and Holmes felt more inclined to accept the "boilers on stilts" comparison he had heard on the street. Even as he read the telegrams, all information from Surrey ceased abruptly. The operator told Holmes that telegraphic communication had broken down and that railway service was disrupted.

He swiftly made his way home. There he packed two valises and wrote a note to Watson, spiking it to the mantelpiece with his report. As he did so, a knock sounded. He opened the door to Sir Percy Phelps.

"Come in, my dear fellow," said Holmes. "I am just on my way from town, and I strongly advise you to go as well. The news here is of continual disaster."

"But you must not leave," said Sir Percy, his voice shakily earnest. "I have brought you a most important secret commission."

He handed a folded paper to Holmes, who spread it out and read it at a glance. He frowned in concentration over it.

"Dear me," he said after a moment. "This appears to give me the most sweeping powers and responsibilities."

"The Government itself is leaving for Birmingham," said Sir Percy. "We are asking you, Holmes, in the name of your country – nay, in the name of all human-kind – to be our observer here in London, help to plan for whatever can be done. You cannot leave."

"But I must," said Holmes flatly. "I have another important duty in Norfolk, which I consider to be as important as this assignment you offer. What is my brother Mycroft doing? He reasons profitably in an armchair, which may well be exactly the place in which to resolve this matter."

"Your brother has accompanied the Royal Family up to Balmoral Castle in Scotland," replied Sir Percy. "No, Holmes, there is no living man better fitted, none more worthy, of this important and dangerous commission than yourself. Surely someone else is able to represent you in Norfolk."

"I must ago there in person," insisted Holmes. "But I promise you to come back as soon as I can."

"Back to London, Holmes? In the face of the Martians?"

"I do not despair of successfully accomplishing that return. Meanwhile let me communicate with you by wire at Birmingham, and you may say that I can be relied upon to return and do my best duty here."

"Thank you, Holmes, thank you in the name of the Government itself." Sir Percy wrung his friend's hand. "Let me say one thing more. If you and I survive this crisis, if England and humanity survive it, a fitting reward will be given you for your services. I am in a position to speak for people in the highest places. There will be recognition for you. A knighthood."

"Knighthood?" repeated Holmes, smiling and shaking his head. "Well, that is very handsome, but I must decline, with deep gratitude and respect to those who make the offer."

"But, my dear Holmes!" cried Sir Percy. "You deserve to be knighted. The title will be conferred upon you by His Majesty the King. Such a title would be gratifying to you and to your friends. It would cause you to emerge from your seclusion, come into high society, as your services and gifts so richly merit."

"That is exactly what motivates me to decline." Holmes' smile widened. "If I were knighted, people would have to call me Sir Sherlock. Can you think, offhand, of a worse tongue twister? Not at all easy to say, like Sir Percy. No, I say, I shall be better off, and so shall all my acquaintances, if I remain simply Mr Sherlock Holmes."

Nine

When at last the train brought Holmes and Martha into Donnithorpe shortly before midnight, the village inn blazed with lights. Its main hall seemed charged with an excitement that reminded Holmes of that day years before when Hudson, the blackmailing butler, and his scapegrace son Morse had fled the home of Squire Trevor, leaving their master dying of a stroke. Martha's aunt and uncle gave her a glad welcome, asked questions about the invasion, and blinked uncomprehendingly at Holmes' guarded replies. Holmes slept well in the small room they gave him. At nine o'clock Monday morning, Martha brought in a tray with bacon, scrambled eggs, toast, and tea. As they ate together she gave him more news.

"The Squire has called a meeting here at the inn to discuss the situation and how to meet it," she said.

"Of course, that is my old university friend, Victor Trevor," said Holmes. "We have not seen each other since he returned from the East Indies to his family estate. Probably I should attend that meeting."

He found half a dozen grave-faced men in the inn parlour. Victor Trevor greeted him and introduced him to the rector of the parish church, the postmaster, the sturdy, bearded blacksmith, and other community leaders. At Trevor's request, Holmes told them what he knew about the Martians but omitted all mention of his government assignment.

"I say, we must form a volunteer company of defence," said Trevor when Holmes had finished. "Every able-bodied man in the place. Let each bring what weapon he may have — a sporting rifle, a fowling piece. We shall meet war with war if we must, even die if we must. Die fighting."

"Hear, hear!" applauded the blacksmith. "Every one of us is with you, Squire."

But Holmes held up his hand.

"Gentlemen, the regular army has tried to fight and was hopelessly defeated," he reminded them. "The invaders saw at once how we gave battle and brought that sort of resistance to less than nothing. Their heat-ray weapon wipes out whole crowds at a single flash. It destroys houses and guns like wisps of straw. There is also a rumour of some sort of vapour, called black smoke, that smothers any living thing it touches, like bees smoked from a hive. To try to draw up in ranks against them would be suicidal."

"How then would you have us deal with them?" asked Trevor. "Run like sheep before them, and be slaughtered like sheep by them?"

"As of now I would favour scattering before them, which is not quite the same as running. But they are not here yet, nor near, and I hope for more useful information shortly. Meanwhile, I advocate the gathering of supplies in homes and keeping a close watch to southward."

Several looked dubious, but Trevor nodded agreement.

"Thank you, Holmes, you give us something of a basis on which to plan," he said. "Let us ponder all these matters, gentlemen, and meet here again at noon."

"Telegrams for Mr Holmes," called a clerk from the door to the front hall.

Holmes went out and took the messages. He saw at once that they were in a cipher Sir Percy had not given him, and he studied them for a moment to puzzle it out. Then he was aware of Trevor at his elbow, and with Trevor stood a stranger.

"Holmes, this is Lord John Roxton," said Trevor. "His name is familiar throughout the whole world of exploration and big-game hunting. He has adventured in every wild and dangerous land on Earth. I consider it fortunate that he is visiting me at Donnithorpe at this time of critical action."

Lord John Roxton was tall and lean, not unlike Holmes in figure. His strong features were deeply tanned, and he had gingery hair, a crisp moustache, and a pointed beard. Holmes judged him to be in his mid-thirties.

"I say, I got here a thought late for your meetin', and I was outside the door when you spoke, Mr Holmes," he said without preliminaries. "I've heard of you, of course. You're the big thinker of Scotland Yard."

"Not exactly," said Holmes. "I have never served with the police, although on occasion I have been able to help a trifle."

"I see. Well, sir, I'm takin' the liberty to say that I think action, not talk, is the best ticket here. I plump for that volunteer company of defence, don't you know. I happen to have some fine long-range rifles – I only came up here for the trout fishin' with Trevor, but I never travel anywhere without my guns. I could arm several good men who were worth lendin' such things to."

"Your guns might serve against a rhinoceros," said Holmes, "but the rhinoceros wouldn't be using the heat-ray or the black smoke."

"Now, Mr Holmes," said Lord John, a touch of irritation coming into his voice, "I agree with you that we'd be fools to meet these Martian devils in the open, try to make a standup fight of it. But we could shikar and stalk, set up ambushes, flankin' movements and all that. I've had such things to do myself, here and there in Asia and Africa, and among man-eatin' tribes in the South Pacific when they got pressin' with their attentions. A cool hand and a sure eye are what we need to do the trick.

That's the English way, what?"

"If you heard what I said of their methods when they are opened on with guns," said Holmes, "you know that I consider any such muster against them as only asking for death."

Lord John's eye glittered. "You seem to think that I'm afraid of death, Mr Holmes," he said coldly.

"I think nothing of the sort," Holmes replied, "nor have you any right to think it of me. Dying in battle may be dramatic, but it does not always win. Surrey and the south of London are full of those who died in battle to no avail. If the Martians should come here, I say that I advocate a retreat before them, but a well-planned retreat that will draw them away from Donni-thorpe and other towns. A fight near any village means it will be destroyed in a flash of the heat-ray."

"Retreat," said Lord John after him. "Retreat where, may I ask?"

"Into the roughest country hereabouts, where there is cover and the protection of dunes and banks. Whatever the power of the invaders, just now they are few – far too few to occupy all England at present. That gives us some chance, some time to prepare. You, Lord John, will be useful in observing the country here and choosing proper lines for an ordered retirement such as I suggest. Meanwhile, they are not here yet. And they may not come at all."

"Pray heaven they do not," said Trevor, as from a full heart.

Lord John Roxton raked Holmes with his brilliant eyes.

"You speak with some penetration, don't you know," he said at last. "You have it right. I venture to say that I was more or less going on instinct, had some idea of a last stand of the Scots Greys. But you've made me think twice, and thinkin' twice never yet harmed a fightin' man. Very well, Mr Holmes, I'll do as you say – help form the company here, and look out lines of retreat."

And he gave Holmes his hard, brown hand.

Alone in his room again, Holmes studied out the messages and solved the mystery of the code fairly quickly. The news from Sir Percy was of widespread, unreasoning panic throughout London as the invaders had come their terrible way up the Surrey side below the Thames. All organised military resistance in the area was at an end. Nobody could estimate the number of dead. A fourth cylinder had fallen in Surrey. Chiefs of staff at Birmingham were pondering the chances of reaching it with high explosives to destroy it.

Holmes sat with the telegrams in his hand, pondering this intelligence. The invaders seemed to be in a position of triumphant conquest in whatever part of England they ranged. Did they plan to exterminate all men? If not, why not? Using the cipher he had just decoded, he wrote out an answer:

Available facts indicate enemy concentration in relatively small area. invader attention now fixed on London. Six more cylinders on way, doubtless to land on sites chosen by precise instruments on Mars. If arrivals continue to show close pattern in Surrey, localised occupation manifest. Full intentions of Martians may clarify, whether extermination of mankind or exploitation.

At the village post office, the telegrapher stared at the coded message, but sent it. Holmes returned to the inn and found Martha waiting in the shadowed rose garden behind.

"You were gone so long," she said. "What have you been doing?"

"Little enough of any real consequence, I fear. You haven't lost faith in me, I hope."

"Never that," said Martha. "Nor must our world lose faith in you."

It occurred to Holmes that Challenger would have puffed up importantly had those words been addressed to him.

He went into the parlour and studied several morning papers. None had come from London, of course. The Norwich and Cambridge journals were crazily printed and gave disjointed accounts of the destruction in the London suburbs. The heat ray and the black smoke were mentioned, but with no explanatory details.

Martha's uncle said that train service to Donnithorpe had ceased. "Are any running southward through Langmere?" asked Holmes.

"Southward, Mr Holmes?" echoed the innkeeper. "Bless you, sir, no train in all these parts even dares point its nose south. The last ones up from London came packed with people like salt herring in a Dutchman's pail. Those I've spoken to, I can't make aught of their stories. They seem fair stunned by what was going on in London. Nor can I blame them."

By evening the inn was crowded with pale, unstrung refugees, and the overflow paid high prices for beds and food in cottages throughout Donnithorpe. Out on the street, Holmes met Dr Fordham and remembered him at once from that visit long ago. Fordham was elderly and plump, with a daunted, sidewhiskered face.

"I was in London myself, I had planned a pleasant weekend at the theaters," he said moodily. "Then those. Martians tramped all through town, killing street after street with their black smoke – killing's the only word for it – and came following on as everyone, myself included, took to running. I was lucky to get home here, jammed aboard a goods train last night."

"So far, I have heard only the scantiest reports of the black smoke," said Holmes. "But if they came following through it, as you say, I daresay it moved at too low an elevation to do them any hurt in their tall machines."

"And you are right, Mr Holmes. "They use great blasts of steam to precipitate their gas into black grains, like soot, after it has done its deadly work."

"Thank you," said Holmes. "You have given me some useful information. It shows, first, that the Martians are not really bent on exterminating us, since they nullify their deadly vapour when it has routed opposition; and, second, that steam is a counter-agent, something that perhaps men can use."

He sought the post office at once, to wire these observations to Sir Percy Phelps at Birmingham and to his brother Mycroft in Scotland. Back from Mycroft came congratulations for having escaped from London. Reading this reply, Holmes reflected that, if the Martians were occupying London as reported, the black smoke could hardly be rampant there any longer. He wired another promise to Sir Percy that he would make an effort to return and told Martha of that promise as they walked together among the flowers in the garden.

She clasped his hand in both of hers. He could feel her trembling.

"Please stay here," she pleaded, a hint of tears in her blue eyes. "What could I do, alone here without you?"

"You might pray, perhaps," he said, speaking cheerfully to comfort her. "Prayer would seem indicated. My time here is not wholly wasted, my dear, but it is my sworn duty to observe the enemy at closer hand than Donnithorpe."

Tuesday found him busy interviewing refugees, assessing information and communicating it to Birmingham. Early on Wednesday morning, news arrived at the inn from Cambridge that not one but two cylinders had fallen overnight, one of them somewhere close to Wimbledon in Surrey, the other directly upon Primrose Hill in north-east London, making six arrivals in all. Holmes and Dr Fordham discussed these reports as they ate breakfast together in the inn parlour.

"But how could two of them strike almost at once?" wondered Fordham, plaintive in his mystification. "We know now that there were ten cylinders shot from Mars, at twenty-four hour intervals. The thing's downright incomprehensible, Mr Holmes."

"My dear Dr Fordham, you sound to me like another medical man, my old friend Dr John H. Watson," said Holmes, buttering a muffin. "It is always a capital mistake to theorise before one has data, but I think it should be manifest by now that these cylinders are not launched from Mars by anything as simple as a giant gun. They are not mere bullets aimed at a target millions of miles away. The closeness of their earlier landings strongly suggests that they have deliberately concentrated their points of arrival. Undoubtedly they are able to control speed and direction of flight while in space."

"But if they have been making their landings in Surrey, why now in London?"

"That, too, is susceptible of explanation, and helps us to understand their reasoning. The first landings were in relatively open country, where they could quickly estimate their situation and its possible hazards. But by now, with London in their possession, they can come down safely within its limits. Primrose Hill would be a logical point to establish a command post, rising as it does above all surrounding districts in town."

Fordham chewed and thought. "I am obliged to say, Mr Holmes, you make all these things sound simple. Simple, that is, after you have explained them to me."

"Again you remind me of Watson. I hope he is safe somewhere." Holmes sipped coffee. "After witnessing only the heat-ray, I deduced a second weapon, which turns out to be the black smoke. What, I now ask myself, will their third device be?"

"Their third?" Fordham almost squealed.

"The heat-ray mechanism arrived in the very first cylinder. The black smoke of which you told me was also in use by Sunday, and seems a compact bit of freight, also a practical arrival in any cylinder. But by now, as we are aware, there are six cylinders on Earth. I take leave to wonder if something larger, more complex, might have been brought here in several shipments, to be assembled against us."

Fordham sank back in his chair, his sidewhiskers drooping. Trevor entered and came to sit at their table.

"You look shocked, Dr Fordham," he said. "Not bad news, I hope."

"It's what Mr Holmes has been saying," said Fordham. "Now I wait to hear what this terrible new weapon may be."

"I hesitate to go into speculation," said Holmes, "but I would suggest something that flies."

Fordham moved so violently in his chair that the dishes clinked before him.

"A flying-machine? My dear sir, that's impossible."

"Not to the Martians," said Holmes. "They have already flown through millions of miles, landing at their own time and place. If they can accomplish that, why not a machine that would course over the Earth, spying us out, striking us?"

"You have seen such a thing?" asked Trevor.

"Not as yet. I remind you, I said I was going into speculation."

Trevor shook his head. "But I came here with an answer to another of your questions, Holmes. A train is being made up, here in Norfolk, to approach London in hopes of gathering refugees. It will stop at Langmere. Since you seem determined to go, I am ready to drive you there to board it." He looked earnestly at Holmes. "You are acting with your usual recklessness, I think, but I tell myself that I can only trust your judgement. I learned to do that long ago, when we two were students together at the university."

"Thank you for that trust," said Holmes, rising. "Let's be off."

The refugee train was a long string of cars, but Holmes, wearing a soft hat and a checked cape, was the only one aboard other than the volunteer crew. They chugged down to Cambridge. Holmes heard from men at the station there that the Martians had taken complete possession of London and that some of their hurrying machines had pursued frightened crowds all the way to the sea. What use, he wondered, did these monsters have for men?

As they trundled on, his thoughts were banished by a baleful shadow above the train. He leaned from the open window to look. Against the cloudless June sky soared a distant round object like a saucer in flight. It made a sweeping turn and glided above them again. The train speeded up and the flying-machine sailed out of sight beyond the horizon.

Silently he congratulated himself. He had foreseen another weapon, and this could be a terrible one. But foreseeing it gave him new confidence in his reasoning powers.

The train scraped to a halt at Ware. Its crew fairly sprang out upon the station platform. As Holmes, too, stepped down, several of the men came together, all talking excitedly. The engineer was there, sweaty-faced and wide-eyed, loudly proclaiming that the crew would approach London no closer, that the train would seek a siding, turn itself around and flee northward again.

"What of your duty to find refugees and bring them back?" Holmes asked him.

"There's a plenty of refugees to take on, right here in Ware," mouthed the engineer, "and I've got a wife and nippers at home. No more of that flying thing, sir, not for me. It hung over us like a bloody great hawk, ready to pounce on a poor running hare."

"If it happened to want you, it could come back and get you as you ran," said Holmes coldly. "Well, if you're running away, goodbye to you."

"But what will you do, sir? Bide here at Ware?"

"No," snapped Holmes over his shoulder as he turned away. "I am going to London."

He strode quickly off along the platform. Beyond, he followed a grassy lane beside the railroad tracks, with hedge growing close at hand. He could dart in there to hide should the flying thing come back. Nobody passed him, and nobody peered from the doors and windows of silent houses. As he walked, he ate the sandwiches Martha had disconsolately made for his lunch. By late evening he reached Cheshunt. The railroad station was empty, but he found food and water in its restaurant. He rested on a bench, until twilight, he took the way to London once again.

The stars came winking out overhead, and a new moon like a curved blade. On trudged Holmes, and on. In the deep darkness he crossed the bridge over Hackney Marsh and entered among the dark, deserted streets of London. He heard no sound other than his own tireless footsteps on the pavement until, distant but shrill and piercing, rose a burst of noise like a steam siren. Holmes stood still under a shop awnings to listen. Another howl rose, as though in reply. The invaders, he decided, signalling to each other. That meant that they could hear, though not keenly if they needed such strident voices for signals.

At any rate, there was no movement anywhere in those streets by those giant machines. Perhaps, like men, they preferred to hunt by daylight. But hunt what? If man was their prey, how would they use him? He pondered several possibilities as he resumed his journey.

He began to feel increasingly weary as he negotiated square after square. On his way through Hoxton he heard a clatter of metal, at a remote distance. No human contrivance could make such a noise as that. He wished he were close enough to observe without being observed.

As dawn came, he slowed his journey. The voices of the invaders were loud to the north of him. They must be on patrol again. He was shrewdly careful at crossing a street whenever he came to a corner, and he stopped again and again to look both ways before he ventured into the open. One strident clanging came near at hand, and he slipped inside a tobacconist's to wait until it departed. From the counter he took two pouches of shag.

It was fairly late on Thursday evening when once more he mounted the stairs at 221B Baker Street.

He counted the seventeen steps – it had become a habit with him over the years. Unlocking his door, he entered his quarters. It was dark inside, but he made no light as he explored. His sheaf of notes and the message to Watson were still undisturbed, there on the blade of the knife at the mantel. He tested the taps and found that a small stream of water still ran in the pipes. He drew a cold bath and washed himself quickly, feeling much the better for it. Then, at last, he kindled his spirit stove and set a kettle of water to boil. A supper of tea and sweet biscuits gave him a further sense of refreshment. After eating, he lay down in his old blue dressing gown and slept fitfully. Now and then he wakened to the sound of metallic stirrings, not unthinkably far away. But finally his weariness lulled him soundly to sleep, and he did not waken until early morning.

He went along the corridor to Martha's rooms, let himself in with his pass key, and from her kitchen took potted ham, marmalade, a plate of stale scones, and a saucer of radishes. With these and some more strong tea he made his breakfast. He peered from behind his window curtains, but saw nothing outside to dismay him. The prolonged scream of an invader's siren rose, but this time far away, somewhere well to northward, as he judged.

Suddenly he was startled by the sound of the bell at his front door. He hurried to open and saw young Stanley Hopkins, his chief friend and reliance at Scotland Yard. Hopkins's usually neat clothing looked sadly rumpled, and his square jaw was stubbled with several days' growth of dark beard.

"You're alive, Mr Holmes," Hopkins stammered. "Thank God for that! I've been to the Yard, but found nobody there – nobody much anywhere. Nobody but those damnable Martians, tramping around in their great machines, like constables on their beats."

Holmes stepped back to let his friend in, studying him closely. "I can see that you have been riding horseback, and at a fast pace," he commented after a moment.

"Yes, so I have," said Hopkins, amazed. "That is quite true. But how can you know? I left the beast miles away, out on the eastern edge of town."

"It is quite simple. I see traces of dried foam on your trouser knee and on the skirt of your coat. And I will add that, if you dismounted at the eastern limits, you came from considerably farther beyond in that direction. Perhaps as far as the sea."

"Mr Holmes, you are right, as usual. Yes, I have been to the coast."

"Sit down, Hopkins," Holmes invited him. "Please have something to eat. There is plenty here."

Hopkins sank gratefully into a chair, helped himself, and ate eagerly. Holmes busied himself making more tea. "And now," he said at last, filling a cup for Hopkins and pouring a fresh one for himself, "if you have been east of town, you can fill in some of my deductions. Tell me how far you went, and what you saw."

"I went east on Monday, with the main retreat of people from town." Hopkins told him between mouthfuls. "The Martians came up from the west and south, and the impulse was to get away to the east. I got hold of a bicycle, but even then it was an ordeal—a great, wild scramble, like rats from a burning house," He drew up his broad shoulders, almost shuddering. "I never want to go through such an experience again. I reached the coast by Tuesday afternoon, and there was a tremendous crowd already on the beach, at the mouth of the Blackwater, growing and growing with every hour. On Wednesday, all sorts of shipping gathered offshore to take away the refugees. And then—" He paused, trembling. "Then those Martians came rushing in."

"I see," said Holmes, quiet in his deep interest. "Were you able to observe much about them?"

"I had climbed a tall church steeple to watch. Three of them came into view, in their machines a hundred feet high. They went wading out to sea, to head off those refugee ships; but then a naval ironclad, one of those old torpedo-rams – the Thunder Child, I think it was – came steaming up to fight them. That was a glorious fight, Mr Holmes."

"Undoubtedly, but how successful a fight?"

"The poor ship was blown up with all on board. The Martians set fire to it somehow. But first it smashed two of their machines, and that gained time so that the refugee craft had all gone too far out for the third one to follow. That third one shot black smoke at them, and then came a flying-machine and put down more, all along the beach where people had been left. You may find that hard to believe, what I say about a flying-machine."

"Not I," Holmes assured him. "I have seen it myself. Tell me about the black smoke, so far, I have heard only rumours."

"For one thing, it is heavier by far than any smoke I have ever seen. It is so heavy that it pours down along the ground, almost like liquid. Fortunately, that steeple from which I watched was so high that it could not rise to me, or I would not be here. At last it settled. It made the ground all sooty. When I came down, I saw only dead in all directions about me. Hundreds of dead, I should think."

Hopkins's face looked drawn. Holmes poured him more strong tea.

"Then it was dusk," Hopkins continued. "Two or three more Martians came to join the one that was left, and they tinkered with the two wrecked ones. I headed for London once again, taking advantage of any cover I could find, sometimes hiding and resting, all of Wednesday night. I scrounged for food and found a little – not much."

"I had much the same experience, coming down from Norfolk."

"On Thursday morning, between Tillingham and Chelmsford, I found a horse," said Hopkins. "A spotted horse, all ready saddled and bridled. He was a good horse." At last Hopkins smiled. "Nobody was with him. So I rode him back to town; rode him into a lather, as you saw. By dawn today we were at Great Ilford, on the eastern town limit. Then I took off his bridle and saddle and left him grazing on a lawn. And I made the rest of the way here on foot."

He set down his teacup with a sigh. "And now, Mr Holmes, tell me what we are to do."

"We are to keep our heads, to begin with," was Holmes' prompt rejoinder. "For my own part, as I just said, I have been in the north, up at Donnithorpe in Norfolk."

"A problem, no doubt?"

"A problem of a sort. I got back here yesterday, walking part of the way. What I have been able to see and surmise of the Martians is dismaying, I must confess. Yet you yourself have seen that they are not omnipotent, that it is possible to fight and destroy them. And I have been trying to establish some facts about their weapons — their offensive weapons, I mean."

"And very offensive they are," Hopkins said, and Holmes smiled because his friend could make a small joke.

"As for their defences," he elaborated, "they may well prove to have some interesting chinks."

"Surely you don't mean to stay in London, Mr Holmes."

"But that is precisely what I mean to do. Why not? They seem to have ceased their wholesale destruction here in town, and in any case it was not as terrible as what they wreaked upon Surrey. You and I can be circumspect, Hopkins. We can stay tactfully out of sight and make a profitable investigation of their motives and behavior."

"Investigation?" The word made Hopkins sit up straight. "You speak as though you were studying a crime, Mr Holmes."

"And so I am, Hopkins, the most infamous crime ever perpetrated upon Earth and against Earth. But just now, why not freshen yourself in the bathroom yonder? You will find soap, towels, and a razor, and I believe some water runs as yet in the taps. Then come down and have a rest on the sofa here."

Holmes' calm confidence had had a good effect upon the young inspector. He shaved and washed thoroughly, then came back to the sitting room to take off his boots and fall into a deep sleep on the sofa. Holmes sat alone at his desk, thinking and now and then jotting down a note. After a while, he dressed and ventured down the stairs.

There was no sound or motion in empty Baker Street. Holmes went across to Camden House that stood next to Dolamore's wine and spirits establishment, directly opposite 221B. Camden House had remained untenanted since the arrest there of Colonel Sebastian Moran in 1895, but the door sagged open. Holmes entered and mounted four flights of dusty stairs, then climbed a ladder to a trapdoor in the roof. He crept cautiously into the open and peered over the parapet.

The smudgy vapour that so long had poured from London's countless chimneys had vanished, and the air was as clear and bright as that of Donnithorpe. To the northward Holmes saw the green trees of Regent's Park, strangely peaceful in that captured city. There was no sound in the streets between, those streets once so thronged and busy. He looked past the trees of the park toward Primrose Hill, rising two miles distant. Metal glinted in the morning sun there, and something moved, probably one of the invaders' machines that Hopkins had likened to tramping constables on their beats. Holmes looked this way and that. There was nothing nearer at hand to hint of the enemy abroad. At last he went down the ladder again, and down the stairs and back across the street, meditating.

Ten

Seven cylinders had landed in the London area before he had come down from Donnithorpe, and undoubtedly an eighth had arrived at midnight of Thursday, very probably not any great distance from its fellows. That meant that two more were still on the way, making ten in all, with a total of fifty of the invaders and their machines and weapons. The heat-ray and the black smoke were as terrible as the destructions in the Book of Revelations; but to produce them must take method and materials, and these might be in limited supply on Earth, so far from the base on Mars. What if the invaders were to run out of ammunition? But in the meantime, it remained to define the exact purposes of the deadly assault, to rationalise and oppose those purposes.

Hopkins stirred at noon and then woke up, much refreshed. He was able to describe, more calmly and fully, the things he had seen at the sea coast.

"Those Martians could have wiped out everyone on the shore had they so chosen," he said. "But there was no wholesale killing, except at the last when they put down their black smoke. Before that, I saw them scoop up some people into cages that they carried at their backs."

"They captured people alive?" exclaimed Holmes. "If they did, it proves that they have a special interest in us. I deduced as much when I saw they had more or less spared London after taking it." He frowned. "Disregarding several possibilities, I would suggest that they might consider men as edible."

"As if we were animals!" cried Hudson, shocked.

"Well, we are neither vegetable nor mineral. But reflect, lower animals have outwitted, even outfought, men ere this. Baboons may not understand the hunter's rifle, but sometimes they trick a hunter into an ambush and kill him. The same is true, as I have heard, of the Cape buffalo. And in the United States, the timber wolf has been almost exterminated, but the cunning coyote is more numerous in these days than ever before. It refuses to be stalked or trapped or poisoned. And our common rats, for all our efforts to wipe them out, still swarm in the basements and cellars of our cities. Some of them are so wise that they might be called animal geniuses."

"Like yourself, Mr Holmes."

"Like me, if you care to say so. Observing and deducing, in their animal fashion, comprehending abstracts and infinities, solving problems and escaping dangers."

"Marvellous," said Hopkins, almost raptly, "and please don't say elementary."

"But the elementary is the foundation upon which all structures, concrete or abstract, must be founded," Holmes said with a smile. "Yes, our task is hard and dangerous, but by no means hopeless. Come now, we can have lunch and then go calling on a friend of mine – Professor-Challenger, an excellent rationality."

They made themselves sandwiches and drank wine. Hopkins washed their dishes. Then after carefully studying the street from the windows, they went down stairs and moved along empty, silent streets westward, into Hyde Park and beyond into Kensington Gardens. Once Hopkins climbed a tall tree and descended to report that three machines were in sight, miles away above Primrose Hill. He and Holmes walked on, at the side of a brook that was choked with a great mass of murky-red weed. "What is that, Mr Holmes?" asked Hopkins. "I have never seen its like before."

"Nor have I," confessed Holmes. "To me it proves that more than one sort of life has crossed space to take a foothold here on Earth."

He plucked a fleshy sprout and examined it with a magnifying glass.

"It has grown and spread quickly in these few days, but see this brown wilt upon it," he said. "Very interesting, Hopkins, and I venture to say, encouraging."

"Encouraging, Mr Holmes?"

"Quite manifestly it spreads with bewildering swiftness, but then it dies with equal rapidity. I give myself to doubt if it grows and perishes so fast on its home planet. Indeed, I surmise – no, I cease to surmise and begin to deduce again. Our terrestrial climate seems strangely unhealthy to confident, invading organisms such as this red weed."

Emerging from the Gardens, they stole along Kensington Road below. "The invaders have been here," pointed out Holmes. "The provision shop yonder has been broken into."

They stopped to look. The exposed interior was violently disordered. Entering, Holmes looked here and there. "The shelves have been almost stripped," he remarked. "Here, however, are still a few tins of meat and some biscuits. Put them into your pockets, Hopkins. And here, two bottles of ale. They carried off the rest of the stock."

"Do you mean the Martians?" asked Hopkins, taking the tins from the shelf. "Might they not have been taken by hungry men?"

"No, the whole front was smashed in by a blow more powerful than any man could achieve."

"But why would the Martians take food? To eat and and drink, I suppose."

"More probably they will supply their captives with these provisions. I wonder increasingly if they themselves do not eat and drink something vastly different."

This time he did not elaborate upon his suggestion.

Reaching Challenger's home, they mounted the broad steps. A front window had been shattered, but the door was locked, and repeated pushes on the bell brought no answer.

"I begin to fear that Challenger died with those others at Woking," said Holmes. "Someone said that he suspected that the invaders might not be Martians at all, that Mars was but an advance base to which they came from a more distant world. That might be related in some way to their primitive means of crossing space to Earth."

"Would you call those cylinders primitive, Mr Holmes?"

"Decidedly. I would compare their use to a human crossing of a ford or river in rowboats or on makeshift rafts."

He fished a notebook and pencil from his pocket, sat down on the top step, and began to write swiftly. He filled one page, another, and a third. Then he tore them out, folded them, and gave them to Hopkins.

"Off you go," he said. "Find your way to Birmingham. Report to Sir Percy Phelps of the Foreign Office."

"Birmingham's a walk of a hundred miles and more," protested Hopkins.

"Approximately, yes. But once you're out of London, you will find people and transportation. As a police official you can requisition a horse and carriage, and if you travel cautiously you probably will avoid any embarrassing attention by the Martians. No, Hopkins, I must insist that you go. What I have given you for Sir Percy is a written summary of our views and findings to date, matters of the utmost value to the defence effort which soon will be mounted."

"And you, Mr Holmes, why do you not come, too?"

"My clear duty is to continue my observations here. Good-bye Hopkins, and good luck."

They parted. Hopkins headed westward along the street, then turned north at the corner. Holmes returned the way they had come, ever alert for any sound or motion anywhere.

As he retraced his steps, Holmes told himself that never had his mind worked more powerfully or profitably upon a case. He might well know more about these invaders, whether they came from Mars or not, than anyone else now trying to study them. Again he took cover among the trees on his way through Kensington Gardens – Peter Pan lurked there, he remembered – and then through Hyde Park. He came out at the Cumberland Gate and was doubly furtive when crossing the broad open stretches of Uxbridge Road and Edgware Road. He kept to the narrower streets beyond. In the distance he heard the howling of an invader's siren, but could see nothing of the machine.

It was evening when he entered his rooms again. His first action was to explore his larder. After giving food to the famished Hopkins, he had little left for supper except jam and sweet biscuits. He would do well to go out and forage before darkness came.

He put on a shooting coat with capacious pockets and his deerstalker cap. Outside again, he went silently along Baker Street. At Portman Square he turned upon another street with many shops.

At once he saw the door of a public house that had been kicked in. A man had done that, and Holmes meditated that here was proof that London had not been wholly deserted. As at the shop he and Hopkins had entered, there seemed very little worth his taking. He pocketed three oranges and returned to the broken door. There he paused and peered out in his usual prudent manner.

At about a block's distance toward Baker Street, a human figure was approaching.

His impulse was to step into plain view and wave in welcome, but he paused and peered again. It was a stout, dark-clad man who carried some sort of long blade that gleamed in the evening sun.

Holmes drew back, well inside the broken door. The man walked toward him with swift, heavy purpose. Holmes took several steps more, to the center of the barroom floor. When the man came in, Holmes recognised him at once.

"As I live, it is Morse Hudson," he said. "Years since, I was at your shop in Kennington Road, tracing the Six Napoleons. At that time, I told you aside that you had best shut up business and vanish, like your unhappy father. And again, last December, we met and I gave you another friendly warning. Where may you be lodging now?"

"Never you mind where I lodge," sniffed Hudson. His short, broad body was dressed in filthy clothes. His grey hair bristled untidily and his face flamed red. In one had he posed his weapon, an old basket-hilted sabre. He sneezed violently.

"Yes," he muttered rheumily, "I've been following you about, ever since I saw you come back to London. Earlier today someone was with you and I stayed out of sight. Now we are alone, face to face, and you're going to tell me where Martha is – Martha, my wife."

"Speak roughly to your little boy, and beat him when he sneezes," quoted Holmes mockingly. "You have a very bad cold, Hudson. If Dr Watson were here, he could prescribe for you. But as for Martha, I can tell you roundly that she wants never to see you or hear your name again. She is where you cannot follow or find her."

Hudson trembled all over, as with pent rage. "I'll make you tell me," he said, and took a shambling step forward. The sabre rose threateningly. "No, Holmes, don't reach for a pocket."

"Oh, I am not armed. Reflect, Hudson; if you should kill me, you'd never find Martha."

"I'll find her." Hudson's breath rattled as he spoke. "She is my lawful wife, I say, and I love her—"

He broke off, his voice dying away. He took a deep breath.

"If you loved her, you demonstrated your love most strangely."

"I did love her, and I love her still. She loved me, too. She married me."

"Martha was only a trusting girl at Donnithorpe. And you left her, without one word of farewell." Holmes watched the sabre in Hudson's hand, ready for any move to attack.

"My father begged me to come with him, to help him escape," Hudson burst out. "I didn't have any other choice."

"Yes." Holmes saw the sabre make a quivering motion. "You fled with your father when he was unmasked as an extortionist and a former pirate. If the law should be consulted, those things would weigh against him and against you. You sacrificed Martha's love for you. You abrogated it, and she has nothing but contempt for you now."

"Words, words," mouthed Hudson. "Why do you speak of the law? There is no law any more. You and I shall settle this business alone!"

"Not quite alone, I suspect," said Holmes evenly. "Someone else is coming this way to join us — or something. Hark!"

Something clanked outside, clanked again. The noise grew louder as Holmes spoke.

"I daresay it is a Martian fighting-machine," said Holmes. "I was careful as I came along this street, but you were too intent on following me and making your threats. What if an invader has spied you and is coming after you?"

Clank, clank, just outside the building.

"That's nothing," cried Hudson wildly. "An awning, creaking in the wind. Your tricks can't make me afraid. Tell me where Martha is!"

He took another heavy step, the sabre whipped up high. Holmes seized a bar stool. Hudson cut savagely at him, and the sabre's edge bit deeply into the wooden seat of the stool as Holmes warded off the blow. At that moment, there was a sudden heavy crash outside. The windows and the door drove violently inward in a clatter of fragments.

Dropping the stool, Holmes slid quickly backwards toward a rear door that stood partially open. Hudson wheeled, just as a loud jangling crack and hum sounded through the barroom and the domed superstructure of a fighting-machine lowered itself into view among the wreckage of glass and broken wood.

Like a shadow, Holmes moved through that open rear door. He went down four or five dark stairs inside and turned again to look into the barroom.

Hudson shrieked a curse. A tentacle, gleaming darkly, came writhing toward him. He ran half a dozen paces across the floor and made a desperate slash with the sabre. Its edge glanced from the tentacle with a metallic clang, and it fell from his hand to rattle upon the floor.

Hudson screamed. The tentacle had snapped two coils around his body, swift as thought, like a python seizing a prey. Hudson struggled and screamed again. His captor lifted him effortlessly and bore him away outside.

Holmes tiptoed down the rest of the stairs, his hand on the wall to support him. Small windows gave a faint wash of light in the cellar. From the barroom overhead came tappings, scrapings, a tinkling crash of glass or crockery. Having secured Hudson, the invader had reached back its tentacles to search for food, the sort of food mankind ate. Holmes stood like a statue. At last the heavy humming clank resumed, like the fall of mighty feet. The invader was departing.

Up the stairs he headed again, and to the smashed front of the shop. The gigantic enemy stood hardly a block away. Its cowl turned from side to side. It swung around and came rushing back to the shop. Holmes faintly glimpsed a steel basket on the monster's back, and a struggling figure inside – Hudson.

He raced back through the shop and down into the cellar. As he ran, he heard a heavy booming sound like an explosion, as though the whole front of the building had been driven in. The floor above him shook with the crash of broken lumber and masonry.

Then, silence again. If the monster had meant to capture him, too, it was defeated by the violence of its own attack on the building. The whole structure must have collapsed, trapping him in the cellar.

Moving silently, he explored the dark basement, by what light the window gave. This was a stone-flagged storage space. There were kegs of what seemed to be salt fish, and crates of dried vegetables; and, on a side shelf, some tinned and potted delicacies. He stuffed the great pockets of his coat with tins of lobster, sardines, tongue, liver pâté. Now to get out again—but not the way he had come.

For that invader who had taken Hudson might still be in view of the smashed front door. Holmes moved as quietly as possible to a coal bin at the rear of the cellar. A square trap showed above it. He climbed upon the coal, shoved the trap upward, and climbed through. He found himself emerging upon a paved court, with a plank roof overhead and a narrow alleyway beyond.

He prowled across and through a fenced area opposite the back door of a haberdasher's. It was locked, but he produced a pick and expertly sprung the catch. On through he went, to the front. No sign of lurking menace in the street, nor anywhere all the way home.

Eleven

In the morning he came out again to observe, first from the top of his own building, then from the parapet of Camden House, looking through powerful field glasses. For some hours he probed the distances of London, clear to see in all directions now with the smoke of industry blown away. Once or twice he heard remote siren voices, but he saw no movement of the enemy except miles away to the northeast. He considered, and this time discarded, a scouting adventure toward Primrose Hill.

Again that night he lighted no lamp, but he brought out his violin and played softly to himself to help his thoughts, the composition that Martha had remembered and liked. Then he made more notes to add to his sheaf, until it was too dark to see the page.

On Sunday morning he wakened to remind himself that the tenth and last of the cylinders from Mars must have found its landing place on Earth overnight. But again, there were no menacing sounds of machines outside his windows. Holmes studied the case on the mantelpiece that for years had held his hypodermic needle, studied the bottles of cocaine and morphine, so long unused. But he felt no impulse to take any such stimulant now, not with a problem itself so stimulating, so energizing, that it brought out the best in him. He pondered the mental processes of the invaders. He had been wont to say, whimsically, that he himself was principally a brain, that the rest of his body was no more than an appendage. That brain of his might not be despicable in comparison with those of his adversaries.

After a while, he went out and down to steal along Baker Street, almost all the way to Regent's Park with its shadowing trees. Primrose Hill and enemy headquarters lay beyond, no more than a mile or so. As he lounged within a doorway to estimate the situation, a prolonged cry rang out above the treetops of Regent's Park, and Sherlock Holmes listened.

That cry was not so strident, not so dominating, this time. It sounded like a true voice, not a metallic note, and it seemed pleading, even troubled. Holmes gazed at the trees of the park. Above and away from them hovered a thread of a paler green colour, the vapour the invaders emitted from their mechanical devices. It hung there in place. Whatever gave it form did not move. Again rose the plaintive cry, almost as though it begged for compassion.

Holmes frowned over the mystery. After several more moments he headed back home again, as circumspectly as he had come forth. The cry sounded no more behind him.

In his sitting room, he glanced at his watch. It was nearly noon, and he would do well to eat something. As before, he boiled water to make tea, while he opened a box of cracknels and two tins of choice Italian sardines. He partook of these things sparingly, then sat down in his armchair, his knees drawn up and his fingertips together, to rationalise what had happened and what still would happen.

The invaders apparently patrolled London less freely. Their feet fell with heavy impact on the pavements, but their hold on the city seemed less arrogantly sure. That information he had sent to Birmingham – and by now Hopkins must have reached there – would help. So would later findings – if he could manage some way of sending them – help form new policies to help mankind deal with its danger.

The red weed had given him a clue. It offered evidence to replace conjecture. Overwhelmingly swift in its growth, yet it perished almost as swiftly, fell to pieces, and washed away in the water. It could not face the conditions Earth imposed for survival. Might this analogy be applied to the masters of those machines with their heat-rays and black smoke?

Very likely.

Holmes reflected deeply on certain aspects of world history, in which this race or that had been assailed by deadly plagues. Stalwart Indian warriors, for instance, had caught measles from white frontiersmen in America and had died by whole tribes from what Europe considered a mild childhood disorder. On South Pacific islands, splendid physical specimens of native races had perished from nothing more deadly than the common cold. Their systems had not been conditioned to resist it, and it had destroyed them.

Morse Hudson had been sick with a cold when he was snatched away from before Holmes' very eyes by the tentacle of an invader. Whatever they did with Hudson, what would they do with, or against, his disease?

What could they do?

Flying from Mars, they had assembled here in conquered London. If a plague sprang up among them, none would escape it. Those fifty invaders would suffer and languish, would perish. Sherlock Holmes felt suddenly certain of that.

Outside the open window, a bird sang. Holmes' saturnine face relaxed as he listened. He wished he had a companion with whom to discuss these concepts. Not that he wished Martha here, he was grateful that she was a comparatively safe distance apart from London. But it was too bad that Moriarty had been a menace, to be killed in the grapple at

Reichenbach Falls. Holmes had overcome him by Oriental wrestling, what his Oriental coach had called baritsu, or jiu-jitsu, or judo. It used an opponent's strength against him; let his fierce overconfident aggression channel itself into a headlong fall to disaster. The same thing might happen now, if man could be found to apply the baritsu principle and not collapse themselves in unreasoning panic.

Had Moriarty been an ally, he would have had the mind and courage to help. Challenger, if he had survived the invaders' assault, might yet join Holmes and help to plan a campaign. But the man Holmes wished for above all others was loyal, dependable Watson, wherever he might be.

The lean face smiled. How often Holmes had teased Watson about not understanding the science of deduction. As a joke, that was all very well, and Watson took it in good part. But Watson was a scientist himself, would grasp and help rationalise this proposition of earthly diseases striking the invaders. He would see that, even if the first battles had been lost, the war was not lost.

For this was not simply a war of humanity against strangers from beyond space, it was a true War of the Worlds. Mother Earth herself would prevail against these unbidden, unwanted intruders.

Watson? Was he still alive? Would he come home again?

Holmes took up his cherrywood pipe and bent down to fill it with tobacco from the Persian slipper beside his chair.

The door opened and Watson stumbled in.

III

⁓

GEORGE E. CHALLENGER VERSUS MARS
BY EDWARD DUNN MALONE

Twelve

Friday's twilight was falling over West Kensington when Challenger came home to Enmore Park. He lumbered in, slamming the door so fiercely that the whole house vibrated. Little Mrs Challenger hurried into the hall to meet him.

"Foolishness on every hand, arrant foolishness that brought disaster at Woking," he erupted before she could question him. "The Martians came out of their cylinder and struck down a whole crowd of people who came too close."

"Thank heaven you have escaped, George," his wife quavered.

"They would not listen to me," he went on angrily. "I came there with the one device that would have served, this crystal egg." From a side pocket of his tweed jacket he rummaged the thing, a blue light shining from it as he held it out. "I told Stent, the Astronomer Royal, and his stupid friend Ogilvy that it had power to communicate with those creatures – that I had seen them by its agency, and that they certainly must have seen me. I pleaded with the two fools, earnestly, eloquently!" His great voice rose to a roar. "And they? They brushed me aside, like a thing of no account, ignored my warnings of manifest danger, and formed a party under a white flag."

"What is this crystal?" asked Mrs Challenger, eyeing it timidly.

"Oh, I don't believe I have mentioned it to you, Jessie. Sherlock Holmes and I have been observing the Martians in it. But I was speaking of the arrant stupidity of their flag of truce. Why should they think that a white flag would seem a peace overture to such alien observers? To these invaders – which is what I take them to be – it might well have seemed the very opposite."

He strode off down the hall to his study and set the crystal on his table. His wife trotted at his heels.

"You said that people were killed," she reminded him. "A whole crowd of them."

"I saw that from a distance, after I had turned my back on Stent and Ogilvy. It was some sort of flashing light, which I judge burned as it struck. Those who survived ran. I heard about it from them."

His brow furrowed. "Nor was that all, my dear. Some poor devil was shoved into the pit when the cylinder opened, pushed into it by fools crowding eagerly to see the invaders, and I thought I saw him caught by some sort of mechanical contrivance. There was no possible chance to go to his aid. Later, at a distance, I saw his head bob up and down, heard him cry out as though he struggled. No doubt they dragged him into the cylinder. Almost at once, they brought their weapon into play. I now wonder what they will do to their first prisoner of war."

"You call it a war," she said softly.

"I foresee that it will be a war between worlds." He gazed at his wife, and his scowling face relaxed. "Yes, my dear, G.E.C. has been spared to you, and to an undeserving nation which will need him badly. I am glad to be home, and I begin to realise that I have had no dinner. Might there be something in the kitchen that may be readily prepared?"

"I'll ask Austin to bring you something."

She pattered out. Left alone, Challenger stared down into the crystal. After a moment, he dragged out the black cloth to screen away the light. He was able to get a view of dust and shadows, where several bladdery bodies sprawled. They seemed to work with their tentacles, fitting together lengths and pieces of bright metal.

"The thing moves," he grunted to himself. "It is articulated, after the manner of the jointed leg of a living creature. No slightest sign of a wheel anywhere."

He turned his swivel chair and rose, walking out into the hall to where the telephone was fixed to the wall. He rang and asked for a number. Nobody answered and he hung up, fuming.

"Holmes!" he snorted the name aloud. "What is he doing away from home at a time like this?"

Back he went to his study. Austin appeared, quiet and leathery-faced, bearing a tray set with dishes. Challenger tucked a napkin under his bearded chin.

"Hot roast pork, I see," he remarked. "And Brussels sprouts and scones, and gooseberry, tart. Capital, Austin."

He ate with good appetite, and Austin carried the dishes away. Again Challenger tried to telephone Holmes, and again there was no answer. He shook his great head unhappily. A newsboy cried shrilly outside, and Challenger hurried out to buy a copy of the the special edition offered for sale. Standing in the street, he read the headlines and the leader article, then stormed into the house again.

"Imbecility compounded!" he bellowed, flourishing the paper in his wife's startled face. "The inaccuracy of England's pressmen is rivaled only by the foolish misdirection of the scientific pundits."

He jabbed at the page with his mighty forefinger. "Here it is stated, with complete certitude, that the Martians are harmless beyond the direct range of their weapons, and that they can scarcely crawl. Dolt, simpleton! Does he think—if thinking is not impossible to a journalist — that they came among us with no means of transportation? They will have mechanical devices beyond anything that our Earth has ever conceived. I question even if they are hindered by our gravity. For that matter, they may not be Martians. I tried to explain that to Stent, but the idiot refused to listen."

Yet again he tried to call Holmes, and hung up with a wheezing sigh of discontent.

"Holmes, at least, has caution and can understand the presence of danger," he said. "You tell me he went to Woking. I give myself to hope that he was not one of the fools who died there."

She gave a little cry of protest. "Oh, George, how can you be so callous when those scientists died so miserably?"

"Their loss, my dear, may be a tragedy considered from a conservative human standpoint," he admitted, more quietly. "For my part, I will seek to bear it with fortitude. But I value Holmes more than Stent, Ogilvy, and all their colleagues together, and my principal concern is for him. Our researches together with the crystal were rewarding."

She still lingered, her wide eyes upon him. "George, I have a right to ask you why you never hinted to me of all these things until now. Did you believe I would be frightened to distraction?"

He put the newspaper aside.

"That, my dear, is exactly what I believed," he said, smiling in his beard. "Had I taken you into my confidence about this communication with Mars, and this knowledge that they were on their way to Earth, you would never have slept at night and you would have worried by day, which in turn would have worried me. But now there is no reason to keep anything from you."

And he bent his shaggy face to kiss her.

Early on Saturday morning, he rang up Holmes again, and when there was no answer, he went out to buy newspapers.

These were full of tremendous headlines and very little news. It was plain to see that the advent of the invaders – another cylinder had landed, not far from the first – tremendously excited the British Government, without any suggestion of how to receive such a visitation. Troops had encircled the Martian positions, heavy guns were moving up, but strict orders had been issued not to attack. Efforts must be made, said the authorities, to signal the Martians in their pit; and nobody seemed vastly to fear the emergence of any dangerous Martian technology. One witness was quoted as saying that the Martians wielded their heat-ray from a mechanical vehicle, "like a moving dish-cover." Challenger shook his head over these.

"Typical journalistic garblings of hysterical reports," he said to Mrs Challenger at breakfast. "Those creatures might laugh, if they could laugh, over these things. Why do the papers not tell us something of true importance–the fate of Holmes, for instance?"

But by late morning, a letter came by special messenger. Challenger tore it open eagerly.

"He has escaped, and is back in London," he said happily to his wife. "But hear what he says, to the effect that 'Very likely they consider us lower animals.'" He crumpled the sheet in his great paw. "Lower animals, indeed; how much lower, does Holmes think? This was the conclusion he did not divulge to me, just as I did not develop to him my suspicion that the creatures observed on Mars are not native to Mars."

"George, why do you say that?"

"Because only now have I given it serious meditation. Well, I wonder if Holmes is right about lower animals. I have felt that we are better compared to savage tribesmen than to lower animals."

"At least Mr Holmes was fortunate to escape," offered Mrs Challenger.

"Fortunate be damned! He was wise and prudent. He tells about it modestly. Modesty is a trait which Holmes shares with myself."

Austin brought in more special editions of the newspapers as the day went along. They reported that the Martians were busily working in their first pit. The town of Woking had been badly damaged, many of its buildings having been set ablaze by the heat-ray. Troops were concentrating in Surrey – infantry, artillery, cavalry, and engineers – and their commanding officers confidently predicted a swift destruction of the invaders. Challenger wondered what Holmes would say.

Again he tried to telephone to 221B Baker Street, but service was disrupted and he could not achieve a connection. He tried Martha Hudson's number, but in vain. At last he brought out the the crystal in his study and tented himself in the black cloth to look into it.

He saw a gouged, tumbled place in the earth. In the background a machine moved and revolved, stacking what appeared to be bars of pale metal. Several invaders crept and slumped there, and in their midst Challenger made out a struggling something, a human figure– undoubtedly the man who had been shoved into the pit and captured.

The fellow strove helplessly against a myriad of metal tentacles that cross-latched upon his body. He was naked, and his mouth gaped wide open as though he screamed in terror. One invader hunched above him. Challenger saw a wink of light on metal, something like a long slender pipestem. A steel tentacle drove this down into the struggling victim. The bladder-bulk stooped close above it, making contact at the free end of the pipe.

Challenger forced himself to watch the process through. Now he knew how the invading monsters fed.

"A drawing of living blood," he muttered. "Living blood, from a living victim. Holmes is right. We are lower animals, and to them we mean food."

"Jessie," he called out, "we must make plans to leave London soon."

She came from the drawing room. "Why leave London?" she asked.

"Those invaders may well be heading this way," he said soberly. "I, for one, have no intention of serving on a reception committee. I have just seen, in the crystal, their way of treating us – and I prefer not to elaborate upon it, even to you. I shall keep in touch with events, and we must plan on being gone when those events approach too embarrassingly near."

"You have heard from Mr Holmes. Is he at home now?"

"He was when he wrote to me."

"Will you go to visit him?"

"Not now. I would do well to be reachable here."

Thirteen

Night came, and with it a great torrent of rain and the crashing of thunder. Challenger wondered how invaders from arid Mars, if indeed they were native to that planet, might deal with such a storm. The telephone rang. Someone was calling Professor Challenger from London University, but the connection was so faulty that he could not tell who the speaker was or what he wanted. Then the sound of the nervous voice broke off. Challenger spoke disdainfully into the dead instrument and hung up the receiver.

Sunday morning was bright again, and the street outside was thronged with excited people. Challenger came out and approached a knot of men, all of them talking at once.

"Have you any news of the invaders?" he addressed them, and his ringing bass voice riveted their attention.

"Here's my mate, what was there at the time and place, guv'ner," said one of the group, pointing at a pallid-faced oldster in a checked coat and cloth cap.

"It's the truth, sir, and I don't never want to go back there no more," said this man earnestly. "Swelp me, they can set the 'ole world afire, they can."

"Yes, yes, I saw the beginning of that," said Challenger. "What can you tell me of their operations?"

"Operations?" repeated the other. "Bless you, sir, all I can say is, I don't want them operatin' on me, and that's whatever. I caught the mornin' train in from Woking, and be'ind me I seen my old 'ouse blazin' away like a fire in a grate. Thank the Lord I ain't got no wife nor child to 'old me back. Now I'm for catchin' another train, as it might be for Glasgow."

"When I spoke of operations," said Challenger, with what he thought was patient calm, "I meant their *modus operandi*. How they move and fight, how they manoeuvre."

The old man blinked at him. "I don't understand you, sir."

"As Dr Samuel Johnson said in a conversation similar to this, I am not obliged to provide you with an understanding. Tell me what you saw of their machines in action."

"I seen only a little of that, and it was ample. They go walkin' round in great tall things, taller than church steeples, with three legs—"

"Three legs?" repeated Challenger.

"Like a milkin' stool, with a hood at the top, turnin' here and there and flashin' their devilish heat-rays, I 'eard say they wiped out a whole regiment. I'm fair glad I wasn't there to see that."

Challenger turned heavily away and returned to his telephone. Once more he tried to call Holmes, then rang up the War Office, intent on offering his services. The overworked operators could put him through to neither. As he hung up the receiver with an angry snort, church bells tolled outside. Austin came to Challenger's study with a special edition of a newspaper, shakily printed and with big screaming headlines. A third cylinder was reported as having arrived, also in Surrey. The Martians were abroad in their vaguely described machines, of which the paper said only that they were towering structures of intricate workmanship and operation, running on three jointed legs with the speed of an express train. Artillery units had been obliterated by the incomprehensible heat-ray. Not much more could be learned from anything in the journal.

In the afternoon, Challenger walked the street, trying to learn something from those who had come up from Surrey. He talked to a young man, who stopped to wipe sweat and rest in front of the house. At Challenger's word, Austin fetched out bread and beef and a glass of ale, and the man told of his adventures, shakily but understandably.

He was an attorney's clerk and had been visiting friends at a country house in Surrey for the weekend. He said that he had seen the Martians in action and that he counted himself fortunate in being able to flee back to London. The Martians, he told Challenger, had effortlessly and mercilessly struck houses and villages, but had seemed rather to concentrate their attention on various communications. Railroads and telegraph lines had been systematically destroyed.

"To be brief," summed up Challenger, "they seek to disrupt us rather than exterminate us outright."

"From what little I saw, that seems to be their policy," said the clerk, eating the last of the sandwich.

"Thank you sir, for your kindness. I had best be getting along now, my rooms are near Promise Hill."

He mumbled his thanks and walked away. Challenger walked slowly along the street, then back. When he returned home, it was time for the evening meal, and he was thoughtful as he ate.

"George," said his wife at last, "what are we to do?"

"I am coming to a decision on that, Jessie. By this time in our relationship, you have learned to depend on my decisions. Tomorrow morning we leave London."

"To go where, George?"

"That is still problematical. Please pack a change of clothes for us and bring your valuables – your jewels and so forth."

He himself was awake in the early summer dawn, dressing himself in comfortable tweeds. He filled his pocket case with banknotes and into his trousers pockets dropped twenty gold guineas along with silver and copper coins. When he had finished with breakfast, he went to the door. Austin had stepped out at the cry of a newspaper hawker, and Challenger saw him standing on the pavement, the paper in his hand, talking to a short, heavyset man with grey sidewhiskers and a visored cap. Beside them at the curb waited a spotted horse in the shafts of a two-wheeled cart.

Austin handed Challenger the paper. Challenger glanced at the front page, while people hastened past him, jabbering to each other. LONDON IN PERIL, said the big black headline, and there was an account of military units wiped out at Kempton and Richmond and great destruction of suburban communities, also a new perilous weapon, which the paper called black smoke. This was described as a discharge of "enormous clouds of a black and poisonous vapour by means of rockets."

Challenger turned to where Austin was arguing with the man in the cap. "I can't go without Professor Challenger's word," said Austin.

"Go where?" Challenger demanded.

"I'm an old friend of Austin's, sir," said the strange man, touching his visor in something of a military salute. "Knew him when we was both railroad men. Now the train crews are refusing to work, and we're getting up a volunteer crew to carry off these crowds of frightened folk to the north."

"My duty is to you and Mrs Challenger, Professor," said Austin, but Challenger waved the words away.

"Go with him, Austin, if he needs you. You can be of great use in helping with the train. But," and he faced the railroad man, "if you take Austin from me, you leave your horse and cart."

He looked at the horse. It was a gelding, perhaps eight years old at a guess, short-limbed but seemingly healthy and strong.

"What's his name?" asked Challenger.

"Dapple, sir. But it wouldn't hardly be regular if–"

"Nonsense!" Challenger broke in, so loudly that a passerby turned to stare over his shoulder. "What regularity is there in the present situation? These are excessively irregular times, my good man, and a certain irregularity is implicit in the meeting of them. Come now, you want Austin, I want your horse and cart. I call it more than a fair exchange!"

Again his voice rose to a roar as he spoke the last words. The railroad man almost quailed before him and held out a palm.

"Well then, sir, shall we say ten pounds?"

Challenger fished out a banknote and handed it over.

"Go pack whatever you need, Austin," he directed his manservant. "Take cook with you, and Jane the maid, and may all of you have good luck and find safety."

"Won't Mrs Challenger go on the train with us, Professor?" Austin asked.

"On an overcrowded, overworked train, manned by volunteers?" Challenger blared at him. "I value her too much for that. But ask her to step out here for a word with me. Hurry along, now."

Austin trotted in, and after a moment Mrs Challenger appeared. Her husband smiled triumphantly at her.

"Observe the equipage with which we will take our little jaunt into the country," he said. "Now, I must stand by here with our new friend Dapple; someone might be tempted to drive him away. Can you manage to bring out our bags, and my straw hat and those Alpine boots? Pack us a dinner basket, too. Cold meat for today, and tinned things for later – sausages, perhaps, and sardines and pickles. Off with you, my dear, we must be quick."

She bustled away obediently. Austin came out carrying a battered satchel and accompanied by the two women servants, and they departed with the trainman. Challenger examined the cart. It was lightly and plainly made, but serviceable, the sort of vehicle used around railroad stations to carry luggage and express packages. The floor of the bed was lined with straw, and the seat could hold two. He stroked Dapple's flecked nose, and Dapple responded with a soft whinny.

"You and I begin to know each other already," said Challenger.

Minutes passed, and Mrs Challenger appeared again, weighted down with a wicker picnic basket. Challenger met her on the steps and bore the basket to set in the cart.

"I must ask pardon for sending you to carry heavy things," he said, "but I cannot leave our conveyance alone."

He gestured to the growing stream of bustling pedestrians.

"Might you be in danger if someone wants to take the horse?"

"Let someone try! But I dislike to see you struggling with burdens."

"I don't ask for apologies," she said. "I have always tried to act upon your judgement of things."

"And with good reason," he nodded, with a smile of approval. "There are husbands in this world upon whose judgements it is folly to act my dear, but I am not one of them. Now, the clothing."

"I have already packed it. I will go and fetch it."

She went back into the house. Challenger bent and examined the basket with dignified relish. It was filled with sandwiches and fruit, some tinned things, and two bottles of wine. Mrs Challenger came out again with a satchel, returned, and brought another. Into the cart went the stout boots Challenger had specified, and upon his head he set a round, stiff hat of straw with a bright ribbon. Mrs Challenger herself wore a sensible brown dress and sturdy walking shoes. She bound down her hat with a veil that tied under her chin and flung a cape around her. Once more, at her husband's direction, she went into the house and filled a gallon earthenware jug with water.

"Now we are ready, as I judge," he said as he stowed this with the other supplies. "Up you get, my dear. It has been five years and more, if memory serves me, since I have taken you on a drive."

He helped her to the seat and mounted ponderously to sit beside her. The springs creaked beneath his weight. "Gee up, Dapple," he commanded, flicking the reins.

Away they rolled, sitting together like a massive tame bear and a gazelle. They had to wait at a crossing while a close-jammed throng of people passed, feet hurrying and faces frightened. Then they continued, along the Uxbridge Road. They fared westward, slowed down by traffic both on the street and on the sidewalks. Challenger drove with careful attention, his great hairy hand light but authoritatively firm on the reins. The sun was well up, and the crowds were thicker at every crossing. Policemen tried to control the rush, but the policemen, too, looked frightened.

"I hazard the speculation that our Martian visitors are closer at hand," said Challenger. "Whatever they are doing, it stimulates the desire to stay well away from them."

Checking his horse, he leaned down to call to one of the crowd. "What news have you?" he asked.

"It's all up with the soldiers," was the panting reply. "And they're scorching the whole country with their heat-ray, and drowning it with their black smoke."

Waiting no longer, the man ran ahead to northward along a cross street, Challenger clucked Dapple into a trot.

"Heat-ray," he rumbled. "Black smoke. I have seen something of the one and have heard something of the other, and Holmes suggests that they may have deadlier weapons. I doubt if Holmes is being unduly pessimistic. Well, these considerations impel me not to seek a possible ship on the Thames. We'll keep going out of town. Perhaps we can get beyond this rush."

"If we stayed in London, George—"

"If we did, it would be like staying in a burning house, or possibly worse than that."

Her dark eyes were wider than ever. "Oh, George, what must England's scientists be thinking?"

"I can tell you, my dear Jessie, exactly what they are thinking, if we may flatteringly apply such a term to their inadequate mental processes. They are thinking that they were wrong again, and that G. E. C. was right again, and they hope that they have not begun to think too late in the game."

"Too late?" she repeated, her voice hushed in terror. "Is disaster upon humanity?"

Challenger reined Dapple into the middle of the street to avoid a hastening wheelbarrow.

"That, Jessie, is a question not susceptible of any but a qualified reply. It is quite plain that humanity has fought and lost its first battle and is in demoralised flight. But I reflect that such things have happened in past wars. Frederick the Great was obliged to fly from his first battle. So was Sherman, the American general, at Bull Run. Yet both of them proved victorious later."

"Later," Mrs Challenger said, almost dreamily. "Later."

"We shall see what happens later. At present, suppose we emulate those other brilliant tacticians in the orderly swiftness of our retreat."

But it was with no great swiftness that they drove westward into Clerkenwell. The sidewalks at the crossings were full of people, and a stream of vehicles clattered in the streets – cabs, private carriages, carts, heavy wagons, bicycles. The air shook with the roar of wheels, the louder roar of voices. Once a bulbously fat man in a derby hat tried to catch hold of the cart and climb up behind, and Challenger cut him across the face with the whip to make him let go. Beyond Clerkenwell they came into

Shoreditch, and at last, as the sun rose to high noon in a hot blue sky, they found themselves on Mile End Road, on their way out of London.

"Good horse, then," Challenger praised Dapple. "You have done nobly. How old are you, do you suppose? Jessie, it is fifty miles and better to the east coast and possible safety. Prepare for a long summer jaunt of it."

"I feel perfectly safe with you, George dear."

"And you do well to trust to me. But I believe I said something like that earlier today."

Though they had come well past the center of town, traffic was heavier. The road seemed jammed from side to side, with horses and carriages all going eastward at a nervous trot.

"I do hope that this great crowd of travel will grow thin again," said Mrs Challenger, pressing her little body close to her husband's side.

"A vain hope, Jessie," was his bleak reply. "Look there ahead."

Pedestrians also moved into the road, so thickly pressed together that Challenger had to rein Dapple to a walk. People shoved pushcarts, trundled perambulators heaped with cluttered possessions. As Challenger tried to make a way through without striking anyone on foot, a great carriage drawn by two glossy bays came rolling from behind and would have run upon the little cart had not Challenger swung around where he sat and whipped the nearer horse with all his strength. The animal emitted a startled, squealing neigh and reared so abruptly that the carriage was almost overturned. Challenger won through a knot of people, and beyond turned to the right along a side road, little more than a grassy-bordered lane.

"Where are you taking us?" Mrs Challenger cried out. "That is the direction of danger."

"The direction of what may be better progress," he half snapped. "The main thoroughfare is too cluttered. At any moment, it could become impossible to travel there. Country ways may be better."

He drove a full mile before turning again and travelling toward the east, through the outlying cottages of a little hamlet. As he had foreseen, it was less crowded, though vehicles moved here, too. Several hurrying people cried out to be taken into the cart, but Challenger paid them no attention.

At last he drew out his watch. It was three o'clock, and they had made gratifying progress. He allowed himself to wonder how the invaders fared, how closely they might be pressing this tremendous retreat from London. A look into the crystal—

"Oh, abomination!" he cried aloud, in something between a furious yell and a groan of self-accusation. "I left it in my study, in an old tea canister!"

"In your study?" echoed his wife anxiously. "What, George?"

"Oh, no matter now," he wheezed. "I suppose even the greatest, the most advanced of intellects, must sometimes overlook a matter."

"George, you were too concerned in bringing me to safety."

At that, he mustered a smile that stirred his beard like a wind in a dark forest.

"Bringing you to safety, Jessie, is a measure that must assume precedence over all else. Do not concern yourself."

Ahead of them showed a bit of green meadow, with flowers fenced in beyond. He turned the cart from the road and upon the grass.

"We will stop for a time," he declared. "Poor Dapple has been going long and faithfully, and he should rest. So, when it comes to that, should I. And so, by making a scientific judgement, I think should you as well."

"Would it not be better to keep going along, George?"

"Not if we are to see our excellent little horse able to take us to the ocean."

Mrs Challenger fell silent, as she had learned to do when her husband spoke with such determination. Challenger got heavily down and went to pat Dapple's cheek. He was answered by a soft whinny.

"It is good that you and I are on such friendly terms," Challenger said, unhitching Dapple from between the shafts. He took off the bridle and used a rein to tether Dapple to a wheel. At once Dapple began cropping lush June grass.

"We have not eaten since early this morning, Jessie," said Challenger. "Perhaps you will look out materials to give us a pleasant *al fresco* dinner. I shall go find water for Dapple."

He walked off toward the fence with the flowers. On the far side showed the roof and windows of a brown cottage. Mrs Challenger lifted out the big basket, spread a blue-checked cloth on the ground, and set it with two plates and some sandwiches and fruit. She had finished drawing the cork on a bottle of Burgundy when Challenger came tramping back, a bucket of water in either hand, and, slung across his broad shoulder, a crumpled dark fabric.

"The house is deserted," he informed her. "Sensible people – they have fled before the report of danger. I found a pump, and here is water for us and for Dapple as well."

"And what else have you there?"

"Two blankets. I found them hanging on a clothesline. It may be a chilly night for this time of year, and we must camp here."

He gave the horse water and watched it drink gratefully. Then he came to sit cross-legged on the ground and eat with hearty appetite. Mrs Challenger barely bit into her sandwich and swallowed a few grapes. Challenger coaxed her to drink a glass of wine with him.

"Here is a toast to our present situation," he said, lifting his own glass. "Confusion to these importunate visitors, and a safe journey to us."

She, too, sipped. "But so much of disaster has come already," she said, her voice hushed with gloomy foreboding. "I keep thinking of those scientists you say died so horribly – Mr Stent, and Mr Ogilvy. Surely you mourn them, too, the more because our Earth could use their knowledge and advice today."

"As to their knowledge and advice, I can find nothing in those things to feel great deprivation in their loss," replied her husband gravely. "I regard the scientific attainments of both Stent and Ogilvy with an indifference that partakes of professional disdain. But you are right, dear Jessie, in reminding me that I should be sorry that they have died. It was a wretched death, let me assure you, and an entirely unnecessary one."

This condescension seemed to relieve Mrs Challenger, who ate another sandwich of roast chicken and had a second glass of wine. They sat at ease and talked, while Dapple grazed near the cart. The sun set at last, and peace seemed to abide in the cloudless sky as it darkened.

"I am getting sleepy, George," said Mrs Challenger at last, yawning behind her tiny hand. "That is strange, don't you think? Last night I slept barely at all."

"Which is the exact reason you feel like resting now. Let me arrange these blankets for you. Wait, before we spread them. I shall hollow you a bed."

Powerfully he scooped away soft lumps of turf, to make a depression that would fit her body. Then he tramped here and there, picking up dry wood under trees that fringed the grassy plot. He brought back a great armful and then another.

"This is enough for a small fire to take the chill off, and with careful supervision it will last out the night," he said in his lecturer's voice.

"But will you not lie down, too?"

"Later, my dear."

She crept among the folds of the blankets. He sat by the fire crooning a favourite song of his:

> *Ring out, wild bells, to the wild sky*
> *Ring out the old, ring in the new*

His wife seemed to be comforted, as by a lullaby. At last he heard her breathing gently and regularly in slumber. But he sat awake in deep thought.

He wished he had brought the crystal, and ventured the hope that it would stay safe, with his house safe as well, while the invaders moved through on their way up from Surrey. If Holmes were here, there might be profitable discussion of the dire situation. He remembered what he had seen the last time in the crystal and clamped his teeth beneath his beard. Despite his repeatedly expressed contempt for humanity in general, the thought of a fellow man given to such a fate made his blood run cold.

Again he remembered Holmes' letter and the suggestion that man was but a lower animal in the harsh view of the invaders. Did Holmes suggest that the invaders, then, represented an advanced form of life developed by evolution from the human form? Did humanoid creatures exist, or had they existed, on other worlds of the universe?

As he asked himself these things, a night bird sang close by, its voice strangely sweet in a world so terribly threatened. What might the invaders think of birds? He took the bottle from the basket and drank another glass of wine, then rinsed the glass in the bucket and walked through the night to fetch more water from the well in the cottage yard.

It was nearly midnight, as his watch told him, when the sky suddenly glowed with a racing streak of green light, like the path of a flying meteor. Surely another cylinder, he knew as he watched it drop to the western horizon and wink out of sight. Very likely it was landing in Surrey, near the others. Quickly he counted in his head. Midnight of Monday – this would be the fifth arrival. Five more were hurtling earthward on their way. They would find their fellows triumphantly in possession of Earth's largest city.

At last he lay down on the blankets and slept.

He was awake at sunrise, brushing dew from his beard. He carried the buckets to the well beside the cottage. A cyclist in dusty clothes stopped in the front yard, and Challenger let him drink gratefully from the bucket.

"What is happening?" Challenger asked.

The cyclist dully told him about flight from London, of riding desperately all the afternoon and most of the night. The Martians had cloaked the Thames and its banks with their black smoke, killing crowds of helpless people who had not been able to get away. But no fighting-machines had seemed to come eastward out of town so far.

"Perhaps they'll be satisfied with London," croaked the cyclist, wiping his dirty face.

"No longer than time enough to establish themselves there," said Challenger authoritatively. "Afterwards, they will range further."

"And what will they do?"

"It will take some perception to divine their future tactics."

The man mounted his bicycle and pedalled away. Challenger carried the buckets to his own campsite and held one for Dapple to drink. Mrs Challenger, too, was awake. She had tucked back her hair and folded the blankets. They dipped a cloth to wash their faces and hands, and made a breakfast of bread and fruit and tinned herring. She took a little copper pot from the basket to boil tea for them.

"And now?" she said. "It seems so peaceful here."

"It seemed more or less peaceful in Enmore Park, only last Thursday. Shall we go along?"

He reharnessed Dapple and they rolled off on the road.

"Such a good horse," said Mrs Challenger. "Dapple – it is a good name, I think."

"A common name, and a fairly descriptive one," Challenger replied. "But thus far, he has shown some evidence of being an uncommon horse in an uncommon situation. He is strong, willing, and docile. Our relationship with him is uncommon, in more ways than one."

"Uncommon, George? How so, apart from the crisis, the emergency?"

"A question well worth the asking, my dear," he lectured. "I have been giving some considerations to the problem of what these invaders think. And I agree with Holmes that to them mankind is a mere race of lower animals. They may well regard horses as a different species in a broad category of inferior creatures. But as to Dapple, should he be as extraordinary among horses as myself, or even Holmes, among men, then he will nobly serve our needs. I hope that he will bring us to the Channel coast before nightfall."

They found carriages and hurrying pedestrians on the road. One huge dray wagon came thundering from behind, making the little cart wheel far to the side to avoid being hit. Challenger's blue eyes shone dangerously, but he said nothing to the driver. They fared on their way for some hours. Occasionally, at crossroads, they caught glimpses of the main road to the north, jammed with traffic.

"How wonderfully wise you were, George, in deciding to take us along by these side ways," Mrs Challenger said.

"The same thought occurred to me independently," he returned.

At noon they pulled into the dooryard of a deserted inn to eat a hasty lunch. Challenger went inside to look for possible fresh supplies, but found nothing other than two bottles of ale, which he fetched to the cart. They let Dapple rest for an hour, then drove along.

By mid-afternoon they found the traffic much thinner about them and approached a scatter of houses that Challenger took to be in the southern part of Chelmsford. From the yard of one of the houses a group of men came running out across the road as though to stop them, holding up their hands. Challenger reined in.

"What is it?" he growled. "What do you want?"

The men closed in around Dapple, four of them. Three were sturdy fellows, dressed in rough clothes like laborers. The fourth, a sinewy little man with top boots and a peaked cap, might have been a jockey or a groom. His sharp face grinned toothily.

"We're the Committee of Supply of the town of Chelmsford," he proclaimed. "We'll just be taking this horse, sir."

Challenger leaned his huge body forward above the reins. "Will you, indeed?" he asked dangerously. "And why do you presume to do that?"

"For provisions," said the little man, his hand on Dapple's bridle rein. "To eat. Since it's your horse, you can have a slice if you like."

"I have been told by Frenchmen that horseflesh is succulent and nutritious," said Challenger, setting himself to rise quickly. "I cannot speak to that of my own experience. But you must immediately disabuse yourself of any notion that we will give up this horse."

"Hold hard, whoever you are," spoke up the biggest of the others, moving close beside the wheel. "We mean business."

"Exactly," nodded Challenger, with something of baleful cheer in his manner. "Business. And I suggest you attend to your business elsewhere." With ungainly swiftness, he sprang down from the cart. "Be off with you!"

He gave the little man a shove that sent him staggering half a dozen paces away. The others, too, fell back into a knot, scowling. Challenger hunched his shoulders massively and bent his thick knees as though for a spring. His two hands spread themselves, their fingers like hooks.

"Don't talk to him, rush him!" bawled the little man who seemed to be the leader. "He's just one against us, for all his blathering!"

So saying, he drew a step or two apart. The other three advanced upon Challenger.

Challenger's teeth shone like fangs through his beard. Again he made a swift, heavy movement. Slipping past the three men as they charged at him, he clamped his big hands on their leader. The little fellow bawled in sudden terror as Challenger clutched him by shoulder and belt and whirled him bodily aloft, then threw him. The struggling body fairly sang through the air, struck two of the others and mowed them down like a scythe. Challenger wheeled to face the man still on his feet.

"So that's it," growled the man, a broadly built tough with a stubble of roan whiskers on his jaw. Out of his pocket he dragged a huge clasp knife, which he opened with a snap.

Mrs Challenger screamed as the man rushed. Challenger caught the knife wrist in his left hand and with his broad open right palm struck the stubbled face. The blow rang like a pistol shot, and the man went floundering down on the grass at the roadside. He lay as silent as though in sudden deep sleep. Challenger stooped and caught up the knife. He held it in his hand as he turned to face the others, just then struggling to their feet again.

But they only goggled at him, with wide, frightened eyes. Challenger confronted them, a terrible figure, squat, bearded, deadly. As though by a common impulse, they whirled from him and went dashing away among the houses. Challenger watched them go, then closed the knife and put it in his trousers pocket. He picked up his straw hat, which had fallen from his head in the scuffle, and put it on again. Heavily he climbed back to the seat of the cart and took up the reins. His wife gazed at him as though thunderstruck.

"Oh, how awful," she said under her breath.

"Awe is the precise emotion I intended to impart to them, my dear," he wheezed happily. "Gee up, Dapple."

As they trundled away again, he glanced back once. The man he had struck still lay motionless beside the road.

"When he revives again, perhaps he will be more circumspect, Jessie," said Challenger. "I seldom need to appeal to that particular talent of mine for physical combat. But when I was a boy at Largs, and later when I was at the University at Edinburgh, I was more or less preeminent at wrestling. I boxed once, too."

"Once?" she said, her voice still soft and timid.

"Yes, my dear, once. After that single bout, none of the other students were at all interested in trying me."

But his mood of self-congratulation faded when the front wheel on his side began to wobble and creak. He checked Dapple and got down to look.

"I should have foreseen," he said unhappily. "A person of my particularly impressive figure can put too much weight upon a light vehicle. Please change places with me, Jessie."

The cart ran better for a while with Challenger's bulk on the other side. But soon the damaged wheel began again to shake and scrape. Challenger drove at a walk to keep Dapple from striving too hard. By evening they drew into little Tillingham. The whole town seemed deserted, except for two or three figures that prowled at a distance, as though foraging for food in the empty houses. Challenger drove into the yard of a silent cottage.

"We shall stay here for the night," he decreed. "I fought once today for Dapple, but he has been fighting for many hours, on our behalf and he is nearly exhausted. See, there's a barn, and, if I mistake not, hay in the manger. He can spend the night luxuriously, under shelter."

Mrs Challenger stared timorously over her shoulder, but he patted her and actually chuckled in an effort at reassurance.

"Jessie, if the invaders are abroad, they are not many as yet. They will concentrate their attention on the main body of refugees, to the north of here on the main roads. Suppose they should come tonight; they will pass us by unless we officiously attract their attention."

Unhitching Dapple, Challenger led him into the stable and saw that he was provided with hay and water. Then he came and tried the front door of the cottage. It was locked, but a great heave of his shoulder broke it open. They walked into a modest, neat parlour with a leather couch and chairs. A tea service stood on a dresser. Through an inner door was a kitchen.

"Splendid, splendid," pronounced Challenger. He poked his bearded face into a cupboard. "The householders sensibly took away all food, but we have ample provisions for supper. Here is a spirit lamp, over which we can brew our tea. You are used to better quarters than these, Jessie, but I know that you will be more comfortable inside than in the open."

His wife busied herself in setting the kitchen table with bread, potted meat, tea, and some jam tarts, but she was still nervous. Challenger did his best to cheer her up, telling jokes and laughing loudly at them.

"I wish we could have lights tonight, but that might seem an invitation to any possible prowling invaders," he said. "Come, I'll help make you a bed here in this little room, it has the aspect of a boudoir. I'll lie down on the couch on the parlour."

But first he went out to see that no hungry lurkers were disturbing Dapple. He examined the damaged wheel of the cart as best he could in the night, and shook his great head over it. Bringing in their luggage, he thought again of the crystal and wished he had not left it behind. Finally he loosened his neckband and removed his shoes and socks and lay down on the sofa. Its springs creaked under his great weight.

He wakened in the morning. His wife was making tea in the kitchen. Challenger put on his stout alpine boots and walked out to look again at the cart. It was plainly beyond any repair he could make. But he felt better when, entering the stable, he saw a saddle on a rail and a bridle hanging on the wall. These he strapped upon Dapple, who seemed to accept them well.

"You have been ridden as well as driven, it is plain," Challenger addressed the animal. "'Well, now you will carry someone I value most highly. See that you are worthy of the task."

Returning to the house, he ate breakfast with his wife. Then he gathered what food remained into a napkin. He led Mrs Challenger out, helped her into the saddle, and handed her a grip to hold across the pommel. Then he took the reins and led Dapple away through the deserted streets of Tillingham.

No more than two miles beyond, they made their way around a high hill of rock-studded sand, at the top of which showed a small stone house among trees and brush. Just beyond, they came in sight of the shore.

It curved away north and south, with the bright waves lapping a sandy beach directly in front of them and mud flats showing far southward to the right. And the shore itself was thronged with a great dark crowd of people, and the water farther out was full of shipping. Challenger saw liners and cargo vessels well away in deeper water while, closer in, lay a multitude of smaller craft, like a great flock of all manner of sea birds at rest. Among these were tenders, launches, fishing smacks with sails furled at their masts, pleasure boats. At the shore itself hung open skiffs and dories, and the people were bunched at these, trying to scramble into them.

Challenger helped his wife down and drew Dapple's head back to westward. "Away you go now, my boy," he said. "But I advise you to avoid Chelmsford; they evince an ungrateful attitude to horses in those parts."

So saying, he slapped Dapple's spotted flank smartly. Dapple went trotting away on the path around the hill. Challenger stooped to pick up the satchel and the package of food.

"A considerable embarkment is taking place here, Jessie," he said. "We would do well to see what arrangements may be made for taking ship."

Together they walked on down to the sandy beach. Challenger led the way toward one knot of people who seemed to be chaffering all at once with two sailors in a lifeboat, and for a moment his wife feared that he would elbow his way through and bellow for passage. But just then a voice rose from a point farther down the beach.

"Professor Challenger! Professor Challenger!"

A sturdy, grey-whiskered little man with a peaked officer's cap was running toward them. Challenger wheeled to meet him.

"Upon my soul," he boomed, "it's Mr Blake." Out came his big hand to take the other's. "You were mate aboard the British Museum's Poinsettia in '92, when I was on the expedition to Labrador to measure cephalic indexes of the natives."

"Yes indeed, sir," said Blake. "And now I've my own boat – there she is yonder, Professor." He gestured to where, farther offshore, rolled a big grey steam launch, a puff of smoke rising from the funnel. "These six years I've been master of her, making runs with passengers and goods to France. Now I'm making a run. There's room for one more aboard her – no, for two, if this is your lady."

"My dear, this is my friend Howard Blake, now Captain Blake," Challenger made the introductions. "Well, suppose we come down to the shore with you. Is that your dory? Nobody seems to be going with you."

"Because I've told them, no room for more than one passenger, we're loaded heavy now," said Blake, trotting alongside. "But you're a different case, Professor, you're such a cargo as a man gets very seldom in his life."

"Where are you bound?"

"Calais," said Captain Blake. "It's a run we've often made from the London docks, and the sea, thank God, is a calm one today. You'll have a fine voyage of it, Professor. Under other conditions, it would be even a pleasant one;"

They were at the waterside. Two sailors sat in the dory, oars poised. Challenger put a hand into his pocket.

"What is your fare?" he asked.

"We've been asking ten guineas – gold, just now. But in your case–"

"Here are fifteen." Challenger counted the coins into his hand, then swung around to gaze earnestly into his wife's dark eyes.

"Jessie," he said commandingly, "you will go with Captain Blake to Calais. When you come into port, he will see you into the hands of Professor Anton Marigny – he and I were students together at the university and have corresponded on mutually rewarding terms. Marigny, in his turn, will get you to Paris, to Monsieur Jean de Corbier of the Zoological Institute there. You will remember when we entertained him."

"But George," she wailed, "you speak as though you will not be coming."

"You will do as I say, Jessie," he assured her masterfully. "My place is here. Among other things, I must recover a valuable scientific instrument, which, in one of the few rare moments of carelessness remarkable in my whole career, I forgot to bring along with us. I am certain of my duty, and do you be certain also. Nor must you worry above me. That duty of which I spoke is one for which I was trained, and one for which, I need not argue, I am eminently fitted."

He handed Blake the napkinful of eatables and hugged Mrs Challenger to him. "And so, Jessie," he said briskly, "aboard with you."

She was shedding tears, but obediently she got into the dory. He watched in silence as they pulled out toward the launch and stood there while the sturdy craft got steam up and began to make for open sea. At last he turned and walked back across the sand to where coarse grass grew.

Fourteen

A stringily built man stood there, hands in his trousers pockets, gazing gloomily seaward.

"I saw you come back when you 'ad a chance to leave, sir." he said as Challenger came near. "Might I ask why?"

Challenger surveyed the speaker. He saw an active figure, clad in a smudged army shirt, breeches, and scuffed boots, with a gaunt stubbled face.

"You presume, I think," he said in tones like the bass of an organ. "However, I shall tell you why I did not go. The war is going to be fought here, and I am going to help fight it. That's enough for you."

He moved past as though to go inland but stopped when the other raised a sort of protesting cry.

"War, sir? Help fight a war? We can't fight them, we're beat!"

Challenger turned, beard thrust out aggressively.

"I was in Surrey," stammered the fellow. "I saw us beat!"

"You seem to have accepted the fact very decisively," said Challenger in cold, measured tones. "I have heard how a sea captain, one John Paul

Jones, said in a similar critical situation that he had just begun to fight. Your words and behavior, my good man, suggest that you do scant credit to the vestings of the uniform you wear." He drew himself up grandly. "I take leave to inform you that I am Professor George Edward Challenger."

But the name seemed to mean nothing whatever to the trembling soldier.

"My name's Tovey, sir, Luke Tovey," he said in his turn. "I am – I was – a trooper of the Eighth Hussars. I saw the fighting on Sunday. Our artillery got one of them – just one, a shell right in the ugly face of one of their machines – before their heat-ray wiped the battery out entire. I got away to London and had a ride here in a dray. But no money, not a shilling, for a ship to sail on, and I'm wonderin' what is to happen to us all." He flung out his hands. "The Martians are goin' to kill us all, every mother's son and daughter!"

"Not all, I can assure you. I have been able to learn something of their plans for humanity. And now, Tovey, I bid you a very good morning."

Again he stalked away toward the tree-tufted hill which he and Mrs Challenger had passed on their way to the beach. Tovey came trotting after him.

"You've got a plan, sir – Professor, you called yourself. You've thought about it. Won't you tell me what you think?"

"Thinking is a process with which a dismaying majority of the human race is utterly unfamiliar," returned Challenger bleakly. "It demands recognition of a state of affairs, an estimate of its directions and effects, and a sane decision on how to deal with it. I am in the midst of these considerations at present, and I will be obliged if you do not interrupt my mental processes."

On he walked, and toward the hill. A sort of lane, steep but well worked, led up its rocky side. With considerable assurance he followed it and made his way to the top. The stone house among the trees was old but excellently built. Apparently it was a seaside retreat. Challenger went to the door, tried it, and found it locked. "A window, then," he muttered to himself, and inspected one in front. It, too, was locked. He returned to the doorstep, bent over the iron foot scraper, and wrenched it away with a single sudden exertion of his great strength. One end of this he jammed under the lower sash of the window as he heaved on the other. The clasp of the sills gave way and the window went up.

A rustle behind him, and he spun, the scraper lifted. It was Tovey, the hussar, apologetic but determined.

"I want to be with you, Professor, if you don't mind," he said. "Maybe if you think out some goodish plan, we'll both come clear of this, but why are you staying here? You don't know nothing of these Martians on the way here. They've got a black smoke they put down, and it kills like a plague of Egypt."

"It so happens that I have heard something of that black smoke," Challenger lectured him, "and I feel able to rationalise something of its action and effect. Their machines are said to be a hundred feet high."

"Yes, sir, more or less."

"Then the black smoke must be of strikingly heavy composition, not rising to threaten the operators at the tops of these machines. Therefore a hill as high as this one – seventy feet, as I estimate – would be a refuge of sorts. I confidently expect the invaders to come in pursuit of these crowds of refugees. It will be of the utmost value to hold an unostentatious observation point up here and study their operations at comparatively close quarters."

Tovey grinned suddenly. "I say, Professor, that's topping!" he cried. "You're one of the ones, you are."

"One of what ones?" returned Challenger austerely. "I have told you that I am George Edward Challenger. I give myself to doubt that I am to be classified carelessly in any category of informed reasoning."

He walked majestically out through the trees to where he had a good view of the beach. It was as he had come to it, clustered masses of frightened people and small boats plying with passengers to the craft waiting out at sea. He fished out his watch.

"Noon, or nearly," he said to the goggling Tovey. "I have opened a way into that stone house. Suppose we see if its occupants have left us anything from which we can make a meal."

Entering at the window, they found the kitchen, but its shelves were almost entirely stripped. Apparently the vanished occupants had taken most of the supplies. Challenger found several eggs in a bowl, and then Tovey, exploring a cupboard, turned up half a loaf of bread. On the floor was a keg with beer in it and a sack of onions. Tovey lit an oil-burning range and broke the eggs into a frying pan with a lump of butter from somewhere. Into the omelette he sliced onions. From these things they made a luncheon and then walked out again to survey the coast. With him Challenger carried a pair of opera glasses he found on a mantelpiece.

To northward stood a jumble of cottages, and among them a white-painted church with a lofty steeple. Challenger peered, then focused his glasses. He made out a human figure in that steeple, someone else on watch.

He turned the glasses out to sea, studying a long, dark vessel lying low in the water well out beyond the various craft taking on passengers. "Here, Tovey, what would you call that?" he asked, pointing.

Tovey took the glasses and gazed intently. "Naval ship, sir," he said after a moment. "I've seen the like at off-coast manoeuveres. Torpedo rams, they're called. That one was in the Thames when I came through town, I fancy. Someone said it's named the Thunder Child."

"And here to help, I surmise," Challenger walked back through the trees and beyond the house. There the high ground narrowed into a slope landward, with a driveway of sorts upon it that led to a broader road beyond. Just now more people, in vehicles or afoot, were crowding along that road as though toward the shore, but not masses as large as he had seen earlier. Back he went to the front, and again scanned the craft at sea. Captain Blake's launch which had taken his wife was nowhere in sight. He permitted himself a sigh of relief about that.

"You're calm, Professor," said Tovey, hovering near. "The one calm man I've seen since all this began. Like as if you, at least knowed what you're doing."

"I have had the opportunity of spying upon these invaders", said Challenger.

"Blimey now, have you? However did you manage that?"

"I doubt if I could explain in terms simple enough for your comprehension. Suffice it to say, I have watched them at fairly close hand and am building a realization of their actions and intentions."

"Reconnaissance, that's the word!" cried Tovey. "So 'elp me God, Professor, it's what we need. If we could read them out, then we might deal with them, right?"

"Over-simply expressed, but right."

They went back among the trees at the house. Challenger sat on a root beside the lane toward the sea. He watched for hours as the various craft, large and small, loaded themselves to the railings with passengers. Fortunes were being made aboard those vessels, he reflected; but what would money mean if all human civilisation was to fall? The sun sank toward the west. It was nearly five o'clock, his watch told him.

Then, far off to southward, he heard guns. Up above the torpedo ram rose a string of bright signal flags. The ships inshore began to stir, to move as though making way outward. Challenger shifted as he sat and looked in the direction of the gunfire.

There it was, emerging into view and tramping three-legged across the mud flats, a towering fighting-machine.

Even so far away, it seemed to approach with terrifying assurance. As he watched, another appeared from the west nearer at hand, and then a third, not more than a quarter of a mile away. Challenger set his glasses upon this closest machine. It walked smoothly and rapidly upon those three wonderfully jointed legs. They upheld its ovid carriage of metal, surmounted by a triangular superstructure that turned this way and that, like a great head in a cowl. Behind the carriage was slung an openwork cage of bright metal like aluminum. Here and there stirred long, supple tentacles, and close to the cowl jutted a sort of articulated arm like a crane, bearing some sort of a case. That, Challenger told himself, must house the heat-ray.

All three of the monsters moved in open order toward the shore. The one nearest Challenger stooped a trifle. Two of its tentacles caught up little fleeing men and flipped them into the cage at its back. Then all three machines waded confidently into the sea toward the ships.

They did not hesitate at entering the water, Challenger meditated. Surely there were no such waters as this on Mars. They knew oceans from another world. He nodded to himself, a trifle smugly.

From one machine rose a penetrating, prolonged shriek, like a steam siren. Another machine answered it. The three of them were like gigantic, grotesque children on a holiday, shouting back and forth as they sought treasures at the seaside. Now they closed the distances between them. Manifestly they meant to cut off the flight of the vessels.

"Not a chance for them poor beasts," half-moaned Tovey behind Challenger. "I've told you, sir, they mean to kill us all."

"And I have told you that they do not mean to kill us all," reminded Challenger, the glasses to his eyes. "You will do well to take note of the things I say, Tovey."

The machines were all wading swiftly out, moving faster, even in the water, than the retreating swarm of craft could pull away. Challenger shifted his glasses and saw something else.

It was the Thunder Child, full steam up and smoke pouring from its funnels as it fairly flew through the water toward the invaders. And all three machines paused, their cowled heads turning as though they stared at this onrushing curiosity. Motionless they stood, hip-deep in the water, so to speak, and stared.

"Upon my word, they're caught off guard," muttered Challenger.

"But what can that ship do?" Tovey gabbled.

If the invaders were deadly, so was the Thunder Child. Straight for the trio it drove. They separated and retreated, actually retreated toward the shore. Now they were like seaside venturers when some unknown monster from the deep comes swimming close. One of them lifted a tubelike object in its tentacles and seemed to aim.

Out from the tube flew a small bright projectile, which struck the approaching ram on the side and glanced off. As it struck the water it burst into a cloud of jet-black vapour, which abruptly shrouded the surface. But the Thunder Child had driven clear before the cloud could involve it.

"That there's their black smoke, sir," Tovey was saying.

One of the machines shifted its arm with the heat-ray chamber. A lean, pale beam of light flashed from it. Steam rose from the water against the ship's side. Above the steam rose a sudden, swift tongue of flame.

"She's done for now," groaned Tovey.

"Not yet, Tovey, not yet!" cried Challenger.

For the Thunder Child had fired her guns, even as she won free from the steam and the black smoke. Down went the machine that had used the heat-ray, a gigantic splashing sprawl into the ocean, with foam flying high and then more clouds of steam. More guns went off, a whole salvo of them. The Thunder Child was ablaze, flames spouting from ventilators and funnels, but she put about and charged at a second fighting-machine as it backed away toward shore.

She was within a hundred yards when the invader's heat-ray jabbed its pale beam into her. The explosion shook the sea, and the Thunder

Child's upper works rose into the air in jagged, flying fragments. She was finished, but not alone. The machine that had destroyed her reeled in the water, and a moment later the still hurtling wreck smashed into it. The machine caved in and went down in the water. More steam, great clouds of it, hid everything. Only the third invader could be dimly seen, actually striving back toward land.

"Oh, strike me blind, what a fight that was," gasped Tovey.

"A brilliant action, a valiant one," said Challenger. "She was blown up, brave ship, but she took two of them with her. And you told me that the artillery got one in Surrey—"

"Just the one, sir, that's all."

"But now, two more!" Challenger caught Tovey's arm so powerfully that the hussar flinched. "My good man, don't you see that they aren't invulnerable? They destroy but, upon my word, they've found that they too, can be destroyed. And see, the Thunder Child sacrificed herself to save that whole fleet of rescue craft."

For all the boats, large and small, were standing well out to sea. Down on the shore, knots and swirls of people seemed to caper back and forth. The third invader stepped over their heads and retreated swiftly inland.

"He, at least, has had enough," said Challenger grimly. "He will have an embarrassing tale to tell his fellows."

"And he won't half cop it from his commander," added Tovey.

"An interesting, and edifying, experience. I could wish that my friend, Mr Sherlock Holmes, had been here to witness it."

"Coo, Professor, do you know Sherlock Holmes?" asked Tovey, in tones of awe that irritated Challenger.

"You sound as though you have heard of him."

"Who ain't heard of him, or anyway read of him?"

"Had you read more advanced publications than the popular magazines, you might know the names of those with greater claim to celebration. But let us think of supper, and perhaps find supplies for breakfast."

Over the haphazard meal, Challenger spoke with authority.

"You may like it here, Tovey, and for all of me you may stay, perhaps thrive. But I am going back to London."

"London, sir, on foot? But it's fifty miles and more."

"You remind me that you are a cavalryman. It happens that my chief recreation has been in taking long walks and climbing mountains. I see you have found a box of captain's biscuits." Challenger took a huge handful. "These will help me on my way."

Out through the open window he climbed as evening fell. A shadow flickered overhead. Looking up, he saw a soaring disk, dark against the greying sky. As he looked, it dipped down in a sweeping glide above the beach where people still stood in huddles. It dropped something. Up sprang an inky cloud of vapour, and another. They spread, cloaking the beach.

"The black smoke." Tovey was saying again.

Fifteen

Challenger stood and watched. The vapour spread, hiding the roofs of the cottages but not rising to the church steeple. He lifted the opera glasses. The figure was still up there, so apparently at least one man would escape. He walked back to the yard, Tovey at his heels.

"Professor," said Tovey, "asking your pardon, but could I take your hand?"

Grandly Challenger's massive paw obliged. "Be of good cheer," he bade Tovey. "Ponder on what I have said about this situation, and see if you cannot profit by my words. And now, I am going."

He headed around the house, then purposefully to the high ground at the west. It would be above that black smoke, he felt sure, and evening was coming, with a scrap of moon already risen. He could make good progress, with as much safety as anybody could hope for with invaders abroad.

The way beyond the height curved to the northwest, toward the main road on which the pell-mell retreat of thousands had gone. As Challenger walked toward that thoroughfare, he saw nobody upon it. The myriads of fugitives had gone to the shore, some of them had been left, and there at the last the black smoke must have smothered them, or most of them. He stayed close to roadside trees and looked again and again into the dusky sky, but saw nothing of that flying disk that had brought its dark death.

Once on the main road, he took up the steady, knowledgeable gait that eats up distances. Rambling walks had been his pleasure ever since his boyhood in Scotland, and he knew how to pace himself for a long journey. On he trudged toward the sinking sun, and on. When he judged that twenty minutes had passed, he stopped and sat on a fence to rest. He ate a broad, hard biscuit, and washed out his mouth at the spout of a pump. Then he went on.

As he travelled the road he saw wreckage upon it. A dog cart stood on the far side, a little bay horse lying motionless between the shafts. Someone had driven it to death. A laden wheelbarrow stood abandoned, a velocipede with a broken wheel slumped in the ditch. Here and there lay scattered garments, hats, parcels, abandoned in flight. Challenger watched the last of the sunset fade. A spatter of stars appeared in the night, and the quarter moon rose behind him. He walked on, with intervals of rest. The miles fell away behind him. He went through Chelmsford, passing dark, silent homes. It was past midnight when he stopped and ate the last of his biscuits. He judged that he had accomplished fifteen miles.

Again he walked. He felt sweat trickling upon his great body, but the hard-muscled pillars of his legs did not tire. At three o'clock or so, he began to forage in dark houses. Most of them had been stripped of all food by their departed owners, or perhaps by fugitives from London. At last, in a homely little cottage, he found a dozen potatoes in a bin, with a pump at the sink. Striking a match, he built a small fire in a grate, then pumped water into a kettle and hung the potatoes on a crane to boil. After half an hour, he fished out three of the largest, mashed them on a plate beside a window where faint moonlight came in, put on salt and pepper and olive oil from a cruet. He ate them ravenously. Finally he slumped down in a creaky armchair and slept.

The sun was well up when he woke. He ate a cold potato and filled his pockets with others. Cautiously he peered outdoors, scanning the horizons for stalking machines, the heavens for that flying disk. Nothing moved except a figure far to the westward on the road. No, two figures, a man leading a spotted horse.

Was it Dapple? Challenger hastened his steps. But the man was mounting the horse. He rode off at an amble, around a bend of the road and put of sight. Challenger scowled as he set off for London again.

Town after little town he passed. They were silent as though Judgement Day had come and gone. Making his way along a stretch of the road with an open field to the left, he heard a cry. Looking that way, he saw someone rushing clumsily toward him. It was a plump, bald man with rumpled clothes who came near and wheezed inarticulately.

"If you have lived this long, you should know better than to show yourself in the open," Challenger scolded him.

"I was wondering if anybody else was left alive in England," the man panted out.

"Your eyes should convince you that somebody else is very much alive," said Challenger, tapping his huge chest.

"Where are you bound?"

"To London," said Challenger.

"Never say that, sir! London's full of the Martians. I ran from there, I saw them."

"Hardly full of them, though," Challenger corrected him. "Ten of their cylinders were launched, each with five or six at most. That is no tremendous number. They will need all their manifest efficiency to patrol London."

The plump man wiped his nose and complained that he was

hungry. Challenger gave him two potatoes and left him spluttering thanks as he munched.

By noon, Challenger estimated that he had finished fully half of his journey. He found himself among gatherings of suburban homes, empty and silent. Again he foraged for food, and in one house discovered the end of a flitch of bacon and some slices of stale bread. This time he decided against a fire to send up betraying smoke. With the great knife he had taken from the tough in Chelmsford he cut slices of bacon which he put on bread and ate. Another house yielded a bottle of claret – not of particularly good quality, decided Challenger as he walked along drinking from it.

He began to take longer rests. At one stopping place, on a bench before a silent shop, he took off his heavy boots and turned his socks inside out to ease his now tingling feet. That gave relief as he resumed his journey.

Late in the night he knew he was close to London. It gave him new reserves of determined strength. West Kensington – he would go there, would find the crystal in his study and consult it. Into the town he tramped, along deserted streets. The hush was awesome until he heard, far away in the darkness, the bellowing siren of an invader on patrol. At last he dragged himself into a shop, a clothier's shop as well as he could tell in the dark, stretched out upon the counter, and slept again with the soundness of exhaustion.

He roused, with the sun well up once more. His muscles ached, but not too painfully. In a rear room of the establishment he found a tap that still ran a trickle of water, in which he washed his hands and face and under his bearded chin. His last cold potato made his breakfast. Out he ventured in the bright morning.

Again, no hint of enemy machines peering above the buildings. He judged that he was not far from Bethnal Green Road, perhaps seven miles or so from his own home in Kensington, but he must move with care. He crossed the Cambridge Road into Whitechapel. Off to the northwest, like a grotesque toy in the distance, showed a stalking machine monster. He watched from a basement door until it moved on east and out of sight. His feet were sore and his legs tired, but he trudged on in the direction of Hyde Park and, beyond that, Kensington.

The streets toward the Thames were sprinkled and sheeted with dusty black grains. That would be the black smoke, precipitated and harmless, judged Challenger. He avoided touching the stuff, though birds sang cheerfully there and two dogs romped in a game of their own. He walked with cautiously steady steps, now and then hearing distant sirenlike whoops. He made his way through Grosvenor Square. To the north was Baker Street. He would go looking for Holmes there, but not just now. In among the trees of Hyde Park he moved, and furtively on the bridge across the Serpentine. A strange rank growth of red weed showed itself there, and broken tufts of it floated. Challenger had never seen such a growth before. It, too, was an aspect of the invasion. Had it been planted by design or by accident? Beyond Hyde Park he walked through Kensington Gardens.

Miles to the southwest rose sooty clouds that looked like fire. Undoubtedly the blaze had been set by the heat-rays during the battles in Surrey. Entering his own street, he saw with weary exultation the massive portico of his Enmore Park home. Up the steps he climbed, and set his big key in the lock.

Just then, a shadow fell across him. A towering fighting-machine came stalking along the street toward the house.

Instantly Challenger was inside, locking the door behind him. He heard a metallic racket at the front of the house. He looked quickly through the open door to the front parlour. The window glass broke with a crash, and a snaky tentacle came creeping in.

Challenger tiptoed back through the hall, into the kitchen beyond, and out at a back door into the rose garden. But he did not flee away. Instead he crept along the wall toward the street and gingerly poked his bearded face around the corner of the house.

The metal machine crouched down there. He took a fleeting moment to admire the intricate mechanism of the joints of its legs, set at half a dozen places along the metal rods. It had lowered its oval body almost to ground level, and the cowled housing in which the operator lay pushed close to the window. Its tentacles groped within. At any moment, it might turn the heat-ray upon his house.

Challenger wheezed as he bent down and wrenched a brick from the border of the side path. Then he straightened, drew his hand back and, with all the strength of his brawny arm, hurled the brick. It clanged loudly against the metal shield just below the cowl and glanced away.

At once that cowl swung toward him, as though to stare. He whipped around and, for all his weariness, ran like a huge hare along the way he had come. He dodged around the house, scrambled through the garden and into the door to the kitchen. A moment later the gigantic mechanism came rushing past between his house and the next, then away between two a more houses that faced on the street beyond. He looked up and saw its cowl, turning this way and that.

It thought that he had run for his life, perhaps toward the Gardens. He leaned against the door jamb, breathing hard.

His first consideration was that, as usual, he had done well. But then it occurred to him that human affairs, even when directed by a supremely brilliant intelligence, sometimes needed luck to prosper them.

Sixteen

Again he looked out at the door. The thing was prowling more distantly, looming high above the housetops on streets to the north. Challenger closed the door stealthily, walked up the hall to his study, and sat down. Weariness flowed over him like dark water, and he stayed there, motionless, for long minutes before he went again to peer from a back window. His pursuer was no longer in sight. He grinned triumphantly through the forest of his beard and again sought the kitchen to explore for food.

There was plenty on the shelves, and he ate a great deal of it. There was still a slow trickle of water in the taps here, as in the store he had visited earlier. He drank a glassful and set a small kettle to catch more, while he returned to his study. There, just where he had left it on his table, was the lead tea canister with the crystal egg.

Quickly he draped himself with the black cloth and looked into the blue glow. A few shifts of the crystal suddenly gave him a clear view.

He saw the interior of a great excavation, larger than that pit made by the cylinder he remembered at Woking. It was almost full of machinery, fighting-machines and handling-machines, as well as other elaborate assemblages he could not identify. And on the gravelly floor of the crater were grouped invaders, grossly swollen, with something in the midst of them that struggled and fought unavailingly.

He slammed the lid of the canister shut and sat back from it. Not without difficulty, he put from his imagination the picture of himself in just that nightmare situation.

He drew out his watch. It was midafternoon. He went and set another kettle to catch the dribble of water, while with the first kettleful he managed to take a sponge bath, clammy cold but refreshing. Then he dressed in clean clothes, pulled on his heavy boots, and again sat in his study. His tired body relaxed gratefully, but his mind was furiously active, and, as so often in the past, he found reason for self-congratulation.

Not only had he escaped the merciless invaders, here and at the shore, but he had actually hoodwinked one of them into running off and leaving him alone. They were gigantically brilliant, but they were not omniscient. Their behavior in the fight with the Thunder Child had seemed to indicate confusion. He, Challenger, felt that he might well be assessing them as well as they assessed humanity.

Their machines were bewildering, but he took refuge in the memory of Robinson Crusoe's sober conclusion: *...as reason is the substance and original of the mathematics, so by stating and squaring everything by reason, and by making the most rational judgement of things, every man may be, in time, master of every mechanic art.* That could be as true in overrun England as on that island where Robinson Crusoe had survived and prevailed. Intelligence could solve the mysteries of invader mechanisms, could even, God willing, capture them, use them. As he thought of these things, he fell asleep.

He wakened after night had fallen and decided to venture out. No hint of the enemy could be discovered. Again he found his way through Kensington Gardens and Regent's Park to Baker Street. His own footfalls seemed to ring in the stillness. He found Holmes' stairs and went up to the door above, but it was locked and no sound could be detected in the dark. Again he returned, as cautiously as ever, to Enmore Park, stopping here and there to forage in stores and public houses. At home he set a light under a chafing dish and heated some canned peas and some turtle soup. It was his first satisfying hot meal since he and his wife had driven away on Monday morning. That night he slept soundly in his own room.

Next morning he climbed to an attic window and surveyed London to the northward. In the distance, somewhat east of north, rose green fumes. That might well be the main station of the enemy, the great cavity he had seen in the crystal the day before.

He thought of breakfast. There were eggs in the kitchen, but he sagely decided against those after they had lain in the basket a week, and opened a can of smelts. Finally he went to his study and opened the canister with the crystal. Spreading his black cloth, he concentrated upon it.

There they were, revealed to his gaze, the invaders in their pit. He could make out more than a dozen, slumped at various tasks. Handling-machines moved here and there. A sort of furnace gave off grey-green smoke, and one machine shovelled in earth, then pulled out a shiny bar of pale metal that looked like aluminum. Thus the invaders set up industries, consolidated their gains.

In the midst of his observations, a pair of round, brilliant eyes came close as though to stare from the crystal into his face. Then they were gone and the viewpoint of the crystal seemed to change abruptly and utterly. Now Challenger seemed to be looking down from a height. He instantly closed the lid of the canister. The invaders had taken their own crystal that which was attuned to his, into the cockpit of a machine.

It was not many minutes before he heard the clank and whirr of a mechanism from the street in front of the house. Taking the canister, he stepped into the hall. As before, there was the smash of breaking glass, then the sound of furniture being overturned. Inquiring tentacles had come into the parlour.

But Challenger had made up his mind what to do. He was at the kitchen door and out of it within brief seconds. Moving furtively under the garden shrubbery, he gained the alley beyond. There he moved along eastwards, keeping close to the shade and the fences lest the invader spy him from above the roofs. He did not venture out into the street, but plunged into a yard on the far side of the alley and sought cover in the midst of some prickly ornamental bushes. For many minutes he lay there, then ventured on across more yards and at last into Kensington Gardens.

Crouching under a tree, he saw his pursuer still hulking against the sky, back at the place from which Challenger had fled. No tricking it away from Enmore Park this time, he told himself. He struck off through the trees and thickets, reached Hyde Park and then Baker Street. Again he went upstairs to Holmes' door, and again found it locked, with silence beyond it. He frowned, asking himself if Holmes had managed to escape from London, and if he had, whether he would be back. Walking across Regent Street, he looked north and again saw the green haze that must mark the enemy headquarters.

The afternoon he spent wandering here and there, looking for food. Many stores had been broken open. and their contents plundered. In a confectionery he found a jar of smoked turkey slices and some currant buns for his supper. Then he lay back in an armchair behind a desk. It was Saturday night. The Martians had subdued London in twelve days; how far beyond had their rule been extended? He speculated on chances of heading north, of reaching some place where mankind still planned defence, giving that plan the benefit of his observations. Sleep rode down upon him.

He wakened to hear excited voices outside, a dozen at once. Hurriedly he rose and walked out. It was dark. A knot of men jabbered and laughed there.

"What is happening?" he thundered, so loudly that all swung around to look at him.

"Look yonder, mate," cried one, pointing westward. Light came from somewhere in that direction, white light and not the green radiance that hung around the devices of the invaders.

"Somebody's got the lights goin' again," said another, apparently far gone in drink. "Come on, chums, let's have a look."

Regent Street was a broad blaze of light. It gave Challenger a chance to see his watch—it was just past four o'clock. Soon the midsummer sun would be rising. To the right he made out Oxford Circus, with the Langham Hotel standing tall, and in the other direction was Piccadilly. People flowed here and there across the pavement, raucously calling and laughing. Through the din came a shrill spatter of music, like the pipes at a Punch and Judy show. Some of the celebrants danced clumsily to its measure. Everywhere, men and women drank out of bottles.

"It's all over, it's all over," gulped a man in a filthy jacket and cap, weaving toward Challenger.

"What are you trying to say?" Challenger growled.

"They're gone, nobody's seen 'em for hours. They came from nowhere and went back there."

A blowsy woman, wrapped in a scarf and wearing a wide hat with a broken feather, put out a hand to Challenger. "How do you fare ducky?" she hiccoughed. "Coo, I've always liked a big man with a big beard, that's the truth."

"And I have always disliked a drunken women with gold teeth," flung back Challenger, turning and walking off.

Disdainfully he studied the crazy mob. It was a nightmare of revelry. He saw no face, near nor far, that did not disgust him. He shifted his gaze to some tall buildings opposite. The first grey of dawn was making the sky pale behind them.

Something else rose there, taller that the buildings, a great brooding scaffold of metal.

Challenger knew the silhouette at once, the three long, jointed legs, the globe like a body at the top. It tilted itself and down came great tentacles. They caught up struggling bodies, there of them. Others screamed, tried to run, seemed to walk upon each other in sudden unreasoning terror. Again tentacles reached, quested, snatched up others. The fighting-machine tossed its victims into the openwork cage at its back as it stepped into Regent Street among the wavering fugitives. Some of them had fallen down, helpless from drink or fear or both.

The machine stooped. All of its tentacles were at work, picking up its prey like a man gathering wind-fallen apples. Those farther away saw it at last and started screaming in a chorus that deafened, trying to run over each other to shelter.

Challenger went swiftly up a side street, into grateful shadows there. More screams rose in chorus behind him. He gained the door of the confectionery and turned to look toward the lights. The fighting-machine turned this way and that above the roofs, busy at what it did. Surely it was gathering an abundant harvest.

He groped his way back to the chair and sat down. He thought of the victims of the invader on Regent Street, too drunken or too terrified to make more than an effort at flight. Who had turned on the lights there to lure it? And what wild fantasy had spread through the crowd, that they thought that the nightmare was past?

He told himself, in cold, rational terms, that the dozens captured and carried off would be no loss to humanity and its fight for survival. But he had seen the invaders feeding, and he could not fight off a daunting sickness of heart.

The sun rose brightly. He made a breakfast of three shriveled tarts and a bottle of soda, brushed crumbs out of his beard, and once more ventured into the open.

No sign of a menacing machine stalking against the sky, no clanking sound of approaching peril. Why should those machines be patrolling this part of town just now, when it came to that? He reflected that the ten cylinders had brought sixty invaders at most, and that that forager at dawn must have seized provisions for several days in Regent Street. Again he sickened as he pondered this, but shrugged the feeling away-with a great heave of his thick shoulders. He returned to Regent Street. Not a single stir there – he had not expected one. The revellers who had not been carried away must have fled far.

Finding a sunken areaway, he sat down and reviewed his adventures since he had journeyed to Woking. He had been eminently right to lose his temper at the self-important Stent and Ogilvy, to depart before the heat-ray struck. Again he had been right to take that railroad baggage cart, virtually to commandeer it, and to drive with his wife to the shore. Good fortune had attended his encounter with Captain Blake, who had carried Mrs Challenger out of immediate danger, and good fortune had been with him again when he mounted the hill to observe and so had escaped the black smoke. His had been a series of almost miraculous escapes; while thousands around him had perished.

His mind kept going back to the people captured in Regent Street and borne away to be drained of their blood. Offscourings of London, those wretched victims. He remembered Holmes' suggestion that the terrible invaders, against whom mankind's most deadly weapons had availed so little, might perish of simple earthly diseases. And that made him think again of Holmes' quiet but confident rationality, his suggestions that at times had been irritating because he Challenger, should not have needed to be reminded of them.

Twice he had failed to find Holmes at his rooms. Why not look once more? He drew out his watch. It was noon, or nearly.

With watchfulness that had become almost second nature in these days of furtive movement, he set out for Baker Street. At every corner he carefully surveyed the cross street beyond, lest danger be lurking. At last he came along Baker Street, opposite Dolamore's broad frontage with its displays of wine and spirits. Up the stairs he walked and paused in front of Holmes' door.

Voices sounded on the other side of it; Holmes' voice, then one he did not know. Sudden relief flowed through Challenger's big body, like warmth, like stimulating fluid.

"May I come in?" he shouted at the top of his lungs.

IV

❧

THE ADVENTURE OF THE MARTIAN CLIENT
BY JOHN H. WATSON, M.D.

Seventeen

M r H.G. Wells's popular book, *The War of the Worlds*, is a frequently inaccurate chronicle of a known radical and atheist, a boon companion of Frank Harris, George Bernard Shaw, and worse. He exaggerates needlessly and pretends to a scientific knowledge which plainly he does not possess. Yet scientists and laymen alike read and applaud him, even while they scorn the brilliant deductions of Sherlock Holmes and Professor George Edward Challenger.

Wells refers in his book to the magnificent and almost complete specimen of an invader, preserved in spirits at the Natural History Museum, but he carelessly, or perhaps even deliberately, overlooks the history of its capture, examination, and presentation. And both scholarly journals and the popular press almost totally disregard Professor Challenger's striking rationalisation that the invaders were not Martians at all. As for Holmes, he shows little concern over these injustices, but after consulting him, I have decided to put the true facts on record for posterity to judge.

When the invasion began, in bright midsummer of 1902, fear seemed to overwhelm every human being except the two wisest and best men I have ever known. On that Friday morning of June 6, when the first Mars-based cylinder was beginning to open at Woking to disgorge its crew of ruthless destroyers, I was hurrying to Highgate. Poor Murray, my faithful old orderly who had saved my life during the Second Afghan War, lay critically ill in his lodgings there. Even as I came to his door, newspapers and jabbering neighbours reported something about strange beings from Mars landed among the little suburban towns in Surrey. I paid scant attention, for I found Murray very weak and helpless. Almost at once I became sadly sure that he could not be saved, only made as comfortable as possible as he settled into death. Later that night, while I sought to reduce his fever, I half heard more news to the effect that the invaders were striking down helpless crowds of the curious.

If it seems that I was not fully aware of these stirring events that day and on Saturday and Sunday, I must again offer the reminder that all my attention was needed at Murray's bedside. From other people in the house I heard wild stories, which seemed to me only crazy rumours, that these creatures from across space had utterly smashed Woking and Horsell, had utterly wiped out the troops hastily thrown in their way, and were advancing upon London itself. By Monday morning, Murray's fellow lodgers and the people in houses to both sides had fled, I never learned where or to what fate. The entire street was deserted save for my poor patient and myself.

I could have no thought of going away, too, and leaving Murray. Day after day I did what I could for him, as doctor and as friend. Meanwhile, all about us whirled terror and fire, and, in streets below us, dense, clouds of that lethal vapour that has since been called the black smoke.

I heard the ear-shattering howls of the fighting-machines as they signalled each other above London's roofs, and several times I peered cautiously from behind the window curtains to see them far away, scurrying along at tremendous speed on their jointed legs fully a hundred feet high. It was on Tuesday, I think, that their heat-rays knocked nearby houses into exploding flames, but our own shelter had the good fortune to escape.

Through all this, Murray lay only half-conscious in bed. Once or twice he murmured something about guns, and I believe he thought himself back fighting the Afghans. I ranged all the other lodgings in the house to find food for him. It was on the morning of the eighth day, the second Friday of the invasion, that he died, and I could take time to realise that things had become strangely quiet outside our windows.

I straightened out my poor friend's body on his bed and crossed his hands upon his breast. Bowing my head above him, I whispered some sort of prayer. Then I went again to the window, peered out, and asked myself how I might escape.

I could see a cross street down the slope below. It was strewn with sooty dust left when the black smoke had precipitated, and I thanked God that Highgate's elevation spared me that deadly contact. Doing my best to see the state of affairs outside, I made out a dog trotting forlornly along a black-dusted sidewalk. He seemed to show no ill effects, from which I surmised that the vapour had become harmless when it settled. But then, just as I was on the point of going out at the front door, I saw a fighting-machine, too. It galloped along among distant houses, puffs of green steam rising from its joints. That decided me not to venture out in the daylight.

Again I roamed through the house, poking into every larder I could find. Some dried beef and a crust of bread and a lukewarm bottle of beer made my evening meal that Friday, with the silent form of poor dead Murray for company.

At last the late June twilight deepened into dusk. I picked up my medicine kit and emerged from the house, setting my face southward toward Baker Street.

A fairly straight route to my lodgings there would be no more than five miles. But, as I moved through the night toward Primrose Hill, I suddenly saw great shifting sheets of green light there. I had come near the London and north-western tracks at the moment, and upon the earth of the red embankment grew great tussocks of a strange red weed. I did not recognise. At least it would give cover, and I crouched behind it to look toward that unearthly light. I could make out fully half a dozen machines, standing silently together as though in a military formation. At once I decided that there was a formidable central concentration of the enemy, close at hand. Instead of trying to continue southward, I stole away to the east, keeping close to the railroad tracks.

Creeping furtively, I won my way well above Primrose Hill and saw grateful darkness beyond. I dared stand erect and walk beside the rails. But abruptly there rose the ear-splitting peal of a siren voice, a fierce clanking of metal, seemingly close to the other side of the tracks. In cold terror I flung myself flat into a muddy hollow and lay there, not daring to stir, while the monster came clumping fearsomely along, now here, now there. If it had seen me, I told myself, I was doomed. But it went noisily back toward the green lights. Scrambling to my feet again, I fled northward into the deeper gloom.

Today I cannot say exactly where my terrrified feet took me. I stumbled once or twice and panted for breath, but I dared not halt. I found myself fleeing along narrow, mean streets, and once or twice across open spaces among the buildings. When at last I stopped because I was almost exhausted, I judged I must be in Kentish Town. The houses there were deserted; at least, I saw no lights in them and heard no movement except the beating of my own blood in my ears. I sat on a step to rest, but I did not dare wait for long lest a pursuer come on clanging metal feet. Again I took up my journey. I came to a broad highway – Camden Road, I decided – and fared on beyond it, more slowly now. Now and then I paused to listen. Nothing came in pursuit of me, but behind me to my right still rose the green glow from Primrose Hill.

When the early sun peered above roofs in front of me, I was among streets unfamiliar to me. This, I decided, must be Stoke Newington. I fairly staggered with weariness as I followed the pavement along in front of a line of shabby little shops and dwellings. One of the houses was half smashed, the front door hanging from one hinge. In I went, and was glad to find water in a pitcher, though there was no food anywhere. I drank in great gulps, and then lay down on a sofa, to sleep fitfully.

Several times during the day I wakened and went to look out at the shattered windows. No fighting-machines appeared, though once or twice I saw hurrying shadows across the street and the buildings opposite. This may have been the flying-machine that, as I heard later, the invaders had put together to quest through our heavier atmosphere. I finished the water and wished I had more when, at nightfall of Saturday, I went out and sent myself to go southward again.

Now and then I paused to get my bearings. I realised that I was moving east of Kingsland Road, and I took great care whenever I crossed a side street. Suddenly the sound of a human voice made me jump.

Glancing around, I saw a hunched figure in fluttering rags of clothing. He came toward me until I could see him in the darkness. He was old, with an untidy white beard. His eyes glowed rather spectrally.

"I thought that I alone was saved," he croaked.

"You, too, must have the mercy and favour of the Almighty."

"Favour of the Almighty?" I said after him, amazed at the thought. Not for days had I felt any sense of heavenly favour in my plight.

"The destroying angels of the Lord are afoot in this evil town," he said. "For years I have read the Bible and its prophecies, have tried to preach to the scoffers. Judgement Day is at hand, brother, and you can bank on that. You and me's left to witness it together, the judging of the quick and the dead."

I asked if he had seen any invaders, and he replied that they had been roaming the streets earlier in the week, "looking out human souls for judgement," but that for two days he had seen none except at a distance. Again he urged me to stay with him, but I went on southward. My course kept me on the eastern side of Kingsland Road for a number of crossings, until I came to where I could turn my face westward, skirting a great heap of wreckage, to head slowly and furtively for Baker Street.

At midnight, approaching Regent Street, I saw lights. They were white this time, not green. Hastening toward them, I judged that they beat up at their brightest from the direction of Piccadilly. But before I came anywhere near, I spied northward a gleaming metal tower – again one of the fighting-machines – and plunged into a cellarway to hide.

There I cowered, miserably hungry and thirsty, until Sunday noon. There was no sound in abandoned London. At last I slunk, like the hunted animal I had become, to make my way across Regent Street and move west along Piccadilly. I reached Baker Street at last, and saw no sign of destruction there. It gave me a faint feeling of hope. Along the pavement I walked, ready at a moment's warning to dive for shelter, until I came to the door of 221B. The familiar entry seemed strange and hushed. It was as though I had been gone for a year. Up the stairs I fairly crawled, then along the passage to turn the knob of the door. It was unlocked and opened readily. In I tottered, home at last.

There sat Sherlock Holmes in his favourite chair, calmly filling his cherrywood pipe from the Persian slipper. He lifted his lean face to smile at me.

"Thank God you are safe," I muttered, half falling into my own chair across from him.

He was on his feet in an instant and at the sideboard. He poured a stiff drink of brandy into a glass. I took it and drank, slowly and gratefully.

"You have been here all the time?" I managed to ask as he sat down again.

"Not quite all the time," he said, as easily as though we were idly chatting. "On last Sunday night, at the first news of disaster heading up from Surrey into London, I escorted Mrs Hudson to the railroad station. At first I had had some thought of sending her to Norfolk alone, but the crowds were big and unruly, and so I went with her to Donnithorpe, her old home. She has relatives at the inn, and they were glad to welcome her. News came to me there. On Monday, the flight from London moved eastward to the seashore, well below Donnithorpe, with Martians in pursuit of the crowd of fugitives. Then came comparative quiet with no apparent move into Norfolk. On Wednesday I returned here, cautiously, on foot for a good part of the way, to look out for you."

"I was with poor Murray up at Highgate," I said. "He has died. Perhaps it is as well to die, in the face of all this horror."

"Not according to my estimate of the situation," he said. "But to resume. I have hoped for your return ever since I reached here on Thursday evening. I have hoped, too, for word from my friend, Professor Challenger. But you must be hungry, Watson."

I remembered that I was. On the table was a plate of cracknels and a plate of sardines, with a bottle of claret. Eagerly I ate and drank as I told of my adventures.

"You have mentioned Professor Challenger to me, I think," I said between mouthfuls. "Just who is he?"

"One of England's most brilliant zoologists, and vividly aware of his own attainments. He would say, the most brilliant by far."

"You speak as though he is of a tremendous egotism."

"And that is true, though in his case it is pardonable. But do you remember a magazine article some time back, an account of an egg-shaped crystal that reflected strange scenes and creatures?"

"Yes, because you and I looked at it together. I do not care for its author, H. G. Wells, but I read it because young Jacoby Wace, the assistant demonstrator at St Catherine's, was concerned. He said that the crystal had vanished."

"So it had," nodded Holmes, his manner strangely self-satisfied.

"Wace told Wells that before he could secure that crystal from the curiosity shop where it had been taken, a tall, dark man in grey had bought it and vanished beyond reach."

"And what does that tall, dark man in grey suggest to you?" inquired Holmes casually.

"To me? Why, nothing in particular."

"Really, Watson, and you always admired my grey suit I got at Shingleton's."

I almost choked on a bit of cracknel. "Do you mean that you got possession of that crystal?"

"I did indeed. Challenger and I have studied it, and I left it at his home for his further observations. So, you see, we are not wholly unprepared for this voyage across space from Mars to Earth. When the first cylinder struck at Woking, a week ago last Friday, I hurried at once to Challenger's home in West Kensington. His wife said that he had joined the scientists at Woking, but I could not find him when I went there myself. I fear he may have been killed by the heat-ray, along with Ogilvy of the observatory there, and Stent, the Astronomer Royal."

"May I come in?" boomed a great voice from the passage outside.

Eighteen

Swift as thought, Holmes turned and stepped to the door. He opened it, and in tramped a squat, heavy man with the deep chest of a gorilla and the sort of black spade beard that suggests a sculptured Assyrian king. I judged him to be in his late thirties. He wore rumpled dark trousers and a rather boyish tweed jacket. In one huge hairy hand he clamped an oblong leaden case, of the sort in which choice Oriental tea is packed.

"My dear Challenger," Holmes greeted him. "Only this moment we were speaking of you."

"I have been here twice, Holmes, but you were out," said the other, looking somewhat wistfully at the remains of the food on the table.

"I must have been observing the Martians or laying in provisions," said Holmes, "And speaking of provisions, you may care to help yourself to what we have here."

"Thank you very much."

The big man crossed the floor, stepping lightly for all his bulk and the heavy boots he wore. He laid his case on the table, then put two sardines upon a cracknel and opened his black beard to take in the whole arrangement at a bite. Brilliant blue eyes under shaggy brows raked me from head to foot.

"Medium height, well built," the deep voice rolled out oratorically. "Dolichocephalic – a prominent development of the cheekbones. Celtic, undoubtedly. Perhaps Scottish." He forked up two more sardines. "You are kind, Holmes, to give shelter to this poor vagrant."

"No, Challenger," said Holmes, busy at opening another tin. "This is my valued associate, Dr Watson, whose name I have mentioned to you from time to time."

"Indeed?" said Challenger, and suddenly I felt embarrassingly aware of how dirty and unkempt I must look.

"Perhaps I would be better off for a shave and clean linen," I admitted, rising. "If you gentlemen will excuse me."

I headed for my own room. There I soaped away grime and shaved my shaggy chin and washed well. Afterward, I changed clothes and returned to the sitting room, feeling much better.

Challenger had taken a comfortable armchair and was munching cracknels as he talked to Holmes. "On Monday I was able to get a carriage, and I drove with my wife to the channel coast," he was saying. "There, I saw her aboard a ship for France, and then I returned to London on foot."

"Would not the ship take you also?" Holmes asked him.

"Yes, I could have gone with her, but my presence was badly needed here," growled Challenger. "My intelligence – and perhaps yours, too, in a lesser degree – may yet cope successfully with these invaders."

"So far they have driven all before them, but they have not had everything their own way," nodded Holmes. "In Surrey, one was destroyed by a shell. The loss of even one makes a perceptible gap in their ranks, for they can number no more than fifty."

"And they suffered losses at the coast, too," Challenger told us. "I saw it happen. Three of them came wading out to destroy or capture the fugitive shipping, and the ironclad torpedo-ram Thunder Child smashed two of them before she herself blew up. You should have seen that action, Holmes. It was capital."

"I heard a report of that engagement at sea," said Holmes. "It struck me that, if the Martians were so ready to take to the water, they have some experience of it, after all. We did see a waterway with the aid of the crystal, Challenger. Though you seem to feel they were mystified by that attack of the ironclad, it may well be that they understand travel on water, may even have some sort of boats of their own at home."

"Marvellous, Holmes!" cried Challenger, applauding, and Holmes forbore to say that it was elementary.

"In any case, they displayed overconfidence in that situation," he said.

"Two at the sea coast, and the other killed at Woking, before the others there wiped out the men and guns with the heat-ray," went on Challenger, his beard tilting with aggressive assurance. "That makes a total of three out of fifty – a six percent loss, and one which they cannot at once replace. My friends, we may yet survive, we may even fight back against them."

I, too, had sat down. "How can we fight back? I demanded. "They are infinitely superior to us in science, able to cross millions of miles in space. Their armament must be unthinkably greater than ours."

"All that is true, Watson," said Holmes, filling his pipe again. "But reflect, Watson, they are few, as I have said. And they could fetch only relatively simple equipment across space. I keep comparing them to a party of hunters armed with sporting rifles – no really heavy artillery or high explosives – attacking a swarm of baboons. And those baboons are on familiar ground. They can roll huge rocks down slopes to crush their enemies, or perhaps lurk in ambush to charge out at them. I have heard of such things happening. Yes, beasts have fought and defeated men on more occasions than one. Rats evade the trap, foxes outrun and outwit the galloping huntsman—"

"Marvellous, Holmes!" I could not help applauding in my turn, for his calm analysis had suddenly roused a warm flicker of hope within me.

"Elementary," said Challenger, before Holmes had a chance to say it himself. "I take leave to remind you, it is not enough to state the obvious. The feeling that these invaders were less than omnipotent occurred to me strongly before this conversation. I reflected on the matter while at the sea coast. There I watched there machines at a disadvantage when they waded confidently out in the water, and I conjectured that their unfamiliarity with maritime warfare might indicate unfamiliarity with other difficulties upon our Earth." He blew out a deep breath, stirring his beard. "They were truly nonplussed as the Thunder Child came full speed upon them. They were not ready for any such manifestation. They hesitated – and they were lost, two of them." He gestured with his big hands. "They may be destroyed by some other agency than our relatively ineffectual weapons. It remains a simple matter of scientific rationalisation to decide what that agency may be."

And he poured claret for himself and sipped it grandly, as though his own words pleased him.

"Let us begin," he continued, "by saying, once for all, that they are not invulnerable."

"Nor omniscient, by any means," added Holmes, his fingertips together. "I take time to ponder, gentlemen, that all three of us have been afoot here in London these past few days, and never once has any of us fallen into their toils, though I have had a narrow escape."

"And I too," I said, unhappy again as I remembered how near they had come to me.

"When it comes to that," Holmes went on, "I deduce that they do not seek simply to exterminate mankind."

"Why should they show any mercy to us if they want to take our whole world?" I asked.

"It is my privilege to answer that question," put in Challenger grandly. "They have descended upon London as the world's largest center of human population, exactly because they have a practical use for men. Last night I lurked near Regent Street, and in some manner the lights had been turned on. I saw hosts of people out in the open, drinking from bottles and dancing together in a sort of saturnalia. Then, just at the sky was beginning to get pale before dawn, a big machine stepped in among them and scooped them up. It must have captured a hundred or so, and stowed them in a big cage of sorts."

Sickly I remembered those same lights in the street and the lurking monster. "For what purpose, then?" I asked.

"For food," Challenger replied.

I sat up and cried out in protest.

"And I saw some others captured at the sea coast, after I had sent my wife away to France," he continued, again sipping from his glass. "And with the crystal I have observed them twice. Once at what seemed to be their first landing site near Woking, and again at what must be their principal camp. Holmes tells me you have been close to it, Dr Watson, north of here on Primrose Hill."

"Yes, I came almost to that place, "I said. "But at the time I never dreamed that—"

Again I fell silent, with horror hanging over me.

"They esteem us as edible," said Challenger, stroking his beard.

"Yes," agreed Holmes quietly. "No doubt in the world about that. And you say that you have watched them, Challenger."

"Very closely. It is a most interesting process. The victims are held down by the tentacles of smaller machines. I could see their mouths gape open as though to scream. The Martians gather around and pierce their veins with metal pipettes. The living blood is drawn directly into the bodies of the Martians, much as we drink with a straw. Probably it goes into their circulatory systems."

"Horrible!" I could not help exclaiming. "Horrible!" Challenger eyed me expressionlessly. "Permit me to say that in my opinion those drunken fools I saw last night will be no loss to respectable human society," he rumbled. "As for horror, Dr Watson, how do you imagine an intelligent pig would view you or me in our frank relish for the flesh of his species? With alarm and disgust, you may be sure. However, their methods of feeding, together with certain other factors of life on Earth may suggest an effective campaign against them."

"And that?" inquired Holmes.

"Suppose," said Challenger slowly, "that we were to give them diseased victims, to infect their bodies."

Once again I was stricken with icy chills. "Surely you would not deliver our fellow men into their hands."

"Oh," said Challenger reassuringly, "I do not suggest to give them healthy specimens like ourselves. Nor intelligent ones, and all three of us possess, in varying degrees, intelligence. That policy would not be effective to this campaign of which I speak, and in any case men like us – though I estimate men like us to be in relatively small numbers – can do more good to our cause if they avoid being captured and eaten. Holmes, your friend looks quite pale. Suppose I pour him some of this excellent claret."

"I have already had quite enough wine, thank you," I stammered, looking at the bottle. Just then its contents seemed to have the colour of blood.

"Then a glass for you, Holmes," invited Challenger, tilting the bottle. "It is now time for us to consider and accomplish the necessary logistics of our counter-offensive."

He spoke exactly as though the campaign to defeat our enemies had been mounted and was in full swing. I looked questioningly at Holmes.

"Watson is the military veteran among us," said Holmes. "Quite likely he will endorse my own suggestion that we might begin by doing as they do; capture a prisoner and make a profitable study of him."

"Precisely the recommendation I was on the point of making," nodded Challenger. "With certain resources that we can muster here, I venture to trust that we may soon come within reach of one of these creatures."

"And I venture to trust that we may not," I protested stoutly. "When they come racing after men in their machines, all a man can hope to do is get away the best he can. I count myself fortunate in that I was able to stay out of their sight on all occasions. To be approached, even, by a Martian is to be lost."

"Not inevitably," said Holmes, knocking the ashes from his pipe. "Two days ago I was at a shop looking for some things to eat, and a machine burst in at the front and all but stepped on me."

"And you escaped!" I cried.

He smiled and shook his head with an air of friendly sarcasm.

"No, Watson," he mocked me. "I did not escape. The invader captured me and devoured me to the last crumb."

"His presence here demonstrates that he escaped," Challenger boomed at me disdainfully. "The most minor rationality, Doctor, should assure you of that."

"I was able to run back through the shop," Holmes related. "He was groping in at the front of it, but I had dived down into the cellar. At the rear was a coal bin, and I climbed out through the trap into the alley behind. Then on I went through the back door of a house behind, onto the next street, and so safe back here. Nor did I lose the provisions for which I had been foraging. We may be glad to have them in the coming days."

"My dear Holmes, you must have shown great presence of mind," I said.

"Say rather that I showed considerable agility," he said smiling the compliment away. "It was something of a tight squeeze, getting out through the trap there above the coal bin, but the rest was no great problem."

"You were fortunate in doing so," remarked Challenger, his blue eyes studying Holmes' gaunt, sinewy frame. "Your feat might well have been all but impossible to one of more solid, though more impressive, physical proportions. But it strikes me that all three of us have been successful in avoiding capture by the invaders, as Holmes has already pointed out. We have ranged for miles through the very streets of London which they apparently feel that they are in command of."

"At least my adventure demonstrates that we have the advantage of fighting them on familiar ground, ground we know better than they," said Holmes. "But you, Challenger, say that you, too, have avoided capture."

"I did, and brilliantly," Challenger swelled with self-appreciation. "Twice their machines came directly to my house. Both times I slipped away – very cunningly, I may add – while they were reaching in with their tentacles at the front windows. But they did not do any great destruction, fortunately. No heat-ray."

"Possibly they sought an article of value there," Holmes suggested.

"Which I take as a compliment," smiled Challenger, bowing his great, shaggy head. "Although, as you are aware, self-assertion is foreign to my character, I think it obvious that their high intelligence recognises my own particular important position among minds of the human race."

"How would they be able to arrive at that opinion?" I asked.

"By being face to face with me," he replied. "Many times I have looked into the crystal at them, and they have looked at me."

"It was of the crystal I was thinking when I spoke of their searching your house," said Holmes. "You have been observing these Martians with it, then. Have you seen them without their machines?"

"I have, and plainly," Challenger told him. "Here, let me try to sketch one."

Nineteen

He rummaged in his breast pocket for an envelope and a stylographic pencil. Swiftly he drew an oval body, set at one end with round eyes and a V-shaped mouth, between two fringes of whiplike tentacles.

"It is like an octopus," I suggested.

"Somewhat, in its external appearance," granted Challenger. "But this curious body structure is for the most part, more or less a gigantic brain-case, as I think. I discerned the rhythmic movement of what I take to be the operation of lungs. Here at the back," and he shaded a circular area, "is what may well be an eardrum, though perhaps it is not very effective in the dense atmosphere of our planet."

"They do use extremely loud siren blasts to signal each other," commented Holmes, studying the sketch. "Now, Challenger, I suggest that this anatomical specialisation – very little indeed beyond the huge brain and two sets of nimble fingers – argues a far greater evolutionary advance beyond terrestrial man than would be ours beyond, say, those baboons I have mentioned."

"You seem to think that they have developed from an earlier form somewhat like man," said Challenger gruffly, almost as though he made an accusation.

"More or less that, yes. Their machines suggest that they have accomplished some artificial approximation of what they once had naturally, in the way of legs, a torso, tentacle-arms, and a head."

"Those machines have three legs," pointed out Challenger. "Do you think that the primitive race from which the invaders evolved was tripodal?"

"It is not an impossibility. A kangaroo, for instance, uses its tail somewhat as a third supporting limb."

"As did the great saurians of the Mesozoic," added Challenger. "The herbivorous Iguanodon, and the appropriately named Tyrannosaurus Rex, which must have been the most terrible creature in our whole story of life on Earth until these invaders came." He beamed condescendingly upon Holmes. "You may well have the right of it on your side. Again I say, it is really too bad that you did not specialise in the abstract sciences. But if these invaders are so far advanced and specialised, it must follow that the process took whole eons of time."

"Might they not be the result of a highly organised and controlled eugenic specialisation?" I said suddenly. "Stock-breeding has developed some swift strides toward various desired physical forms."

"Now, that is an acceptable analogy, Doctor," approved Challenger, striking his palms together. "The contribution of it by you is useful and, I take leave to add, somewhat surprising. I begin to join Holmes in rejoicing that you were spared to become one of our committee of resistance. But Holmes has indicated that the invaders sought the crystal at my home."

"That crystal was somehow sent to Earth in advance of the invasion, for observation of our planet by way of a similar device that once was on Mars and must now be here," said Holmes. "One crystal, Watson, can make events visible when they occur in the vicinity of its mate. There is a definite rapport that transmits images from one of them to the other."

I must have looked stupid, for Holmes smiled.

"Perhaps somewhat as the telegraph transmits written messages, or the telephone spoken ones," he amplified.

"For lack of a better term, we might call the process television," offered Challenger. "Do not feel ashamed, Dr Watson, if you find it difficult to understand all this. The common run of humanity could no more comprehend the properties of this crystal and what activates them than could monkeys rationalise the way to use a pair of lost binoculars they happened to pick up. But suppose I give you a chance to examine it for yourself."

He opened the tea casket and took out something wrapped in black velvet cloth. Loosening the folds, he revealed a clear, burnished crystal, the shape of an egg and almost as large as his massive fist. I saw a play of light and movement, deep inside the thing. For a moment I thought of those ornamental glass globes in which flakes are suspended in liquid, to simulate a snowstorm.

"You have had this at your home since the start of the invasion," Holmes reminded him. "Why, would you say, did they not come for it at their very first advance into London from Surrey?"

"Why, for that matter, should they not come and seek for it now?" I asked nervously. "Would these Martians not have other crystals, with the same qualities of seeing far distances?"

"Perhaps none like this one, which is able to transmit images far across space to Mars itself," said Challenger. "You and I knew that it showed us Mars, Holmes, for when I observed the landscape there earlier, there were two moons in the night sky. No other planet of the solar system would afford such a spectacle."

"There are more moons than one circling Jupiter," I pointed out. "And more than one moves around Saturn."

"But both Jupiter and Saturn have cloudy atmospheres, as Mars does not," returned Challenger. "In any case, my friends, I suggest that they need this particular crystal with which to set up communication with their home base on Mars."

"But they did not at once come seeking it on their arrival more than a week ago," Holmes pursued. "Gentlemen, this indicates to me a grave necessity with them, even a critical one."

Again I looked into the crystal. Its pulsing light came and went.

"Where are those images you speak of?" I asked.

"We need darkness to see them properly," said Challenger. "A black cloth of some sort is indicated, Holmes."

Holmes stepped across to the sofa and caught up a a dark drapery from it. We three crouched together around the table, drawing the fabric over our heads and shoulders. In the gloom, the light from the crystal waxed and glowed strongly. Movement was discernible in it. Then the mist thinned, and there came a clear image. I saw a sort of crumpled face, with brilliant dark eyes, surrounded by what seemed intricate machinery.

"A Martian?" I whispered.

"Yes, and looking into a crystal of his own that matches its impulses with this one," said Holmes, his own hawk face bending and peering intently.

"Repeatedly I have had such a close view of an invader," said Challenger from where he sat a Holmes' other side. "This one, I should say, is in the cockpit of a machine. He may be travelling in it, on his way to find this crystal of ours."

"I marvel that they did not find it when they came to your house," I said.

"They made a search, but they seemed baffled when I put it into the casket," said Challenger, his beard close to the image. "It happens that the casket is of lead, and the lead can interfere with electrical impulses."

"I daresay we shall soon know about this fellow's errand," commented Holmes. "When he is closer at hand, I mean."

Hurriedly I bobbed out from under the cloth and sprang to my feet. "What! I exclaimed. "Is a Martian coming here now?"

Doubtless the one we have seen is now being guided by the vibrations of our own crystal," said Challenger in the calmest of voices, also casting the drapery aside and leaning back. "Of course, he may be miles away at present."

"But they can move at a mile a minute!" I groaned desperately.

Holmes was striding to the front window and peering up the street. "I take comfort, Challenger," he said, "when you tell me that they did no great damage to your house when they sought the crystal there. Perhaps they will not utterly wreck these premises, as they have wrecked provision shops, for instance."

Cold fear had ridden down upon me. I think I must have swayed on my feet, like a bush blown in a gale.

"How can you both be so calm?" I cried out. "You seem to think that a Martian is even now hurrying to come here to Baker Street."

"Exactly," replied Challenger, running big fingers through his shock of dark hair. "Like a client, seeking help from Holmes."

"And here, Watson, if I mistake not, comes our client now," reported Holmes from where he stood at the window.

I ran shakily to his side and looked along Baker Street toward Portman Square.

A fighting-machine stood on the pavement there, rising high above the buildings to either side. Its three great, jointed legs quivered as though with palsy, while green spurts of vapour issued from them and from the great oval body that housed the machinery. Steel tentacles writhed this way and that. The triangular housing of its pilot swung slowly, like a head peering near-sightedly. I had an impression of sickness, of unsure, unhappy motion.

Challenger, too, had joined us to look. "It must have been fairly close at hand when I brought the crystal out of the case," he commented.

The monster took a slow step forward, then another. It approached creakily on the broad flat pedestals of its feet, nothing like the headlong, confident machines I had watched a week before. I wondered if it was searching its way to us, as a hunter follows the trace of game.

"This is precisely what we have hoped for, Challenger," said Holmes. I stared at him uncomprehendingly.

Challenger stamped back across the room. He put the crystal back inside its leaden case and then carefully arranged the case, its lid open, on the seat of a chair against the rear wall.

"Now," he pronounced in a satisfied tone, "the impulse will operate, but any view must be of your ceiling only." Back he came to us. "Your client, Holmes, very probably will leave his machine to enter at the window, lest he damage the house and perhaps lose the crystal. And we are here to await him."

Holmes stepped to the fireplace. From the corner of the mantel he took a small bottle. He opened a neat morocco case and lifted from it a hypodermic syringe. I was so aghast that I actually forgot the Martian for a moment.

"Holmes!" I protested wretchedly. "Surely you will not use a drug now, after more than a dozen years of total abstinence—"

"I would not use it now except that it is vitally needed," he said, inserting the syringe and drawing back the plunger to fill it.

Metal rang and scraped loudly, just outside. I looked out of the window again. The machine had come opposite the houses only a few doors away, approaching slowly and painfully. The green vapour dimmed the air. I fell back lest it should see me.

"Suppose you stand in the corner, Watson," said Holmes, as quietly as I had ever heard him speak. "But be ready."

Utterly uncomprehending, I moved obediently to the corner of the room next the window. Challenger had returned from setting down the crystal. Holmes gestured to him, and the two of them pressed their bodies to the wall on either side of the window.

The metal clanked fearsomely outside. A shadow fell across the window, shutting away the bright June sunlight. I heard a mechanical drone, like the hum of an unthinkably giant bee. Holmes stood taut and lean as a wire cable. Challenger's mighty frame hunched powerfully. I watched helplessly from where I stood.

There was movement upon the window sill. A cluster of tentacles came gropingly into view there, like dark, searching snakes. These were not metal tentacles. As I stared, holding my breath, a dull-coloured bulk followed them. I could see the strange face that had appeared in the crystal. Its brilliant eyes, with fluttering lids, were fixed on the chair where the casket lay open across the room. Beneath the eyes gaped a triangular mouth, stirring loosely and dripping saliva.

The tentacles extended themselves to the floor, braced there, and heaved laboriously. In came the great bladdery shape, as big as a bear. Its shiny, leathery hide twitched and pulsed, as though with painful breathing. Another effort, and the whole form slid across the sill and thumped heavily down on the floor just inside.

Instantly Challenger leaped, swift as a pouncing cat for all his great size. The tentacles, two bunches of them, writhed up to grapple him. They wound around his arms, and one flung itself to clasp his neck. He tore at them with both hands. For all his tremendous strength, he seemed clamped, strangled. He was like a hairy Hercules, struggling with the Hydra.

"Now, Holmes," he gurgled, his face crimson with effort.

Holmes stooped down quickly and extended his arm. With a perfectly steady hand, he drove the needle of the syringe into the heaving bulb of a body, just behind the face.

The creature's mouth gaped wider and emitted a wild, bubbling cry. Holmes stood up straight again, setting the syringe in the bottle and again drawing it full. He bent down to thrust in the needle and inject a second dose.

Our visitor seemed to flutter all over, and then, abruptly, it subsided into slack submission. Its tentacles drooped around Challenger, its brilliant eyes glazed. Only the heave and fall of its respiration showed that it lived.

Struggling mightily, Challenger won free of the tentacles and gazed at the monster. I, too, left my corner to look. My nostrils were assailed by a musty, sickening odour of decay.

"Gentlemen, this Martian is dying," I stammered out.

"Look, it is far gone in some fatal disease."

"Dying, yes," said Challenger, wiping his broad palms on his tweed jacket. "Of disease, yes. But a Martian–"

He shook his head at me, "No, my dear Watson, no."

Twenty

I was goggling foolishly again. Holmes emitted his quiet chuckle. He turned his aquiline face toward Challenger and nodded in agreement.

"I remember hearing Ogilvy say that you had said something of that sort at Woking," he said.

"But, Professor, we know this creature comes from Mars," I put in. "You yourself told us that what you saw in the crystal proved that. And those fiery blasts reported by astronomers, ten of them, sending the cylinders to us across space."

"Yes, I remarked something of the sort," he agreed cheerfully.

"And at the oppositions of 1894 and 1896," I elaborated. "The telescope showed evidence then of what seemed gigantic artificial constructions on Mars. This creature manifestly comes from there."

"I am not unacquainted with those phenomena you mention," said Challenger, locking his brows as he studied the drugged mass that now breathed only spasmodically. "And I agree wholeheartedly that this specimen and his fellows came here from Mars. But it does not necessarily follow that they are natives of Mars."

"No, Challenger, it does not," agreed Holmes. "Good logic could demonstrate what you say."

"And I shall endeavour to supply the logic." Challenger squared his shoulders and flung back his head in his lecturer's manner. "Bear in mind," he said, "that no evidence of possible construction upon Mars was evident earlier than that 1894 opposition mentioned by Dr Watson."

Holmes returned the bottle to the mantelpiece and the syringe to its case.

"It may be that I have eased the pain the poor creature felt," he said. "Come now, Watson, you are our medical adviser. Of what does it suffer, in your opinion?"

"To judge from the odour, decomposition involves its tissues," I replied. "It rots, even while it still clings to life."

"Precisely so," said Challenger, with a grand air of official endorsement. "Which indicates to me that there are no bacteria of decay on whatever world these invaders have come from to visit us." He gestured with both arms. "Wise as they are, lords of planet after planet, as they seem to consider themselves, they did not foresee this deadly, invisible ally of man. We survive on Earth because our systems have developed resistance to bacteria through all the ages. But they thrust themselves among us, breathing and feeding and drinking, and in so doing they took death unto themselves along with what else they seized of Earth's things."

It was true, and I bowed my head in acknowledgment; in thanksgiving, as well.

"This makes clear the reason that they are sluggish in patrolling our streets," contributed Holmes. "They do not range here and there so freely. I deduce that they are gathered in dismay, at their principal camp on Primrose Hill. This one," and he gestured at the slack form of our visitor, "came stumbling hither in an effort to get hold of the crystal. Undoubtedly they want it to signal back across space, to warn their fellows to send no more cylinders to certain disaster."

"And as to those already here–" I began.

"To sum up briefly, the invasion is doomed," said Holmes, picking up his pipe and filling it. "We need speculate no further on how to meet and resist it."

"I am still in the dark on one matter," I confessed. "Professor Challenger reasons that this is no Martian, though he came here from Mars."

"My reasoning, like that of all brilliant intellectual conclusions, is simplicity itself," Challenger rolled out, stroking his beard. "Mars, with its lesser gravity and comparative nearness to Earth was a most logical base from which to launch the cylinders at us. But this creature's lungs show that Mars was not his native planet."

I looked at the laboured heaving of the bladder-body. "Its lungs move bulkily."

"But for that great mass of flesh – and I would estimate it at four hundred pounds, Earth weight – they are not particularly big," said Challenger. "They would be fatally inadequate in the Martian atmosphere. Are you not acquainted with Stoney's spectroscopic observations of Mars?"

I was ashamed to tell him that I did not know who Stoney was, and so I kept my silence.

"The atmosphere is extremely rare, but with a bare trace of oxygen to support life," Challenger said. "No, these invaders came from another world to build their base on Mars, and on Mars they existed temporarily and artificially. They would need respirators of some sort while they prepared there to accomplish their assault upon Earth."

"Where might they have originated, Challenger?" inquired Holmes. "From a planet more distant than Mars from the sun?"

"From farther across space than that, as I theorise. From a planet in another system in our galaxy. Who can say, who could count, how many habitable worlds the universe holds?"

Holmes gazed at the dying invader with solemn, almost compassionate, attention.

"This doubt of the Martian origin is not offhand with you, Challenger. As I said, poor Ogilvy mentioned your theory to me on the evening of the sixth, only a few minutes before he was killed by the heat-ray. I would judge that the thought had occurred to you even before the arrival of the first cylinder, but that you declined to divulge it to me."

"So I did, Holmes. I forebore, for a reason you yourself should discern – simply because I wasn't sure. You withheld your own suspicion that they viewed us as mere lower animals, farther down the ladder of evolution than themselves."

"All these matters we discuss help me to clarification of one of my own questions," said Holmes, puffing on his pipe. "The year 1894, as Watson has reminded us, was the time when evidences of artificial construction upon Mars were first observed from Earth. Among other importances of that time and event, is probably the sending of the crystal egg at that time, to observe us."

I had been watching the invader. It stirred and breathed no more. Again I stooped close to look at it.

"This invader is quite dead," I said.

"Then suppose we get it down to the cellar below here," said Holmes. "There is a great tub in the floor there, into which it will fit. Afterward, we can venture out – and in some degree of comparative safety, as I believe – to fetch rum and brandy and other spirits from public houses, to fill the tub and preserve this specimen for scientific study."

All three of us bent down to hoist the heavy, evil-smelling carcass.

V

❧

VENUS, MARS, AND BAKER STREET
BY JOHN H. WATSON, M.D.

Twenty-One

$\mathbf{M}$r H.G. Wells apparently chooses to ignore my published comments on his misleading brochure *The War of the Worlds*. A few scientists have derided the brilliant perceptions of Sherlock Holmes and Professor George E. Challenger that the invaders who came so balefully close to destroying our civilisation, and the human race with it, were not native to Mars. In most quarters, that supreme scientific rationalisation seems to be very little known indeed.

Some time ago I visited Holmes at his cottage five miles from Eastbourne on the Sussex Downs overlooking the Channel. It is difficult for me to understand why he retired there, at the very height of his brilliantly useful career as a consulting detective. Holmes had always seemed to me a confirmed Londoner, happy in the busy streets of the city, within easy reach of such enthusiasms as violin concerts, Turkish baths, and gourmet restaurants. I recognise the kindly loyalty of Mrs Martha Hudson, who gave up her prosperous and respected position as landlady in Baker Street to go with Holmes and serve as his housekeeper. Yet I have also wondered why the two of them settled in Sussex when both are North

Country born, with family connections in that part of the kingdom.

Holmes greeted me happily at the door of the picturesque little thatched cottage, around which hung the whispering hum of bees in their hives. Over the teacups he laughingly shrugged away my suggestion that he himself take public notice of Wells's imperfect historical publication.

"No, my dear Watson, his shortcomings strike me as mere trifles, not worthy the dignity of debate," he said, buttering a muffin. "For my part, I am busy writing a book of my own, *Handbook of Bee Culture, with Some Observations on the Segregation of the Queen.*"

Mrs Hudson laughed at that, from where she stood at the door of the kitchen, though I myself saw nothing funny in the title.

More recently I dropped in on Challenger, who likewise scoffs at the scoffers. I found him studying maps and catalogues.

"Human minds, save for a very few like that of Holmes and the only one now existing of my calibre, are absurdly limited," Challenger said, "Decades must pass, my dear Dr Watson, before the public can accept these truths so manifest to us."

"At least Wells should be refuted," I said.

"He is better ignored, as both Holmes and I shall do. To enter any public discussion is irksome to me, as it necessitates a descent to such simple terms as an ignorant audience can grasp. Which brings me to the notion that your own style might better suit the situation. At present, my attention must be given to my forthcoming expedition to the Amazonian jungles, where I propose to study the conclusions of Alfred Russell Wallace and Henry Walter Bates on the racial aspects of savage tribes there. I may be able to verify some of their opinions, and, quite probably, set right what I apprehend to be several glaring inconsistencies. A scientist's manifest duty is to seek out new truths and give them to the world."

With which ringing pronouncement he bent over a great map, and I took my departure. Nevertheless, this supplementary chronicle of mine will now also be offered to the reader in the hope that the findings of my two brilliant friends may be fully vindicated by the more perceptive.

I have already told how, on the afternoon of the tenth day of the "War of the Worlds", we three clustered around the carcass of the invader which had died almost as it crawled through the window into our sitting room at 221B Baker Street. It lay motionless below the sill, a great oval of a body with dull, dead eyes and two limply hanging sprawls of tentacles, eight in each cluster.

"Man may yet live, and perhaps deserve his rule on Earth," rumbled Challenger in the dark thicket of his beard. "As Dr Watson has so accurately suggested, terrestrial bacteria are killing these creatures, when the best weapons we could muster against them have failed."

Squatting down like a giant toad, he tugged at the body. "It is heavy," he grunted, "but the three of us can get it to the basement."

Together we dragged it to the door and down the steps to the ground floor. It taxed our combined strength, and the odour of decay was sickening. We all panted with exertion as we rolled it down another flight of stairs into Mrs Hudson's basement. Holmes lighted a candle and we made out a cement-faced trough in the tiled floor some nine feet by four and more than a yard deep, as I estimated.

"Once a carpet-maker had his establishment here, and this was his vat for the dyeing of fabrics," said Holmes. "Very well, in with our specimen but take care not to damage it."

We found cord and looped it around the slack form to lower it. Then again we mounted to the street door. The great war machine of the invader slumped there against the wall outside, almost blocking the street. We raced across to Dolamore's wine and spirits shop. Challenger drove in the door with a mighty kick of his heavy boot. Inside, Holmes and I took big baskets and filled them with bottles of brandy, whisky, and gin. Challenger hoisted a twenty-gallon keg of rum upon the great ledge of his shoulder. Back across we went and down into the basement again. Carefully we heaped loose tiles and fragments of broken cement here and there around the carcass in the trough and poured in our spirits. Holmes muttered unhappily as I trickled out a bottle of choice Scotch whisky. Several more trips to Dolamore's produced enough liquor of various kinds to submerge our dead invader completely.

It was dusk by the time we left the cellar, went upstairs to our lodgings, and washed thoroughly. Holmes produced a tin of tongue and some excellent cream crackers for supper, while I managed a pot of coffee on our spirit stove. After eating, we had brandy and some of Holmes' excellent cigars.

"Suppose that we take time to attempt an estimate of our situation," said Holmes. "We are now aware that these invaders are dying from disease, and also that they are not Martians after all."

"Because they breathe oxygen, and there is but a trace of that element in the thin atmosphere of Mars," amplified Challenger again. "Wherever they originated, oxygen was present for their breathing, and oxygen, as every schoolboy should know, is a necessity for the production and sustaining of organic life. Remember, too, that only ten cylinders crossed space to us from their launching site on Mars. The last departed before the first landed. That last cylinder must have arrived on Earth only last midnight."

"Then its crew of five should be undiseased as yet," suggested Holmes. "From those late arrivals, we may well look for some menace in the days to come."

"Perhaps not so greatly," I said. "If they have no natural resistance whatever to infection, they will feel damaging effects very promptly indeed. A system not conditioned to resist bacteria of disease and decay will suffer. The one we captured may well be a late arrival, and his companions from the earlier cylinders may even have succumbed ere this."

"My congratulations, Watson," smiled Holmes. "Often in the past I have observed to you that deductive reason is in itself contagious. Your own medical judgement there is a sound one."

"Commonplace," said Challenger, sipping brandy. "Dr Watson states a basic truth, one which undoubtedly was taught him at an early stage of his medical education. I am encouraged that the one that came here has not as yet been followed. He visited us on a desperate, solitary undertaking, to repossess their interplanetary signalling device yonder on the chair."

He gestured with his cigar toward where the crystal lay in its open casket. Holmes rose and walked to where it was. I saw a faint wash of blue light on his hawk face.

"Turn down the lamp, Watson," he said, and I leaned across and did so. "Now," he reported, "I can see what must be the cockpit of this machine just outside our window."

He shifted his head, as though for a clearer view. "There is a light there, and an intricate assembly of what looks like switches and panels on either side. Very well, Watson, you may turn the lamp up again."

He came back to his chair and sat down. We began to speak about the probable bodily structure of the invaders. I knew something of comparative anatomy, and Challenger spoke as though he knew everything.

"Again I wish to speak in endorsement of Dr Watson's suggestion that they have been developed to their present form by special breeding," he said, as though conferring an honour upon me. "As we have discerned, they are for the most part a highly organised but at the same time simplified arrangement of brain and hands. Organically, in some ways, they have evolved as far beyond man as man has evolved beyond four-footed animals but in others they have become rudimentary. They have kept active lungs, their optical processes apparently are quite good, but they would appear to be utterly lacking in the digestive tract. When they feed, they draw living blood from their prey into their circulatory systems."

"To their own destruction," added Holmes.

"Here on Earth, that has been their destruction. But to continue: I have not yet determined whether they sleep, although our specimen's eyes are furnished with lids. Holmes, I must confess that from the very first you had the right of it. Perhaps, in long ages past, their ancestors were not greatly different in physique from some humanoid form."

"And their minds?" I inquired.

"Here, Watson, I appropriate another of your suggestions about them," said Holmes. "I mean, your suggestion that the intelligence differential produced by a specially controlled evolution has been less than the radical difference in organic structure. I have several times drawn an analogy of baboons fighting an attack of human hunters, but perhaps the chimpanzee is a better comparison than the baboon. Chimpanzees are able to learn to ride bicycles and to eat with knives and forks. Who knows?" Again he turned to gaze toward the crystal egg. "We may learn in time to make profitable use of some of their devices."

"We have already done that, with the crystal," said Challenger, and he yawned. "But we are all tired, I think. Our exertions today have been considerable. What do you say to sleeping on it?"

Holmes insisted that Challenger take his bedroom, and he lay down on the sofa in his old blue dressing gown. I went into my own room, and with deep gratitude sought my bed for the first time in ten days. Sleep came soothingly upon me, and I did not even dream.

When I wakened it was sunrise, and Holmes was talking excitedly in the next room.

Instantly I sprang out of bed, my heart racing. I snatched my robe from its hook, hurried it on, and ran out into the sitting room.

Our landlady, Mrs Hudson, was there, her blonde hair disordered and her white shirtwaist and dark skirt crumpled and dusty. Her usually vigourous form drooped weakly. Holmes was helping her to a seat on the sofa.

"Martha!" he cried, the only time I ever remember his using her Christian name. "I told you to stay in Donnithorpe, where you would be safe for a time, at least."

"But I had to find out what had become of you," she said, weeping. "Even if the worst had befallen, I had to know."

Sitting beside her, he held her to him. "Get her some brandy, Watson," he said, and I poured a generous tot. He took it and held it to her trembling lips. She drank gratefully and looked up, as though it had calmed and revived her.

"I had to find out," she said again, more strongly this time.

"You have come more than a hundred miles," Holmes said. "You rode on a velocipede, I perceive. It is quite obvious, the old-fashioned sort kicks up dust on the clothing in just that fashion."

"I started on foot, day before yesterday," she managed. "I found the velocipede by the side of the road, and I came on it into London last evening. Bit by bit, I made my way here."

"Did you see any of the invaders?" rang out the voice of Challenger. He, too, had come into the sitting room. He was in his shirt sleeves, drawing his braces up over the jutting ledges of his shoulders.

"I saw two of them, but far away, thank heaven."

Again tears had come to her eyes, and she bowed her face in her hands. Solicitously Holmes helped her to her feet and led her to the door of his bedroom, from which Challenger had just emerged.

Challenger tapped my shoulder, as authoritatively as a constable. "Come," he said.

"But Mrs Hudson may need my help," I demurred.

"Holmes can look after her very well without any help from you."

"At least let me put on some clothes."

"Nonsense, man. There is nobody on the street to see us, not even an invader. Come as you are, I say."

Grasping my arm, he fairly hustled me out upon the landing, then down the stairs. At the street door we looked carefully, as usual, for any hint of danger. Nothing stirred in the summer morning except a starling.

"Did I not see a stepladder down in the cellar yesterday?" Challenger asked. "Come and help me bring it up. I want to go up into this abandoned machine."

We found the ladder and carried it up to the street. The machine crouched where its operator had left it the previous day. Its gigantic legs were telescoped down to a fraction of their usual height, with their joints doubled so that the oval body was opposite the upper window. I steadied the ladder while Challenger climbed, nimbly for all his bulk. He set a foot on the sill above and crept into the head like pilot chamber from which the invader had crawled to enter our sitting room. There he remained out of sight for well over a minute, while I stood barefoot in the street.

Still no invaders appeared there, though I briefly glimpsed a distant fleck in the blue sky that might have been their flying-machine. At last Challenger dragged himself back into view and descended, with something slung to his back. Standing beside me, he exhibited his find. It was an S-shaped metal arrangement, from which dangled wires. Along its curves showed studs that looked movable. In one bend of the S was set a crystal resembling the one Challenger has brought to our rooms.

"This is exactly the device I expected to find, the one I suggested might be called television," he said. "As you see, there is another crystal egg, furnished with keys and switches to direct its power." Again he slung it to his shoulder by the loose wires. "And now, since we are already downstairs, we can go across to Dolamore's."

He walked across the street, and obediently I followed him. Inside he fumbled in a bind and brought out a tall bottle, which he inspected with satisfaction.

"This is Chambertin, and of what I take to be a very good year," he announced, drawing the cork. "Nor is this too early in the morning for a small sip, would you say?"

On a table stood glasses, and into two of these he poured some wine. I tasted it and found it excellent.

"Why did you climb into the machine from the street, Professor?" I asked. "You could more easily have gone out through our window."

"I preferred not to disturb any researches Holmes might be making," he replied. "But observe this other crystal I have recovered."

It was dim enough in the wine shop for us to make out some details of our familiar sitting-room.

"I see Holmes there, standing with Mrs Hudson," I said gazing. "He is holding her hand, Hullo, it's gone cloudy. I can see nothing now."

"Inadvertently I touched this key," said Challenger. "That must have blurred the transmission of the image. Before we return, let us fetch along more of these very fine wines."

He took excessive care in his selection from bin after bin. It was fully half an hour before we slipped across the street to our door, bearing armfuls of bottles. It seemed to me that Challenger stamped loudly as he mounted the stairs.

Holmes let us in at the door, smiling over his morning pipe. Mrs Hudson, he said, was much more cheerful, and was even then preparing breakfast in her own kitchen. She bore a tray with a great platter of griddle cakes, a dish of butter, and a pitcher of syrup. Coffee was already brewing on the spirit stove. Challenger drew up a fourth chair to the table and insisted almost dictatorially that Mrs Hudson sit and take breakfast with us.

The cakes were excellent and I, at least, relaxed a trifle as I partook of them.

"There seem to be no enemies strolling officiously outside," declared Challenger as he finished his third stack of cakes. "Come, Doctor, I propose to go out and find some fresh clothes. Holmes undoubtedly is eager to examine this communication apparatus I brought out of that machine."

I dressed hastily in my room and went downstairs with him. Nothing moved in the streets save for some twittering sparrows and a forlorn dog that hastened away as we approached. Challenger broke the lock of a haberdasher's and prowled within for shirts to fit his huge frame—he was fifty-four inches around the chest, he told me, and he could find only two shirts large enough. From there we travelled as far as a provision store. It has already been visited by looters, but Challenger found a claw hammer and wrenched open a storage cabinet. From the shelves within we took smoked sausages done up in silver paper, a pineapple cheese, and some tinned vegetables. With these prizes, we returned home at noon.

Holmes sat alone in the sitting room. He told us that Mrs Hudson was asleep in her own quarters.

"I have been looking at both crystals, but now I have covered them in hopes that the invaders cannot locate them here," he said. "Our original crystal shows a considerable camp of them."

Challenger thrust his shaggy head under the covering blanket.

"I verify your observation, Holmes," his muffled voice came out to us. "I see what would seem to be a considerable pit with rough earthen banks all around. There is a fighting-machine, too, against the rampart, not moving. Yes, and two handling-machines, with only a slight stir to their tentacles." He emerged, blinking. "I daresay it is the headquarters Dr Watson approached on Primrose Hill."

"Did you see any of the invaders?" asked Holmes, and again Challenger dived under the fabric.

"Yes," he told us. "One is face to face with me this instant. I see the great, intent eyes. Now it is gone again, and I see the same camp. Several others are in view, lying prone on the ground. They move only slightly, even painfully."

"They suffer from disease," I offered.

"And are probably starving," amplified Holmes, "By now, they must have realised that to drink human blood is to drink death."

"It follows that there are no bacteria on Mars, as well as on their native planet," said Challenger, "or they would have perished on Mars instead of here."

"Professor, at what point did you realise that they were not Martians?" I asked.

"Almost at the very first, at Woking," he replied, standing up. "From my first sight of them as they ventured out of their cylinder and breathed our air. Their slow, hesitant movements impelled Ogilvy to mention Earth's gravity, to remind me and others that it is almost three times that of Mars. But in my mind I ascribed that slowness to the natural caution of sensible aliens venturing into any unfamiliar territory. But I kept my council until I could be sure."

"And when were you sure?" I pursued.

"I became very sure indeed yesterday, when our specimen grappled me so powerfully, even in its dying moments. Wherever it came from, there is quite enough gravity to make it strong and active."

That evening, Mrs Hudson appeared with a good dinner from her kitchen. We drew the curtains and lighted lamps, so confident were we that no attack would come. Holmes brought out his violin to play Strauss waltzes. It was quite a cheerful party. All of us rested well that night.

On both the twelfth and thirteenth days the three of us made more explorations. Mounting the highest roofs in the area, we observed through a pair of powerful binoculars belonging to Holmes. We saw several machines on streets near Primrose Hill, moving slowly in the direction of the main camp.

"They are coming together in their misery," said Holmes. "I am becoming certain, Challenger, that at close quarters they communicate by telepathy. Perhaps they gather in hopes of working out some solution to their desperate plight."

"But any telepathic power might fail as they weaken," said Challenger.

We became bolder in our excursions. Challenger seemed anxious to take me with him as he went scouting here and there. Early on the afternoon of the fifteenth day, he and I determined to push to the very borders of the enemy camp. Northward we stole, up Baker Street and across Park Road through the Clarence Gate into Regent's Park.

As we entered among the green trees, we heard a dreadful wailing just ahead of us. Instantly we crouched to hide for several minutes. Then we dared approach, moving from the shelter of one trunk to another. Finally we saw the source of the long-drawn cry, a motionless fighting-machine toward the western limits of the Park. Keeping ourselves screened from its view, we continued northward.

The sun was beginning to set as we reached Primrose Hill. I did not see the green glow of five days earlier, when first I had started home from Highgate. Machines were visible on Primrose Hill, too apparently standing quietly in their great excavation. None of them moved.

"I shall go on," vowed Challenger, and started up the grassy slope.

His audacity infected me and I followed him. I remember seeing the moon above the eastern horizon as we gained the top of that steep rampart of tossed earth. I paused there, but Challenger valiantly scrambled over the comb of the rampart and stood erect.

"Dead!" he roared, almost deafening me. "They are all dead or dying!"

At once I climbed over to stand beside him.

The wide pit below us was strewn with overturned machines, stacks of metal bars, strange shelters. Against the rampart opposite us lay the circular airship that had terrorized humanity. It looked like a gigantic saucer, flung there by the hand of a Titan. At the deep center of the pit sprawled a dozen collapsed bladdery shapes. One or two stirred feebly and emitted weak wails. I looked up at one of the silent machines. Fluttering birds pecked at the body of an invader, hanging halfway out of the hood.

"It is the end for them," said Challenger. "The end of their adventure. Come, Doctor, we must carry the news."

Down we scrambled and hurried away as fast as our legs could carry us. At St Martin-le-Grand we entered the telegraph office. Challenger inspected the instruments.

"Somehow the power is still turned on," he growled, as he tinkered with the key. I watched as he experimented.

At last – for his resourceful brain seemed capable of anything – he began to tap out a message. Then he paused, tensely waiting. Other tappings sounded.

"We are in touch with Paris," he informed me, and began manipulating the key again. At last he drew himself up impressively.

"There, Dr Watson, you have been present at an historic moment," he proclaimed. "You can tell of it to your children, should you ever have any. As so often in the past, it is George Edward Challenger who gives to the world scientific information of the highest importance. That, sir, is manifest justice. Who is more deserving, better fitted, to announce the end of the war?"

"You seem to set yourself above Holmes," I could not help reproaching him.

"Please do not mistake me," he said unabashed. "I myself admire Holmes to a very high degree. But the highest level of human reason is that of pure science. It transcends even the applied analysis of human behavior.

"There is no way for me to argue with you."

"Naturally not, my dear Doctor. But come, my duty is done here. Let us carry our tidings to Holmes."

Twenty-Two

In happy excitement we set out together again for Baker Street.

I need not rehearse here the familiar detail of England's resolute recovery from the blows dealt by the invasion. Wells's *The War of the Worlds* gives as good a brief account as any of how the nations of Europe and America hurried shiploads of necessary supplies to the sufferers of stricken London and the Home Counties. Commerce and industry returned swiftly to a high volume of activity, and wrecked homes and stores and public buildings were restored. Holmes and Challenger and I helped many returning refugees as best we could.

The preserved body of the captured invader was presented to the Natural History Museum, where it is now on display. Challenger felt, and I was inclined to agree, that Curator James Illingworth was offhandedly cool in his acknowledgment of the gift. But Holmes took little notice of any slight, for among the professions that almost immediately resumed full swing in London was that of organised crime. At the end of June, Holmes solved the cunning deception that I have elsewhere chronicled as *The Adventure of the Three Garridebs*. In assisting Holmes to bring James

Winter, alias Killer Evans, to the justice he so richly deserved, I was slightly wounded in the leg, and at the time I felt a sense of ironic comedy in suffering a hurt at the hands of my fellow man when I had come through the invasion without so much as a scratch.

No sooner was Winter safely in the hands of the police than Holmes became busy helping Scotland Yard trace the bold thieves who had stolen certain crown jewels from the Tower of London.

I saw little of him on that pursuit, for I had become busy on my own part. The privations and exertions of London citizens under those terrible sixteen days of oppression had stricken many with illness. Doctors were much in demand, and I returned to the practice I had all but given up, spending many days and nights in sickrooms and hospitals. It became necessary for me to leave the old lodgings in Baker Street and move to Queen Anne Street, where I could set up a dispensary and consulting room. It would be impossible to list all those who came under my care, but one of them proved a glorious reward to me for whatever useful labours I performed.

She had been Violet Hunter when, a dozen years before, Holmes and I had dealt with another case. She had been a governess like my dear first wife, and after the curious business which I have published under the title of *The Adventure of the Copper Beeches* she had become head of a girls' school at Walsall. Though she was only in her mid-twenties, little more than a young girl herself, she was successful at her post for more than five years. She then married a naval man, the gallant first officer of the Thunder Child, who perished with his shipmates in destroying two invader machines at the mouth of the Blackwater.

His unhappy widow had been forced to flee from their home in Kensington, barely escaping a rush of machines herself. She spent days in a wretched cottage on the outskirts of London, where she contracted a severe fever. It was my fortune to have her as a patient, to bring her back to good health, and to find that she had never forgotten my very minor help to her years earlier. Recovering, she regained the happy, lively charm I myself had remembered so well. She was in the prime of life, with beautiful chestnut hair and a sweet, good-natured face, freckled like a plover's egg.

It came as a dazzling surprise to me that she responded to my admiration. In September, at about the time when Holmes, too, suffered wounds in 'The Adventure of the Illustrious Client', she agreed to be my wife.

On October day I had visited her home in Kensington to take an early tea with her. She was engaged for dinner with some old school friends, and so I said my farewells at five o'clock and departed. Since Enmore Park was near, I decided to call upon Challenger.

Austin answered the door, and little Mrs Challenger appeared behind him to greet me and lead me along the hall. She knocked at a door, a booming voice answered, and I entered the study. Challenger's great bearded head and tremendous shoulders bulked behind a wide table strewn, as usual, with books, papers, and instruments.

"My dear Doctor, you come at an opportune moment," he cried out. "I have been at work on a study, a truly brilliant study, which, as I am confident, will add even greater lustre to my already considerable reputation."

I came to the table. Challenger thrust a sheet of paper under my nose. Frowning, I tried to read what he had scrawled upon it.

"A highly complex mathematical equation," I hazarded.

"It is a correction of some obvious errors in the late Professor Moriarty's *Dynamics of an Asteroid*," said Challenger. "Again and again I have reflected, how unfortunate it was that Holmes felt himself forced to destroy that brilliant intellect, that splendid adventurer among the abstractions of the cosmos. If asked to name a scientist capable of refining and advancing his researches, I can think of only – well, no matter for that, it does not become one to mention one's own gifts and attainments. But for these improvements in his equations, I must gratefully recognise our recent acquaintances."

"Recent acquaintances?" I repeated, uncomprehending.

"The invaders, or rather their fellows. The ones who did not come to Earth and die of our diseases. I am in contact with some of them."

"You are?" I had thought myself beyond amazement at Challenger, but this was something new and startling. "And these figures are theirs? But I see Arabic numerals, such as we use."

"Oh, they almost immediately learned to employ those. I began with pairs and groups of coins to demonstrate simple calculations, that two and two are four and that three from four leaves one, and so forth. Holmes has been here to observe my methods once or twice, and if he did not busy himself at his crime investigations, he might even be of some help. But come with me." He heaved himself out of his chair. "I can show you at this moment how I exchange thoughts with them."

He opened a door at the rear of the study. I followed him into a small, dim chamber with heavy curtains drawn at the windows. A small desk stood in a corner, and from its top shown a familiar gleam of soft blue. As we entered, a young man rose to his feet and faced us expectantly.

"Dr Watson, this is my assistant, Mr Morgan," Challenger made the introductions. "And I see that you have already recognised our crystal egg."

It lay nested on a crumpled piece of black velvet. I nodded.

"I thought it had been presented to the Astronomer Royal," I said, stooping above the desk to look.

"No, he is no great improvement in scientific gifts on Stent," said Challenger. "Holmes and I only turned over the crystal I had taken from that fighting-machine. This is the one that can transmit images across space from planet to planet, and it is far better in my hands than in those of bungling academicians. Morgan, have you seen anything new or interesting to report?"

"Not in particular, Professor," replied the other, his dark eyes upon me. "They've been sending the landscapes again."

"The landscapes of Venus," Challenger said to me.

"Not of Mars?"

"The instrument with which they send their images seems to have travelled past us to Venus, in her orbit closer to the sun. Have you not read in the daily papers that astronomers have reported something about an apparent landing on Venus? No, I suppose not. But sit down, Doctor, and look for yourself."

I dropped into the chair from which Morgan had risen. The crystal reflected a view with no luminous mists to obscure it. It was of a bleak expanse, grey and pallid, with no recognisable growth of vegetation. A haze of dusty clouds drifted in the air, Through this I was able to see a strange assortment of rocks. In the middle distance stood three gaunt pinnacles, like half-dissolved sticks of candy. Beyond them rose a steep bluff, also eroded and worn, and beyond that appeared a murky horizon. Then, as I watched, the whole scene slipped away. I found myself looking into a pair of dark, round eyes with a twitching triangular mouth below them. I had seen such countenances before.

"That is an invader," I said at once.

"You may call him that for lack of a better term," said Challenger. "Although at the present he is invading Venus. What he was exhibiting to us just now is a glimpse of the excessively inhospitable planet where he and his companions are waging a most desperate fight for life."

"How can you know that?" I wondered.

"They are quite adept in conveying information."

The face had vanished in its turn. Now we could see a sort of shelf or table, with what seemed to be a dark cup clamped in a metal stand.

Steamy vapours rose from the cup. A writhing tentacle came into view, pointing. Next moment the scene had abruptly shifted back to the landscape of worn rocks and dusty clouds, and then again to the steaming cup, and at last the peering eyes showed themselves once more.

"You are aware of his information by now," said Challenger.

"I? It was amazing, somehow frightening. Yet I am obliged to confess it did not seem a clear message to me."

"Come now, my dear Doctor," Challenger said in deep organ tones. "I should have thought that you had had some experience of parlour charades and puzzle pictures. Our friend on Venus was offering us a progression of related symbols."

I shook my head. "I saw an outdoor view, and an indoor view, and a glimpse of his face. No more than that."

Challenger fixed his heavy-lidded gaze on Morgan, who remained discreetly silent.

"An outdoor view, yes," he resumed at last. "He showed us the barren surface of the planet Venus. It proves to be a barren world, whipped by dust storms, its very rocks worn to points and knobs by incessant gales. Then there came the steaming container. That, as I gather, signifies an outside temperature exceeding that of boiling water."

"But nothing could live in such a temperature," I said.

"No more it could. Such conditions would destroy life as we know it, or as the invaders know it. Somehow they have built themselves a shelter, insulated so as to allow them to exist within it. But they dare not venture themselves in the open; they can observe only from ports or windows."

Again I looked at the crystal. The image had faded, and blue clouds pulsed within it.

"Professor Challenger, they actually seek to communicate with you," I said, profoundly impressed.

"They do indeed. By now they have come to realise that in me they have by far the most elevated human comprehension in existence on Earth. You can understand now why I have not put this crystal into the hands of the Astronomer Royal or any other incapable blunderer. Well, Morgan, these are things we have seen before. Have they been sending any other messages?"

"They transmitted these," replied Morgan, picking up two sheets of neatly pencilled figures. Challenger took them and studied them.

"I have been pleasantly surprised to find out that Morgan has a truly sound natural sense of mathematics," he said to me. "We have had several such tables as these, decidedly informative about Venus and her drawbacks as a possible abode of life. We have also achieved an exchange of geometrical drawings, and I have made some progress in teaching them the use of our alphabet, with a view toward sending and recieving written messages. All told, we are fast developing a profitable exchange of ideas between our two cultures."

He said all this with a calm assurance that left me with nothing to say in reply. Again I looked at the crystal. The blue mist was clearing from it.

"They seem ready with something fresh, and I myself shall sit here and watch," Challenger decided. "Morgan, will you and Dr Watson go out into the study. I should think you would find him interested in learning of our findings these past few weeks. Meanwhile, I shall try to note down whatever further message our friend on Venus may have for me."

Twenty-Three

Morgan and I went out together into the brighter light of the study. He closed the door and turned to gaze at me. I saw him plainer now. He was middle-sized and slender, thirty years of age or so, with a shrewd, alert face, bright dark eyes, and a respectable height of forehead.

"Are you by any chance the Dr Watson who writes?" he asked.

"Yes, I sometimes write."

"I've read some of your accounts of the cases of Mr Sherlock Holmes."

I waited for him to elaborate on that, but he only sat down in Challenger's chair and began to spread out some papers before him.

"I was serving in the artillery," he said. "My whole regiment was wiped out by the invaders when we tried to fight them down there near Horsell. I escaped by a miracle, more or less, and now I'm on leave while the regiment is reorganising and recruiting."

His manner of speech suggested that he had a better education and more intelligence than the ordinary soldier.

"How came you here?"' I asked.

"Since I was idle and my pay isn't much, I went looking for work. Just by chance I knocked at Professor Challenger's door, and he talked to me a while, then took me on as a helper. It's mostly looking into that crystal he has, trying to make copies of what I see there. Here are some sketches I've made, from what they've been showing us."

He handed me a drawing of a circular flying-machine, such as I had seen at Primrose Hill. It was represented as wrecked among eroded rocks. Another drawing was a diagram of one of the invaders' handling-machines. Both of them were executed with considerable skill and intelligence.

"Did you make those?" I asked. "They seem quite well done."

"Thank you, sir. I do have a bit of a gift with my pencil. The Professor likes me to draw the things that show in the crystal and sometimes to work up his own sketches."

"You seem to feel fortunate to have escaped the invaders," I suggested.

"And so I was. Afterward, there was more fighting, if you care to call it that, and everybody ran before those machines into London. But when I saw the machines were following, to take over there, I stayed where I was and let them go past me. I hid in Putney for days. I looked about me for others who might have escaped and stayed. I thought about living through it – even resistance."

"Resistance?" I said after him. "Against the invaders?"

"Oh, something of that sort. Get together some plucky men and women with sense, was my idea. Hide in the cellars and drains, keep out of sight. Try to find out all we could about those creatures, maybe capture and use their weapons. I found only one man in those parts, and he was with me a day or so, and then he wandered off by himself. I was left alone with my planning."

"But you did plan," I said. "You planned intelligently and with courage. You should have been with Holmes and Challenger and me in London."

"I wish I had been, sir. I wish that very much indeed. But in any case, the invasion collapsed. They all died off."

He said it almost as though he regretted it, as though he would have liked to do some fighting against the alien menace.

"And then?" I prompted him.

"Well, that's more or less my story, sir. As I said, my regiment has to reorganise and refit and recruit from scratch. Meanwhile, I'm working here for Professor Challenger until I go back."

"And you are on good terms with those beings now on Venus."

Morgan smiled. It might have been a joke I had made.

"They're a different sort of creatures now," he said. "They've had to stop thinking of Earth as a place to live, and men as food and drink. And so they're trying their luck on Venus. But the luck is worse for them there, if anything."

"To judge from what I myself saw in the crystal, Venus is hot and lifeless," I said.

"That's the right of it, Dr Watson, hotter than boiling water and nothing alive but those invader people, in whatever shelter they've been able to rig up. The Professor has it that they came from somewhere beyond this solar system of ours, to set up colonies. And their whole try at doing that has failed. Now they're trying to exchange their thoughts with us, as if they want to be friends. They've even passed on some of their scientific knowledge."

"That, at least, would be a profit from an acquaintance with them," I said at once.

Morgan opened the drawer of a side table and rummaged in it.

"We might wind up by learning the secret of their heat-ray," he said. "See here, Dr Watson."

He produced a cylindrical porcelain container, somewhat like a jam pot in size and shape, and carefully screwed off the lid. He set it on the table before me and began to fill an old clay pipe.

"There," said he, "you have the central active element of their heat-ray.

I myself fetched this from one of their machines, up there in that great pit on Primrose Hill."

I looked into the container. At the bottom lay a rounded object, the size of a pea. It had many facets, like a cut gem. To me it seemed to give off a faint light, as did the crystal, but pale pink and ember-like instead of blue.

"I don't understand," I said. "The heat-ray was like a great beacon. I never saw one in action, but I've been told that it sent out an invisible ray that obliterated houses and sent rivers up in steam."

He struck a match for his pipe. "I know," he said. "But what you have there is only the core of the thing. The power it contains is turned on by a switch and directed by a sort of curved reflector. Take it out and look at it closely. Don't be afraid, it's quite harmless."

I gazed at the little pill, hesitating.

"Take it out," he invited me again. "You will be holding in your hand the very essence of their destructive science."

"Don't touch it, Watson!" snapped a voice at the hallway door, and we both looked up.

Sherlock Holmes came striding in. He held a revolver, levelled at Morgan.

Twenty-Four

M y dear Holmes, what brings you here?" I cried, but he paid no attention to me. His narrowed eyes were fixed on my companion.

"If that object is harmless, as you say, take it in your own hand," he ordered Morgan. "Do as I tell you – now, this instant!"

Morgan was out of his chair. He shrank from the table and the container with the object inside. The lid was still in his hand.

"You said that it was harmless," Holmes reminded him icily. "I heard you as I opened the door. Why do you hesitate to touch it?"

Morgan slammed the lid down on the container and backed another step away. "No," he stammered. "N-no, I won't touch it. You can't make me."

"Which signifies that you knew that a touch of that object would kill Dr Watson," Holmes accused. "You would like to kill me, too, I have no doubt."

"What does he mean, Morgan?" I demanded.

"You do not have his name exactly right, Watson," said Holmes, the revolver still pointing. "Drop the *g* and call him Moran. For this is the son of Colonel Sebastian Moran – the second most dangerous man in

London, back in 1894 when you helped me capture him in Camden House, just across from our lodgings."

Moran sagged down in Challenger's chair again.

"This is fantastic," he protested, more strongly. "You have nothing against me, Mr Holmes."

"Which is exactly what all trapped criminals say and very seldom prove. I have just come from tracking down one Ezra Prather."

Moran started involuntarily as Holmes spoke the name.

"Ah, you know who he is, I perceive," said my friend triumphantly. "We walked in upon him just as he was in the act of cutting up certain jewels, to make them easier to sell. Caught red-handed, he readily confessed how you and he stole them from their cases in the Tower, on the very day that Challenger telegraphed to Paris the news that the invasion had collapsed."

Moran stood up again, trembling in every fibre.

"I've been doing my best," he blubbered. "I was a good soldier. I tried to fight the invaders, I was almost killed in action. Here lately I've helped Professor Challenger. He will speak to my helping him. Whatever Prather says—"

"And Prather has said a good deal," said Inspector Stanley Hopkins, also entering through the open door. "He made a full statement to Inspector Lestrade at Scotland Yard and signed it. It tells us all about who you really are, what you did to assist him, and how to find you here."

He produced a pair of handcuffs. "Place your wrists together," he ordered.

The fellow mutely held out his arms. I heard the snap of the irons as they locked upon him.

Challenger came bursting from the inner room. "How can I work profitably with all this commotion?" he growled, staring dangerously at Hopkins. "Who are you, sir, and why are you putting those handcuffs on

Morgan?"

"His name is Moran, Challenger," said Holmes, pocketing his revolver, "and he is a thief and a would-be murderer. He tried to kill Watson just now, because Watson once helped me capture his father. You were wishing it was I, weren't you, Moran?"

"Come along with me," said Hopkins, his hand on Moran's arm. "It is my duty to inform you that anything you say will be taken down in writing and may be used against you."

"Stay," pleaded Moran suddenly. "Hear me out, hear what I can offer – the secret of the invaders' heat-ray and how it is used."

Challenger puffed out his cheeks and locked his brows. "If you know that, you have concealed from me important messages from those creatures on Venus," he charged. "Whatever your crimes have been, this is a worse one still."

"I'll tell you everything," Moran chattered at us. "Yes, I kept some information. I have whole tables of formulas that explain the power. They tell how to direct impulses that will explode atoms."

Holmes' eyes started from his head, and so also must have mine.

"But that is a scientific impossibility," I gasped. "It has baffled the greatest scientific researchers."

"Not quite the greatest," Challenger corrected me. "I have not as yet given the problem my attention." He tramped toward Moran. "If those formulas are operable, then is your price for them your freedom? Show me those figures, at once."

Moran lifted his shackled hands and searched inside his coat. "Here," he said, bringing a sheaf of folded papers into view. "See for yourself, Professor, if you are able to understand."

"You insult me by expressing any doubt of that," Challenger said harshly as he snatched the papers.

He spread them out in both his hands and studied them. His eyes gleamed in his shaggy face. Holmes struck a match.

"By God, you are right," Challenger roared out in his excitement. "To a well-informed, highly capable intellect, this summation – yes, and this, the building upon it–is comprehensible. It is the most amazing–"

Holmes made a lightning-swift stride. In his outstretched hand was the lighted match. He held it to the papers in Challenger's fist.

They blazed up, with a howl Challenger dropped them on the floor. They blazed brightly while, Challenger nursed his burnt fingers.

"Holmes, are you utterly mad?" he yelled.

"Utterly sane, as I hope," replied Holmes evenly. "Sane enough to be disturbed at the sight of a brilliant chimpanzee experimenting with his trainer's loaded pistol."

Challenger knelt beside the burning papers. They fell into grey ashes.

"Lost!" he lamented, rising again. "Morgan... Moran... if that is your right name – do you remember–"

Morgan shook his head in despair. "No, sir, I only wrote down the figures from the crystal. It would be impossible to reproduce them."

"Lost," groaned Challenger again, pressing his hands to his temples.

"Then let man himself find out the secret," said Holmes. "With a weapon such as exploding atoms, he could easily destroy himself and all his world around him. If in future he finds the wisdom to solve the mystery, perhaps he will at the same time achieve for himself the control that having such power must entail."

Challenger breathed heavily for a long moment. I wondered if he would throw himself upon my friend.

"I must endorse that proposition," he said at last. "It should not have been necessary for me to have been reminded by you, Holmes. Now and then I think too much in the abstract. It is a fault I should overcome."

"There, Moran," said Holmes. "You see that we have declined your offer. Take him away, Inspector Hopkins."

Hopkins took Moran by the shoulder and led him out. Challenger carefully screwed the lid back upon the container.

"I must keep this in a far safer place than my drawer," he said. "Now, as for those unfortunate creatures on Venus—"

"You have been in contact with them again, Professor?" I asked.

"And for the last time, I fear. But come and see."

We followed him into the darkened rear room. The crystal egg gleamed softly. Within it we seemed to see what may have been some sort of card or board, and upon it a single large O.

"A zero," I said. "But that means nothing."

"More probably a farewell signal," said Holmes. "The pattern of events is fairly clear. They died on Earth; now they find Venus inhospitable and must flee from there. A tale of failure."

The light died in the crystal. The blue mist faded.

"And as I think, the survivors at the base on Mars must also depart or perish," declared Challenger.

"And begone forever from our latitudes of space?" I suggested.

"Not necessarily forever," said Holmes.

"No," agreed Challenger. "They may well return, better equipped for survival. Since they dare not eat us, they may make scientific studies of us. They may well train us to understand their more fundamental conceptions, as they have already done successfully with me. Now that you have solved your latest case, Holmes, perhaps you will take dinner here and discuss the matter at greater length."

"Thank you, but some other time," said Holmes as we returned to the study. "At present, I have a matter of the utmost importance to attend to at my rooms. Watson, however, will be glad to stay and hear your views. I wish you good-bye for the time being."

He walked out, closing the door behind him.

"A matter of the utmost importance," I mused aloud. "But he

completed his work on the jewel robbers when he arrested Moran, and that was his only case on hand. Why, nobody could be waiting for him at home but Mrs Hudson."

Challenger turned upon me a gaze of the utmost weary pity.

"Cerebral paresis," he said. "Mental inertia. Remarkable!"

"What do you mean?"

"Oh, nothing of great consequence." He turned to the door. "Suppose I tell my wife that you will be our guest at table tonight. For the moment you might like to study my notes and Moran's drawings."

Appendix

A LETTER FROM DR. WATSON

Plum Villa,

Axtellford,

Bucks

April 25, 1909

Mr H. G. Wells,

Spade House,

Sandigate,

Kent

Dear Sir–

I am writing to you personally in order to clarify certain matters which have not been fully dealt with. When my first chronicle was published I received letters from some of your supporters, protesting that the non-Martian origin of the invaders was not demonstrated by the evidence I offered. I therefore wrote a second article, massively proving that the invaders were not native to Mars, and some of my critics wrote to me and retracted. However, no statements by yourself have ever been passed along to me, and I am therefore challenging you directly.

Your supporters have complained that, in calling your book "frequently inaccurate" and full of exaggerations, I have failed to elaborate. Specifically, I meant that you vastly exaggerated your own experiences, resorting sometimes to pure faking. The contents of the 13th chapter of Book I and of the first four chapters of Book II are partially imaginary. Shortly after your book was published, Holmes did research and found that the curate of whom you wrote was your own invention, simply created in order to discredit Christianity. Your atheism is notorious. In your book you portray yourself as a Christian – or, at least, a man who believes in God and in prayer–but this is sheer posturing.

The most blatant piece of fraud in the entire book occurs in the chapter entitled 'What We Saw from the Ruined House'. You report that you saw the invaders trying to raise themselves on their hands, but unable to do so because of the terrestrial gravity. This is sheer fabrication, simply intended to support the view that they were native Martians. In my two articles there is ample evidence that the invaders could move about on our planet as easily as men. The rest of this chapter – apart from the fiction of the curate, since in fact you were alone in the basement – is accurate and informative. But what can be thought of a writer who mixes factual observation with pure invention, just to uphold a questionable thesis? Doubts about the Martian origin of these invaders were being circulated even while the invasion was in progress. You had surely heard about this long before you started writing your book, and in order to refute the suggestion you resorted to dishonesty.

For the rest, I call attention to these errors:

(1) In your account of the battle at St George's Hill, the action immediately preceding the discharge of the black smoke, you write that the invader who had been overthrown crawled out of his hood and repaired his support. This is so absurdly impossible that I should not

even have to refute it, but apparently I must. In point of fact, the machine was repaired by its two companions, the pilot remaining in his cowl. Holmes learned this at Donnithorpe on Tuesday, June 10, 1902, from scouts who had observed it.

(2) In that same chapter, describing the tragedy in Surrey in the night of June 8, you say that none of the artillerymen near Esher survived the black gas. It can be shown, however, that there were many survivors; numerous soldiers realised the danger in time to escape. Holmes interviewed some of them at Donnithorpe, for his presence there was widely rumoured, and survivors of the catastrophe naturally sought him out to relate their experiences and hear his conclusions.

(3) You insist in your book that the slaying of an invader at Weybridge a few hours before the black smoke tragedy was a lucky accident, and you quote Moran to the same effect. All of the troops at Weybridge were wiped out by the ray, but some civilians (notably including yourself) escaped; and several of them contradict you on this point. Their testimony, again given Holmes at Donnithorpe, clearly shows that the pilot was killed by a shrewdly aimed shell. An officer was heard shouting: "Aim for that turning cowl! It's something like a man's head! A shell striking there is like a bullet through the brain!" One gunner absorbed this order and, with swift and expert marksmanship, aimed the fatal shell. If only his name and his officer's were known, they should have statues in their honour, much like the monument which, at Holmes' suggestion, has been built in memory of the crew of the Thunder Child – whose exploits you describe very vividly in the best and most thrilling chapter of your unequal book.

(4) Your first chapter contains a startling mathematical error. You imagine the Mars-based cylinders as moving at several thousand miles per minute. Yet the first one was fired at midnight on May 12, 1902, and landed just after midnight of June 5. If it had been travelling at a speed of

(for instance) about 10,000 miles per minute, it would have crossed the distance in about three days. In fact, it took over three weeks.

(5) The invaders crossed from Mars to Venus shortly after the failure of their expedition to Earth, the Venusian expedition breaking down in October, 1902. This is chronicled in my second essay. Yet you, writing in the year 1908, contend in your *Epilogue* that evidence of the Venusian landing was observed "seven months ago now" by the astronomer Lessing. You therefore disclose a shocking ignorance of the astronomical reporting in the 1902 press, and a gross misunderstanding of what Lessing described in 1907. Lessing, in a letter to Professor Challenger, has retracted his statements, admitting that faulty equipment and hasty judgement were responsible.

I must now correct an error of my own. I wrote my second article without consulting Holmes and quoted an observation of mine which I now realise to be mistaken. When speaking to Holmes and Challenger, I suggested that the captured specimen might be a late arrival, and that his earlier companions might have already succumbed. But Holmes, upon reading my published article, informed me that this was quite wrong, and that he really should have corrected me at the time. The specimen we captured on the afternoon of June 15 was the first disease fatality. All were dead or dying by the evening of the 20th.

If you ignore this letter, I will have it published.

Yours sincerely,
John H. Watson, M.D.

Also Available

the
further
adventures of

SHERLOCK
HOLMES

THE VEILED DETECTIVE

by

DAVID STUART DAVIES

AFGHANISTAN,
THE EVENING OF 27 JUNE 1880

The full moon hovered like a spectral observer over the British camp. The faint cries of the dying and wounded were carried by the warm night breeze out into the arid wastes beyond. John Walker staggered out of the hospital tent, his face begrimed with dried blood and sweat. For a moment he threw his head back and stared at the wide expanse of starless sky as if seeking an answer, an explanation. He had just lost another of his comrades. There were now at least six wounded men whom he had failed to save. He was losing count. And, by God, what was the point of counting in such small numbers anyway? Hundreds of British soldiers had died that day, slaughtered by the Afghan warriors. They had been outnumbered, outflanked and routed by the forces of Ayub Khan in that fatal battle at Maiwand. These cunning tribesmen had truly rubbed the Union Jack into the desert dust. Nearly a third of the company had fallen. It was only the reluctance of the Afghans to carry out further carnage that had prevented the British troops from being completely annihilated. Ayub Khan had his victory. He had made his point. Let the survivors report the news of his invincibility.

For the British, a ragged retreat was the only option. They withdrew into the desert, to lick their wounds and then to limp back to Candahar. They had had to leave their dead littering the bloody scrubland, soon to be prey to the vultures and vermin.

Walker was too tired, too sick to his stomach to feel anger, pain or frustration. All he knew was that when he trained to be a doctor, it had been for the purpose of saving lives. It was not to watch young men's pale, bloody faces grimace with pain and their eyes close gradually as life ebbed away from them, while he stood by, helpless, gazing at a gaping wound spilling out intestines.

He needed a drink. Ducking back into the tent, he grabbed his medical bag. There were still three wounded men lying on makeshift beds in there, but no amount of medical treatment could save them from the grim reaper. He felt guilty to be in their presence. He had instructed his orderly to administer large doses of laudanum to help numb the pain until the inevitable overtook them.

As Walker wandered to the edge of the tattered encampment, he encountered no other officer. Of course, there were very few left. Colonel MacDonald, who had been in charge, had been decapitated by an Afghan blade very early in the battle. Captain Alistair Thornton was now in charge of the ragged remnants of the company of the Berkshire regiment, and he was no doubt in his tent nursing his wound. He had been struck in the shoulder by a jezail bullet which had shattered the bone.

Just beyond the perimeter of the camp, Walker slumped down at the base of a skeletal tree, resting his back against the rough bark. Opening his medical bag, he extracted a bottle of brandy. Uncorking it, he sniffed the neck of the bottle, allowing the alcoholic fumes to drift up his nose. And then he hesitated.

Something deep within his conscience made him pause. Little did this tired army surgeon realise that he was facing a decisive moment of Fate. He was about to commit an act that would alter the course of his life for ever. With a frown, he shook the vague dark unformed thoughts from his mind and returned his attention to the bottle.

The tantalising fumes did their work. They promised comfort and oblivion. He lifted the neck of the bottle to his mouth and took a large gulp. Fire spilled down his throat and raced through his senses. Within moments he felt his body ease and relax, the inner tension melting with the warmth of the brandy. He took another gulp, and the effect increased. He had found an escape from the heat, the blood, the cries of pain and the scenes of slaughter. A blessed escape. He took another drink. Within twenty minutes the bottle was empty and John Walker was floating away on a pleasant, drunken dream. He was also floating away from the life he knew. He had cut himself adrift and was now heading for stormy, unchartered waters.

As consciousness slowly returned to him several hours later, he felt a sudden, sharp stabbing pain in his leg. It came again. And again. He forced his eyes open and bright sunlight seared in. Splinters of yellow light pierced his brain. He clamped his eyes shut, embracing the darkness once more. Again he felt the pain in his leg. This time, it was accompanied by a strident voice: "Walker! Wake up, damn you!"

He recognised the voice. It belonged to Captain Thornton. With some effort he opened his eyes again, but this time he did it more slowly, allowing the brightness to seep in gently so as not to blind him. He saw three figures standing before him, each silhouetted against the vivid blue sky of an Afghan dawn. One of them was kicking his leg viciously in an effort to rouse him.

"You despicable swine, Walker!" cried the middle figure, whose left arm was held in a blood-splattered sling. It was Thornton, his commanding officer.

Walker tried to get to his feet, but his body, still under the thrall of the alcohol, refused to co-operate.

"Get him up," said Thornton.

The two soldiers grabbed Walker and hauled him to his feet. With his good hand, Thornton thrust the empty brandy bottle before his face. For a moment, he thought the captain was going to hit him with it.

"Drunk on duty, Walker. No, by God, worse than that. Drunk while your fellow soldiers were in desperate need of your attention. You left them... left them to die while you... you went to get drunk. I should have you shot for this – but shooting is too good for you. I want you to live... to live with your guilt." Thornton spoke in tortured bursts, so great was his fury.

"There was nothing I could do for them," Walker tried to explain, but his words escaped in a thick and slurred manner. "Nothing I could–"

Thornton threw the bottle down into the sand. "You disgust me, Walker. You realise that this is a court martial offence, and believe me I shall make it my personal duty to see that you are disgraced and kicked out of the army."

Words failed Walker, but it began to sink in to his foggy mind that he had made a very big mistake – a life-changing mistake.

London, 4 October 1880

"Are you sure he can be trusted?" Arthur Sims sniffed and nodded towards the silhouetted figure at the end of the alleyway, standing under a flickering gas lamp.

Badger Johnson, so called because of the vivid white streak that ran through the centre of his dark thatch of hair, nodded and grinned.

"Yeah. He's a bit simple, but he'll be fine for what we want him for. And if he's any trouble..." He paused to retrieve a cut-throat razor from his inside pocket. The blade snapped open, and it swished through the air. "I'll just have to give him a bloody throat, won't I?"

Arthur Sims was not amused. "Where d'you find him?"

"Where d'you think? In The Black Swan. Don't you worry. I've seen him in there before – and I seen him do a bit of dipping. Very nifty he was, an' all. And he's done time. In Wandsworth. He's happy to be our crow for just five sovereigns."

"What did you tell him?"

"Hardly anything. What d'you take me for? Just said we were cracking a little crib in Hanson Lane and we needed a lookout. He's done the work before."

Sims sniffed again. "I'm not sure. You know as well as I do he ought to be vetted by the Man himself before we use him. If something goes wrong, we'll *all* have bloody throats… or worse."

Badger gurgled with merriment. "You scared, are you?"

"Cautious, that's all. This is a big job for us."

"And the pickin's will be very tasty, an' all, don't you worry. If it's cautious you're being, then you know it's in our best interest that we have a little crow keeping his beady eyes wide open. Never mind how much the Man has planned this little jaunt, *we're* the ones putting our heads in the noose."

Sims shuddered at the thought. "All right, you made your point. What's his name?"

"Jordan. Harry Jordan." Badger slipped his razor back into its special pocket and flipped out his watch. "Time to make our move."

Badger giggled as the key slipped neatly into the lock. "It's hardly criminal work if one can just walk in."

Arthur Sims gave his partner a shove. "Come on, get in," he whispered, and then he turned to the shadowy figure standing nearby. "OK, Jordan, you know the business."

Harry Jordan gave a mock salute.

Once inside the building, Badger lit the bull's-eye lantern and consulted the map. "The safe is in the office on the second floor at the far end, up a spiral staircase." He muttered the information, which he knew by heart anyway, as if to reassure himself now that theory had turned into practice.

The two men made their way through the silent premises, the thin yellow beam of the lamp carving a way through the darkness ahead of them. As the spidery metal of the staircase flashed into view, they spied an obstacle on the floor directly below it. The inert body of a bald-headed man.

Arthur Sims knelt by him. "Night watchman. Out like a light. Very special tea he's drunk tonight." Delicately, he lifted the man's eyelids to reveal the whites of his eyes. "He'll not bother us now, Badger. I reckon he'll wake up with a thundering headache around breakfast-time."

Badger giggled. It was all going according to plan.

Once up the staircase, the two men approached the room containing the safe. Again Badger produced the keyring from his pocket and slipped a key into the lock. The door swung open with ease. The bull's-eye soon located the imposing Smith-Anderson safe, a huge impenetrable iron contraption that stood defiantly in the far corner of the room. It was as tall as a man and weighed somewhere around three tons. The men knew from experience that the only way to get into this peter was by using the key – or rather the keys. There were five in all required. Certainly it would take a small army to move the giant safe, and God knows how much dynamite would be needed to blow it open, an act that would create enough noise to reach Scotland Yard itself.

Badger passed the bull's-eye to his confederate, who held the beam steady, centred on the great iron sarcophagus and the five locks. With another gurgle of pleasure, Badger dug deep into his trouser pocket and pulled out a brass ring containing five keys, all cut in a different manner.

Scratched into the head of each key was a number – one that corresponded with the arrangement of locks on the safe.

Kneeling down in the centre of the beam, he slipped in the first key. It turned smoothly, with a decided click. So did the second. And the third. But the fourth refused to budge. Badger cast a worried glance at his confederate, but neither man spoke. Badger withdrew the key and tried again, with the same result. A thin sheen of sweat materialised on his brow. What the hell was wrong here? This certainly wasn't in the plan. The first three keys had been fine. He couldn't believe the Man had made a mistake. It was unheard of.

"Try the fifth key," whispered Arthur, who was equally perplexed and worried.

In the desperate need to take action of some kind, Badger obeyed. Remarkably, the fifth key slipped in easily and turned smoothly, with the same definite click as the first three. A flicker of hope rallied Badger's dampened spirits and he turned the handle of the safe. Nothing happened. It would not budge. He swore and sat back on his haunches. "What the hell now?"

"Try the fourth key again," came his partner's voice from the darkness.

Badger did as he was told and held his breath. The key fitted the aperture without problem. Now his hands were shaking and he paused, fearful of failure again.

"Come on, Badger."

He turned the key. At first there was some resistance, and then... it moved. It revolved. It clicked.

"The bastards," exclaimed Arthur Sims in a harsh whisper. "They've altered the arrangement of the locks so they can't be opened in order. His nibs ain't sussed that out."

Badger was now on his feet and tugging at the large safe door.

"Blimey, it's a weight," he muttered, as the ponderous portal began to move. "It's bigger than my old woman," he observed, his spirits lightening again. The door creaked open with magisterial slowness. It took Badger almost a minute of effort before the safe door was wide open.

At last, Arthur Sims was able to direct the beam of the lantern to illuminate the interior of the safe. When he had done so, his jaw dropped and he let out a strangled gasp.

"What is it?" puffed Badger, sweat now streaming down his face.

"Take a look for yourself," came the reply.

As Badger pulled himself forward and peered round the corner of the massive safe door, a second lantern beam joined theirs. "The cupboard is bare, I am afraid."

The voice, clear, brittle and authoritative, came from behind them, and both felons turned in unison to gaze at the speaker.

The bull's-eye spotlit a tall young man standing in the doorway, a sardonic smile touching his thin lips. It was Harry Jordan. Or was it? He was certainly dressed in the shabby checked suit that Jordan wore – but where was the bulbous nose and large moustache?

"I am afraid the game is no longer afoot, gentlemen. I think the phrase is, 'You've been caught red-handed.' Now, please do not make any rash attempts to escape. The police are outside the building, awaiting my signal."

Arthur Sims and Badger Johnson stared in dumbfounded amazement as the young man took a silver whistle from his jacket pocket and blew on it three times. The shrill sound reverberated in their ears.

Inspector Giles Lestrade of Scotland Yard cradled a tin mug of hot, sweet tea in his hands and smiled contentedly. "I reckon that was a pretty good night's work."

It was an hour later, after the arrest of Badger Johnson and Arthur Sims, and the inspector was ensconced in his cramped office back at the Yard.

The young man sitting opposite him, wearing a disreputable checked suit which had seen better days, did not respond. His silence took the smile from Lestrade's face and replaced it with a furrowed brow.

"You don't agree, Mr Holmes?"

The young man pursed his lips for a moment before replying. "In a manner of speaking, it has been a successful venture. You have two of the niftiest felons under lock and key, and saved the firm of Meredith and Co. the loss of a considerable amount of cash."

"Exactly." The smile returned.

"But there are still questions left unanswered."

"Such as?"

"How did our two friends come into the possession of the key to the building, to the office where the safe was housed – and the five all-important keys to the safe itself?"

"Does that really matter?"

"Indeed it does. It is vital that these questions are answered in order to clear up this matter fully. There was obviously an accomplice involved who obtained the keys and was responsible for drugging the night-watchman. Badger Johnson intimated as much when he engaged my services as lookout, but when I pressed him for further information, he clammed up like a zealous oyster."

Lestrade took a drink of the tea. "Now, you don't bother your head about such inconsequentialities. If there was another bloke involved, he certainly made himself scarce this evening and so it would be nigh on impossible to pin anything on him. No, we are very happy to have caught two of the sharpest petermen in London, thanks to your help, Mr Holmes. From now on, however, it is a job for the professionals."

The young man gave a gracious nod of the head as though in some vague acquiescence to the wisdom of the Scotland Yarder. In reality he thought that, while Lestrade was not quite a fool, he was blinkered to the ramifications of the attempted robbery, and too easily pleased at landing a couple of medium-size fish in his net, while the really big catch swam free. Crime was never quite as cut and dried as Lestrade and his fellow professionals seemed to think. That was why this young man knew that he could never work within the constraints of the organised force as a detective. While at present he was reasonably content to be a help to the police, his ambitions lay elsewhere.

For his own part, Lestrade was unsure what to make of this lean youth with piercing grey eyes and gaunt, hawk-like features that revealed little of what he was thinking. There was something cold and impenetrable about his personality that made the inspector feel uncomfortable. In the last six months, Holmes had brought several cases to the attention of the Yard which he or his fellow officer, Inspector Gregson, had followed up, and a number of arrests had resulted. What Sherlock Holmes achieved from his activities, apart from the satisfaction every good citizen would feel at either preventing or solving a crime, Lestrade could not fathom. Holmes never spoke of personal matters, and the inspector was never tempted to ask.

At the same time as this conversation was taking place in Scotland Yard, in another part of the city the Professor was being informed of the failure of that night's operation at Meredith and Co. by his number two, Colonel Sebastian Moran.

The Professor rose from his chaise-longue, cast aside the mathematical tome he had been studying and walked to the window. Pulling back the curtains, he gazed out on the river below him, its murky surface reflecting the silver of the moon.

"In itself, the matter is of little consequence," he said, in a dark, even voice. "Merely a flea-bite on the body of our organisation. But there have been rather too many of these flea-bites of late. They are now beginning to irritate me." He turned sharply, his eyes flashing with anger. "Where lies the incompetence?"

Moran was initially taken aback by so sudden a change in the Professor's demeanour. "I am not entirely sure," he stuttered.

The Professor's cruelly handsome face darkened with rage. "Well, you should be, Moran. You should be sure. It is your job to know. That is what you are paid for."

"Well… it seems that someone is tipping the police off in advance."

The Professor gave a derisory laugh. "Brilliant deduction, Moran. Your public-school education has stood you in good stead. Unfortunately, it does not take a genius to arrive at that rather obvious conclusion. I had a visit from Scoular earlier this evening, thank goodness there is *one* smart man on whom I can rely."

At the mention of Scoular's name, Moran blanched. Scoular was cunning, very sharp and very ambitious. This upstart was gradually worming his way into the Professor's confidence, assuming the role of court favourite; consequently, Moran felt his own position in jeopardy. He knew there was no demotion in the organisation. If you lost favour, you lost your life also.

"What did he want?"

"He wanted nothing other than to give me information regarding our irritant flea. Apparently, he has been using the persona of Harry Jordan. He's been working out of some of the East End alehouses, The Black Swan in particular, where he latches on to our more gullible agents, like Johnson and Sims, and then narks to the police."

"What's his angle?"

Moriarty shrugged. "I don't know – or at least Scoular doesn't know. We need to find out, don't we? Put Hawkins on to the matter. He's a bright spark and will know what to do. Apprise him of the situation and see what he can come up with. I've no doubt Mr Jordan will return to his lucrative nest at The Black Swan within the next few days. I want information only. This Jordan character must not be harmed. I just want to know all about him before I take any action. Do you think you can organise that without any slip-ups?"

Moran clenched his fists with anger and frustration. He shouldn't be spoken to in such a manner – like an inefficient corporal with muddy boots. He would dearly have liked to wipe that sarcastic smirk off the Professor's face, but he knew that such a rash action would be the ultimate folly.

"I'll get on to it immediately," he said briskly, and left the room.

The Professor chuckled to himself and turned back to the window. His own reflection stared back at him from the night-darkened pane. He was a tall man, with luxuriant black hair and angular features that would have been very attractive were it not for the cruel mouth and the cold, merciless grey eyes.

"Mr Jordan," he said, softly addressing his own reflection, "I am very intrigued by you. I hope it will not be too long before I welcome you into my parlour."

Dawn was just breaking as Sherlock Holmes made his weary way past the British Museum and into Montague Street, where he lodged. He was no longer dressed in the cheap suit that he had used in his persona as Harry Jordan, but while his own clothes were less ostentatious, they were no less shabby. Helping the police as he did was certainly broadening his experience of detective work, but it did not put bread and cheese on the table or pay the rent on his two cramped rooms. He longed for his own private investigation – one of real quality. Since coming to London from university to make his way in the world as a consulting detective, he had managed to attract some clients, but they had been few and far between, and the nature of the cases – an absent husband, the theft of a brooch, a disputed will, and such like – had all been mundane. But, tired as he was, and somewhat dismayed at the short-sightedness of his professional colleagues at Scotland Yard, he did not waver in his belief that one day he would reach his goal and have a solvent and successful detective practice. And it needed to be happening soon. He could not keep borrowing money from his brother, Mycroft, in order to fund his activities.

He entered 14 Montague Street and made his way up the three flights of stairs to his humble quarters. Once inside, with some urgency he threw off his jacket and rolled up the sleeve of his shirt. Crossing to the mantelpiece, he retrieved a small bottle and a hypodermic syringe from a morocco leather case. Breathing heavily with anticipation, he adjusted the delicate needle before thrusting the sharp point home into his sinewy forearm, which was already dotted and scarred with innumerable puncture marks. His long, white, nervous fingers depressed the piston, and he gave a cry of ecstasy as he flopped down in a battered armchair, a broad, vacant smile lighting upon his tired features.

the further adventures of

SHERLOCK HOLMES

THE ECTOPLASMIC MAN

by

DANIEL STASHOWER

Holmes was silent as our four-wheeler sped towards the Savoy, and Lestrade, to his credit, knew better than to probe for the source of the detective's sudden agitation. For my part, I had observed these fits of pique on several previous occasions, and I knew them to be grounded in a personal, rather than professional, vexation. As Holmes now seemed to have regained his composure, I thought it best not to remark upon the matter, for I knew that if my suspicions were accurate, all would be revealed presently.

And so I passed the journey wondering what sort of man it was who could so readily divest himself of canvas strait-jackets and pass through solid brick walls. In my long association with Holmes we had been concerned in a score of mysteries which, at their outsets, seemed to involve spirit beings. Crime aficionados still remark upon the macabre affair of the earl, the ascot, and the heavy feather, which had been the despair of several well-trained investigators. Only Holmes had been able to prove that flesh-and-blood murderers were responsible, rather than the vengeful revenants originally suspected by Scotland Yard.

Would Holmes be as successful in penetrating the mysteries of Houdini, or had Lestrade at last presented him with a problem which had no logical solution? This was the challenge my companion had unwillingly undertaken that afternoon. In Lestrade's defense I must say I rather doubt that he ever truly believed all this spiritualist commotion about Houdini. He was, rather, a man who dearly loved to have a key for every lock, no matter how unwieldy the keys became.

I had not been to the Savoy theatre since the passing of my beloved wife, Mary. Together we had attended many of the comic operas of Gilbert and Sullivan there, and though she had been gone many years, the association was still a painful one. My mood was certainly not lightened by the appearance of the theatre itself, which was dark and grim. The plush lobby, which I was so accustomed to seeing brightly lit and filled with cheery theatre patrons, now appeared shadowy and hollow. Through the far doors I could see rows of empty seats which seemed to stretch forever, creating an impression of eerie expectation. I am not ordinarily given to flights of fancy, but I imagined that I could feel my wife's presence in that opulent crypt, and I acknowledged to myself that if I were ever to see a spirit, it would very likely be in this place.

"Do you see this?" Lestrade was saying. "Do you see this, Holmes?" He pointed to one of the dozens of theatrical posters which covered the walls of the lobby. "Houdini claims to have no interest in spiritualism, and yet he draws attention to himself with a poster like this! There's more here than meets the eye, I tell you!"

The poster showed an ordinary wooden barrel secured with chains and heavy padlocks. Above it hovered a likeness of Houdini, who had evidently just wafted from the barrel as smoke rises from a chimney. His legs, the illustration plainly showed, were still vaporous. To strengthen this supernatural impression, the young man was shown receiving counsel from a small band of red demons who scurried about his form, while in the background a number of befuddled-looking officials stood scratching their heads. Below the illustration was printed the legend: "Houdini!!! The World's Foremost Escape King!!!"

"You are absolutely right, Lestrade," said Holmes. "This is conclusive evidence of the man's spirit capacities. What a fool I have been ever to have doubted you! Now as to the details of this crime you mentioned—"

"Enough of that, Mr Holmes. You'll be able to see for yourself in just a moment. Remember, though, Houdini doesn't yet know that he's a suspect in the crime, so you musn't let on!"

Holmes turned and walked towards the empty theatre. "As of yet I have nothing to let on," he said.

As we gained a view of the stage I could see a group of four workers carrying large packing crates back and forth across the stage. By his resemblance to the poster illustration, I gathered that the man directing the activity was none other than Houdini himself.

Houdini was a small but powerfully built young man. His black, wiry hair was combed out from the centre into two pointed tufts, which combined with the black slashes of his eyebrows to give him a satanic aspect. His every movement was precise and forceful, yet so fluid and full of grace that I was put in mind of the sleek jungle cats I encountered during my Afghan campaigns. He wore a coal-black suit, which contributed to his dramatic appearance, and though he was smaller than any of his workers, he nevertheless insisted on carrying the largest load.

One of Houdini's assistants drew his attention to our arrival. Upon seeing Lestrade, Houdini gave a cry of surprise and set down his burden. He then leapt across the orchestra pit and made his way towards us, skimming across the backs and arms of the theatre seats as if using stepping stones to cross a river. This display of coordination and balance was not mere bravado, but rather the natural course of one whose control over his own body was so complete that such exertions were as natural to him as walking.

"Mr Lestrade!" cried Houdini as he jumped down into the aisle where we stood. "It's good to see you!" He gave the inspector a jovial slap on the back. "I didn't expect to see you snooping around until this evening's performance! You're not still upset about that gaol break, are you?"

"No, no," said Lestrade quickly, "I only wished to introduce you to these two gentlemen. Sherlock Holmes and Dr Watson, allow me to present Mr Harry Houdini."

Upon hearing my friend's name, the young magician was scarcely able to conceal his pleasure. "I am delighted to meet you, sir," he said, grasping Holmes by the hand and shoulder. "I've admired you for years."

"The honour is mine," replied Holmes. "I trust that you have worked out the difficulties with your rope escape?"

"Why yes, I... wait a minute, how did you know I was having trouble with a rope escape?" In his surprise at this observation, Houdini quite forgot to take my hand and slap my shoulder. "I've always read about you doing that, but I never thought I'd actually see it! How did you know?"

"Simplicity itself, my dear fellow. There are several chafing wounds on both your wrists. I have seen identical wounds on the wrists of robbery and kidnap victims who had strained against their bonds for many hours. The natural conclusion is that you have spent some hours attempting to free yourself from a similar restraint, and were, perhaps, less successful than you might have hoped."

"Wonderful!" Houdini cried. "What a trick! But I did get out of that rope tie. I was practising on a new kind of knot. Better to work it out in rehearsal than to have it come at me during a performance." He led us towards the stage. "I sure wish Bess were here to meet you, Mr Holmes." He paused and struck a theatrical pose. "To Harry Houdini," he intoned, "she is always *the* woman."

This brief reference to one of my early Holmes stories[*] was clearly intended to flatter the detective. Houdini could not have known that Holmes seldom remembered anything but the titles of my stories, when he bothered to read them at all, so it meant nothing to him. Instead, Holmes proceeded immediately to the business at hand.

"Tell me, Mr Houdini, is it true that you are able to reduce your body to ectoplasm?"

The American laughed. "Is that why you came here? No, Mr Holmes, as I've been trying to tell Lestrade here, my magic has nothing to do with any witches or ghosts."

"Witches and ghosts have nothing to do with it," Lestrade insisted. "I never said that at all. I merely suggested that if you were a spiritualist you would have to hide your abilities from the public. If it became known that you were able to become immaterial, your escapes would cease to be dramatic. Where's the excitement in an escape artist who can walk right through his chains?"

"On the contrary," Houdini replied, "that would be the greatest act ever staged. People would pay ten bucks a head to see a real live ghost. But I am not a ghost, I'm an escape artist."

Lestrade was not satisfied. "You insist that you are not a psychic, but I still feel that no other explanation is possible for what I have seen on this stage."

Houdini bowed deeply. "Thank you very much, Mr Lestrade. That is the best compliment a magician could receive."

Lestrade turned to Holmes in exasperation. "I get no where with him! Do you see why I wanted you to come down here?"

"Actually, I do not," Holmes answered. "I'm sure you'll forgive me, Lestrade, but your failure to comprehend Houdini's mysteries will not cause me to embrace spiritualism. I submit that some more logical explanation has escaped your notice."

"Are you saying I'm thick, Holmes? Or gullible? I'd like to point out he's not merely pulling rabbits out of a hat; he's walking through solid brick walls!"

"Pray do not grow testy, Lestrade. I did not invite this interview. Nor am I suggesting that you are slow-witted in any way. I merely observe that in this case you are quick to accept the phenomenal where a more strict logician might turn to the somatic. I have no doubt that the same disciplines which govern the science of deduction would lend some insight into the marvels of Mr Houdini."

"Pardon me, Mr Lestrade," Houdini broke in with exaggerated formality. "Did I just understand Mr Holmes to say that my little mysteries would give him no trouble at all?"

"That is more or less what he said."

"Very well," Houdini said. "Let's just see about that." He turned to the stage. "Franz! Come out here!" An enormous bald-headed man appeared from the wings. "Have the boys set up last night's wall." With a nod, the large man withdrew. "Now then, Mr Holmes," Houdini resumed, "I think that even you will have some difficulty explaining this. Please follow me."

He led us up a small flight of steps which brought us onto the stage. "If this were an ordinary performance, my workmen would construct a wall brick by brick while I did some smaller effects out here. That way the audience can be sure that there's nothing tricky about the wall itself. It's absolutely solid." As he spoke his assistants spread a large red carpet across the back of the stage. Onto it they wheeled a low platform which supported, as Houdini had promised, a brick wall. "Observe: The wall is nine feet high, seven feet across, and two feet deep." He slapped the hard surface with the palm of his hand. "Sturdy. Now please note that the wall is positioned so that the top and sides are visible to the audience. If I attempted to slip around or over the wall, the audience would see me."

As he spoke Houdini's conversational tone vanished and was replaced by a practised, resonant mode of speech in which each syllable was carefully accented. His voice travelled out to the farthest reaches of the theatre and came swelling back in waves. One seemed to hear it not just with the ears, but with all the senses.

"I have spread this carpet across the stage in order to rule out the possibility of a trapdoor. You will also note that the platform which holds the wall is only three inches high, far too low to permit me to slip under."

The magician stepped back and gazed searchingly into the distance. "This ancient Hindu mystery has not been performed on any stage for more than two centuries. It was originally part of a sacred rite of passage. The village fakir would prove himself worthy by allowing himself to be sealed inside a deep cave from which he would miraculously emerge. I have brought the effect to England directly from Calcutta, where I was admitted to a holy council of elders—"

"Come, come now," said Holmes.

"What is it?" Houdini snapped, his face darkening.

"Surely if you had come directly from Calcutta you would show some effects of the tropical climate? Instead you are as pale as we are! No, I observe that while your clothing is of an American cut, your collar and bootlaces are German. It seems likely that you have just spent some time in that country, as you were there recently enough to require a new collar, and long enough to have need of new bootlaces."

Houdini paused for a moment and then opened his mouth as if to continue the oration, but immediately he thought better of it. Instead he shouted across to his assistant. "Franz! The screens!" The bald giant reappeared carrying two sections of black screen, each hinged vertically at its centre. These were placed on either side of the wall to create an enclosure which shielded a small portion from view.

"Dr Watson, if you will stand here... Lestrade there... and Mr

Holmes over here... thank you very much." He had positioned us so that the wall was seen from every angle. "Please remember, gentlemen, that I cannot travel over, under, or around the wall. I am stepping behind the screen on this side of the wall. If I appear on the far side, it can only be because I travelled through the wall to get there."

He stopped to let us absorb his words. "Now then, if you are ready, gentlemen. I shall count three. When I am finished counting, a miracle will have occurred. One... two... are you ready?... *three!*"

From the other side of the barrier I heard Lestrade give a cry. "He's done it! He's done it again!" He rushed from behind the wall, dragging Houdini by the arm. The young magician was slightly ruffled, but otherwise no worse for his efforts. I confess that I was thoroughly baffled by the feat, and by the speed and apparent ease with which it was effected.

Holmes must have read my expression, for he asked, "What do you make of it, old fellow?"

"I fear I can make nothing of it," I replied.

"Nothing, Watson? You know my methods, apply them!"

I looked carefully at the American. "His hair is disordered, but I daresay mine would be as well if I passed through a solid wall!"

Houdini smiled broadly and attempted to smooth his unruly hair. "Well, Mr Holmes?"

The detective took his cherry-wood pipe from his pocket and carefully began to fill it. "Watson, you and Lestrade have often heard me assert that when one has eliminated all that is impossible, whatever remains, however improbable, must be the truth."

"Exactly, Holmes," Lestrade said eagerly. "Houdini has shown that he could not get around the wall in any way. Therefore, he must have passed directly through it!"

"I'm afraid that, too, must be eliminated as impossible." Holmes lit his pipe and sent up a cloud of white smoke. "And if Houdini had travelled over, or to either side of the wall, we would have seen him."

"Well, he can't very well have gone under it, Holmes. Even if there were some sort of opening in the platform, there are only three inches between the wall and the stage!"

"And," Houdini could not help but remind us, "I can't have used a trapdoor because this carpet is covering the stage!"

Holmes smiled benignly at him. "Indeed," he said, "you are quite right. Any trapdoor would be covered by the carpet. And yet, I am reminded of a most instructive musical phenomenon, that of the common drum." As he spoke, Holmes stepped down into the orchestra pit where a large set of drums stood. "In effect, every drum is but a hollow cylinder tightly covered by a flexible membrane." Holmes reached up through one of the smaller drums and placed his hand beneath the drumhead. "Observe: If a solid plane is placed below the membrane, the drum makes no sound." With his free hand he struck the drum, producing only a dull thud. "But when there is nothing below the surface, the membrane is allowed its natural flexibility." He withdrew his hand and struck the drum again. A loud beat echoed through the theatre. "In the drum, sound is produced. However, the principle has other applications."

Houdini and Lestrade stood transfixed by this singular discourse. While my companion lacked the resonance and peacockery of Houdini, his narration was made all the more compelling by its quiet logic and absolute self-assurance. I could see Houdini growing restless as Holmes continued.

"Now let us turn our attentions to Houdini himself." Holmes, still in the orchestra pit, walked to the edge of the stage and found himself level with our feet. "I note a long scuff along the inside of the left shoe. This mark was not there a moment ago. Perhaps the shoes dislike transforming into ectoplasm?" He stepped back onto the stage and took

Houdini's arm as if it were a laboratory specimen. "What do we see here? In Houdini's cuff buttons we find strands of red carpeting. This is extremely significant. From this we may–"

"Enough, Holmes!" Houdini snatched his arm away, his face dark purple. "You are mocking me! You are mocking the Great Houdini! You – you – " Houdini then said something in German which had a distinctly unsavoury sound. By Holmes's expression it was clear that the meaning was not lost on him.

"I see that diplomacy is not among your talents, Mr Houdini," said Holmes. "Perhaps you had best concentrate on those abilities which you do possess, for ill-temper is often overlooked in an accomplished performer. *'Est quadam prodire tenus, si non datur ultra.'"*[*]

With this rather obscure quote from Horace, Sherlock Holmes turned and was gone.

---

[*] "Your powers may reach this far, if not beyond."